A Little Twist

USA TODAY BESTSELLING AUTHOR

TIA LOUISE

This book is a work of fiction. Names, characters, places, and incidents are products of the author's imagination or are used fictitiously. Any resemblance to actual events or locales or persons, living or dead, is entirely coincidental.

A Little Twist
Copyright © TLM Productions LLC, 2023
Printed in the United States of America.

Cover design by Y'all that Graphic.

"But I found my family… I found the way home."
—Caroline B. Cooney

For my readers, my friends, my daughters, and Mr. TL, may love surround you.

Prologue

Alex

Sixteen years ago

"**P**ATRICIA, I'M SO SORRY FOR YOUR LOSS." REVEREND SHEPHERD clasps my mother's hand, smiling warmly into her eyes before moving to my dad. "Andrew, Gladys and I are praying for you all."

"Thank you, Jim." My dad shakes the older man's hand, his arm around my mom's narrow shoulder as she clutches a cloth handkerchief to her nose.

I'm standing between my older brother Aiden and my younger brother Adam in a navy suit that makes my neck itch, in front of a stinky flower arrangement.

Stargazers, my mom called them when she lined us up in row. "What a lovely arrangement of stargazers," she'd observed, her nose red from crying.

Stinkgazers is more like it. They're making the pressure in my head worse. Looking over my shoulder, I notice a narrow door with a green *Exit* sign above it, and I wonder if there's any way I can get the hell out of here.

Aiden's jaw is fixed, and at twenty, he only has one year left at Annapolis, the US Naval Academy in Maryland. With his dark suit, short hair, and perfect posture, he already has the look of a future Marine, stoic and unflinching. I guess that'll be me in three more years, when I graduate from high school and follow in his footsteps.

Adam, by contrast, is dressed in a short-sleeved shirt and khakis. His brown hair is a little too long, and it curls around his ears in waves that are bleached caramel from spending all summer surfing.

He's doing his best to fight his tears, roughly wiping away any strays that make it onto his cheeks. But he's only thirteen. He can still get away with crying.

Not me. At fifteen, I'm a young man now. At least, that's what Dad said when he'd helped me with my necktie. The implication being, *men don't cry.* The only problem is when I see Pop lying in that casket, stone cold and unmoving, it pits my stomach and tightens my throat.

He's too thin. His skin is the wrong color, and he never wore suits. He said we had that in common. We'd rather be in our waders fishing in the brackish marsh.

Even when he was so sick with cancer he couldn't get out of bed, I'd sit beside him, and he'd close his eyes. He'd ask me if I could see the redfish swimming in the reeds. I'd hold his hand and say I could. He'd remind me how important it was to be patient, to wait for the fish to come to me, don't rush them. *Good things come to those who wait.*

Now he's gone.

I like to imagine he's found the best fishing hole in heaven, and he's hanging out with all of Jesus's friends, who were also fishermen—as he liked to remind me when Mam-mam would give him a hard time for fishing on Sunday instead of going to God's house. He's probably up there swapping stories and comparing lures.

Pop wouldn't want me to be here trying not to cry. He'd

want me to be out by the water, at our favorite spot, taking in the sunshine and smiling over our memories. He'd say you have to have the clouds, the overcast days, to catch the biggest fish. You don't catch anything on sunny days.

Reverend Shepherd has gone to the back of the room, and Aiden has joined my dad and our uncles around the casket. They're going to carry it out of the church. Adam has his arm around Mom's waist, and the two of them have moved closer to the aisle.

I take a step back, in the direction of that door, as the organ music starts and the men reverently lift my grandfather's casket off the stand. They take another step forward, and I take another step back. Again and again, we move until the entire group is at the top of the aisle, and my hand is on the cold metal barrier leading out of the small sanctuary.

The minute I step out into the muggy afternoon, I start to run. First Presbyterian Church of Eureka, South Carolina, population 3,002, is on the side of town closest to the old neighborhoods, where my family lives. It was designed to be "walkable," but my mom says it's too hot and humid to walk to church in heels.

I run the short distance to the house, and when I get inside, I toss my slick leather loafers in my bedroom, along with my stiff blazer and starched white shirt and tie. Slacks go next, and I snatch a pair of swim trunks off a pile of clean clothes in the corner I was supposed to put away.

In less than ten minutes, I'm riding my bike through the palmettos, out to the closest body of water. Sticking to the dirt paths, my tires thump hollowly over small, wooden footbridges, splash in shallow creeks, and crunch over wet gravel.

When I finally make it to the start of the little lagoon that leads out to the ocean, I abandon my bike and my Vans and take off on bare feet.

In the shade of the Walter pines, it's cooler. The air is still thick with briny moisture, but the pungent odor of lilies is finally out of my nose, replaced with the scent of pine straw and the ocean.

I follow the familiar path as my mind fills with memories of Pop. I can see his calloused fingers attaching the fly to his line and sharing his old stories and wisdom.

"The only place you find *success* coming before *work* is in the dictionary," he once told me.

He'd worked hard all his life as a contractor, but his true joys were his family, fishing, and the smoky bourbon he brewed in our family's distillery.

He'd just started teaching me how to make it. Looks like I'll have to figure out the rest on my own. A hot tear lands on my cheek, and I didn't realize I was crying. I only felt the knot between my shoulders, the ache at the base of my throat, the pain in my chest from longing for days I'll never have again.

The sun shines brightly past the edge of the trees, but I stop short of the water. I stay in the shadows, leaning my head against my forearm as more tears fall. I'm not ugly-crying. I'm just letting the emotion drain from my eyes, my own private memorial to the old man who was my best friend.

Cicadas screech louder. The water ripples past, and I inhale a shaky breath. I'm finding calm when I hear a voice that stills my thoughts. It's sweet and clear as a bell, and like a soothing balm, it quiets my sorrow.

Swallowing a breath, I take a step closer, behind the black trunk of a massive live oak tree to get a better look, and what I see almost knocks me on my ass.

The most beautiful girl I've ever seen is floating on her back in the clear water. Her eyes are closed, and her dark hair floats around her like a mermaid. Only, she doesn't have any clam shells, and my teenage dick jumps to life at the sight of tight, pink nipples. *Shit.*

Reaching down, I try to calm my erection. It's been happening at all kinds of unexpected and embarrassing times these days. I avert my eyes, forcing my brain to think of tobacco juice, stepping on a nail, failing algebra—anything to make my boner go away.

I should go away, but she's still singing the song I sort of recognize, and I can't seem to move.

"I believe in angels…" Her voice goes perfectly high, and it's so pure, I feel like I'm having an out-of-body experience.

I'm not at the little lagoon, I'm in freakin' heaven. Glancing to the side, I don't see Pop anywhere, so maybe it's more of a teenage fantasy. I've found a beautiful, naked angel in the water singing like a siren.

A splash draws my eyes involuntarily to the inlet. She's on her stomach now, and her hands part the water in front of her as she swims. I can't see her body anymore, thank God, and I'm doing my best to forget the sight of her perfectly small breasts and tight nipples.

Dammit. I'll never get rid of my woody this way, but I'm scared if I move, she'll see me. Still, I've got to get out of here.

I take one step, and of course, it's the wrong one. The ground gives way with the sharp crack of branches, and I slide around the oak tree I'd been hugging, splashing into the shallow water at the base.

The girl behind me screams, and I squeeze my eyes shut, not moving from where my stomach is pressed to the tree. My feet are in the water, and I listen as she scampers into the brush.

"Who's there?" Her voice is sharp. "What are you, some kind of Peeping Tom?"

Busted. I release the tree and take a careful step backwards, doing my best not to fall. "Sorry, I didn't know you were here."

When I hear her stomping in my direction, I turn carefully. Thankfully, she's clothed now, but the dress she pulled on clings to her wet body in a way that makes my stomach tight. Her wet hair hangs in thick locks over her chest, and when our eyes meet, it's a punch to the stomach.

Cass Dixon moved to Eureka to live with her aunt Carol at

the beginning of the summer. I noticed her the first day she arrived at the Pak-n-Save, and she stopped me in my tracks.

She's the prettiest girl I've ever seen with long, dark hair and almond-shaped blue eyes. She's tall for a girl, but she has an easy way of moving, like a dancer.

"Hey, Cass." I'm doing my best to be casual, but it's the first time we've ever spoken.

"What are you doing out here, Alex Stone?" Her hands go to her hips, and she's sassy. She tilts her head to the side. "Aren't you supposed to be at a funeral?"

"I ran away."

"How come?"

Shrugging, I look down, shame and guilt twisting together into a knot in my stomach. "I didn't want to be there anymore. I wanted to remember my grandpa like he always was. Not like… that."

Her full lips press together, and she nods, walking over to sit on a log moldering away at the water's edge. "I get that."

Her feet are in the water, and I walk over to sit beside her. "You do?"

We're not looking at each other. We're just sitting side by side, watching the tiny ripples of water rolling in and around the cove.

Her shoulders move up and down. "I've never lost anybody I can remember, but I think if I did, I wouldn't want to see them dead."

The word stings a little, but she's right. "It was all wrong. The flowers and the music, even his clothes—it wasn't anything he would've liked."

Our feet move like white fish in the currents. The soft ripple of water surrounds us, and insect noises fill the air. It's a comforting place, and being here feels safe, familiar. Sitting beside Cass feels familiar, even if we've never talked before. She's easy, like an old soul I've always known.

"What was he like?" Her voice is gentle.

My hands are in my lap, and I think about the old man. "He liked to fish and tell stories. He built houses and made whiskey. He asked me what I thought about things, and he really listened."

It sounds dumb, but with Aiden being the oldest, he always talks to Dad. Adam is the youngest, and everybody talks to him. Pop was the one who made a point of talking to me, like it was important to him to know how I felt about things.

A slim hand covers mine, and my eyes flash to where she's touching me. "I'm sorry he died."

Glancing up, I study her pretty face. "You have a really good voice."

She smiles, full lips parting over straight white teeth, and a pinpoint dimple is at the corner of her mouth. "Thanks. I love to sing."

"What was that song?"

"'I Have a Dream.' It's from the Broadway musical *Mamma Mia*." She tilts her head, taking her hand from mine. "Technically, it's an Abba song, but I love Broadway best."

"Have you ever been?"

She shakes her head. "Maybe one day I'll go. I'd love to see *Phantom* or *Wicked*… I wish I'd gotten to see *West Side Story*, but it's gone now."

Nodding, I'm not sure how to respond. I've never known anybody who knew so much about Broadway shows. "Why are you living with your aunt?" Her brow furrows, and I quickly explain. "I was just wondering what happened to your parents."

"Oh." Her voice goes quiet again. "My mom couldn't take care of us anymore, so Aunt Carol asked if I wanted to come stay with her."

"Us?"

"My little sister Jemima and me."

Again, I'm not sure what to say. I've never known anybody who didn't live with their parents. "I'm sorry."

Her chin lifts, and she smiles. "It's okay. Some people aren't cut out to be parents, I guess. That's what Carol said. As much as they try, they can't get it together. Or keep it together." She adds the last part under her breath. "Doesn't mean she doesn't love me. Or even that she doesn't like me."

My brow furrows, and I can't tell if she's pretending not to care or if she's really okay with her situation.

"I can't imagine anyone not liking you."

She bends her leg, putting her foot on the log and resting her cheek on the top of her knee. Her eyes meet mine, and her smile is back. "You're nice. Your dad's the sheriff, right?"

"And his dad before him."

Her small nose turns up at the end. "You're starting tenth grade?" I nod, and she lifts her head. "I'm only in eighth, but maybe we can be friends."

I don't say anything, but my eyes drift to her full lips. I've never kissed a girl before, and I'm having all kinds of thoughts about things I've never done. I've never been on a date, never held a girl's hand, never seen a girl naked in real life… until now.

"Don't you want to be friends?" Her voice is defiant, and I sit up straighter.

"Uh, sure… I guess." *Do I?*

She stands up quickly, practically jogging in the direction of the forest, and I jump up fast to follow her.

"Where are you going?" I hop over rocks and sticks wishing I had my shoes.

She stops and turns so abruptly, we bump into each other, and I grab her arms to keep us both from falling.

Lifting her arms out of my grip, she shakes her head. "I guess you think you're too good to be my friend. I guess you're too awesome to hang out with a middle schooler who doesn't even have a mom."

"I don't think any of that!" My reply is loud, and I blurt what I was thinking. "I think you're really pretty, and I was thinking how I might like to kiss you."

Her eyes blink wider, then her mouth closes as her brow

lowers. "You spied on me naked, and now you want to kiss me? Are you trying to cop a feel?"

Am I?

Maybe a little.

"No! I like talking to you. And listening to you sing, too."

She studies me a moment longer, her breath coming in quick pants from running. Before I can think, she steps forward and presses her full lips to mine in a closed-mouth kiss.

My heart squeezes in my chest, and heat rushes from my stomach to my groin. Her lips are so soft, and her small breasts press against my chest. My teenage dick is at it again, and I'm trying to decide whether to push it down or wrap my arms around her waist and pull her closer.

Before I can do either, she's gone, running at top speed to where a bike is parked by the path. She jumps on it and pedals away as fast as she can.

She leaves me hot all over. The water ripples behind me, and I'm fighting my second boner in less than thirty minutes— both because of the same girl.

My head is dizzy, and all I can think is one thing: I never want to be *friends* with Cassidy Dixon. Not ever.

Chapter 1

Alex

Present Day

"**H**OLD HER, ALEX!" AIDEN SPLASHES INTO THE DITCH WHERE I'm kneeling, wire cutters in hand.

I'm on my knees clutching a pig the size of a bloodhound, her head scrubbing against my stomach as she struggles to escape, and I lift my chin as he feels around in the dark brown sludge behind the squirming animal.

"It's okay, Myrtle. We've got you." The stench sends a hot surge of bile into my throat, and I do my best to keep calm even as she grinds her muddy snout through my dress shirt to my skin.

"Oh, Myrtle!" Holly Newton, Myrtle's owner, cries from the sidewalk above us. "My sweet piggy! How did this happen?"

The panic in her voice is not helping calm the animal, but I exhale slowly, doing my best to hold on.

Aiden is working fast, his brow furrowed and his jaw set. I imagine as sheriff of our small town he's used to dealing with this kind of thing.

As soon as he left the Marines, he came back and took over our late dad's old job, and it suits his no-nonsense, hands in the dirt, man-of-few-words persona.

As CEO of Stone Cold distillery, producer of the world-renowned Stone Cold original single barrel bourbon, the best single-batch bourbon since Blanton's, I prefer cleaner work.

I spend my days talking to influencers and journalists, carefully crafting fine whiskeys and then helping the people who matter see it's the best on the market. I don't wear a suit to work every day, but I don't mind the days when I do.

Days like today, unfortunately.

While my brother is wearing a thick, canvas uniform and heavy boots similar to what we wore in basic training, I'm in Armani and Italian leather loafers—all of which are now ruined.

How the fuck did I wind up in this ditch covered in mud, bear-hugging a pig?

I blame myself.

It's a lovely summer's day, and I decided to swing by the courthouse after meeting with our accountant to share the mid-year numbers with Aiden.

Besides fishing, Pop taught me how he made his special recipe bourbon in the old distillery he inherited from his father. It's a long, slow process that requires patience and attention to detail, which suits *my* persona.

When I left the Navy, I turned Pop's hobby into a full-time business with our mom, Aiden, and Adam as investors. Stone Cold has had a series of *very* good years, making us millionaires several times over, and it's poised to go even higher.

I'm pretty proud of what we've accomplished in such a short time, but as usual, Aiden simply nods and leaves the business side of things to me.

Our conversation had just drifted to his upcoming wedding, which will be held in our new event space behind the distillery next month, when the call came through that Myrtle, the town's award-winning pig, had escaped her pen and was running down Main Street in a panic and squealing.

As Aiden's sole dispatcher, Holly went into a total meltdown. His one deputy was out of the office—getting Krispy Kreme donuts, no doubt—so without hesitation, my brother grabbed me to help him capture the rogue pig.

Which brings me here, waist-deep in sewage, clinging to Myrtle, and trying not to imagine what else is swimming around in this sludge with us.

"Next time you're coming to me," I grunt, tightening my hold on the squirming animal.

My brother's jaw clenches as he fishes shoulder-deep in the water beneath the pig's ass. A sharp snap of wire cutting, and he quickly rises, pulling away. "Watch out—she's loose."

Myrtle bucks hard against my grip, and I release her, holding my arms in the air as Aiden shoves her rear to help her climb out of the pit.

"My poor baby!" Holly drops to her knees and attaches a leash to the pig's collar. "Are you hurt? Who would do this to you?"

I rise to my full height, looking down at my ruined clothes while Holly continues talking to her pig like it's a person and ranting about teenagers and people having no respect for private property.

"Last year it was my chickens, now this." Her nose wrinkles with a sniff. "Oh, Myrtle, you need a bath. Is it okay if I take the afternoon off, Sheriff?"

"Sure." Aiden holds out his hand to pull me from the muddy trench.

My leather loafers slip on the wet grass, but I finally make it out.

"Those were really nice shoes." He shakes his head, looking down. "Probably not so great for what we just did."

"I'm sure chasing pigs is not what the designer had in mind."

I can't help frowning at the idiotic chain of events, which doesn't really surprise me for Eureka.

Aiden wipes his hands down the front of his uniform pants. "This mud smells like ass."

"No shit. I'm not getting in my car this way. What are you going to do?"

"I have an extra uniform and a shower at the courthouse. Here." He tosses me a set of keys. "Britt's old loft is empty. You can clean up there. I'm pretty sure I left a pair of sweatpants and a few shirts in the dresser."

"Thanks." I catch the keys to his fiancée's now-vacant apartment, and we walk together towards the town square where his office is located in the courthouse. We look like we've been mud wrestling. "I can't believe you had me chasing a pig."

Aiden exhales a short laugh. "She's *some pig.*"

My eyes narrow, but I can't resist. "Possibly humble. *Not* radiant."

He grips my shoulder with a chuckle—a response that's become more frequent since Britt entered his life. Before her, he only smiled at his son. "Walk over when you're done, and we can finish talking about… whatever you were telling me."

Nice. "You mean how well Stone Cold is doing or your pending nuptials?"

"I prefer the latter."

I shake my head. "Can't do it. I've got to pick up Pinky from Mom's. Looks like I'll be a little later than usual."

Aiden's son Owen gave my daughter Penelope her nickname when she was a toddler, and it stuck. He said it's because her strawberry blonde hair is pink. It helps that pink is also her favorite color, and she spends most days wearing or eating something pink or carrying around her stuffed pink piglet.

Mom never complains if I'm late picking her up after work, but I do my best to be on time. It's enough that she dedicates her golden years to babysitting my preschool daughter every day. I try not to monopolize her evenings as well.

"Mom loves her grandkids." Aiden slaps my shoulder. "I'll give her a call and let her know you were helping me out."

He cuts across the square in the direction of the courthouse, and I push through the glass door of a small storefront. To my left is the entrance to the Star Parlor, Britt's mother's tarot-reading studio. In front of me is a flight of stairs leading up to Britt's old loft.

I take the steps two at a time and unlock the door using the keys Aiden gave me. The space is empty except for a few remaining pieces of furniture—a queen-sized bed under large windows, a couch in front of a medium sized flatscreen television, and a dresser against the wall.

Stripping out of my muddy slacks and dress shirt, I leave everything in a pile outside the bathroom door. I'll bag it up after I'm clean and decide if it's even worth trying to salvage.

I'm relieved to find a bar of soap and a bottle of shampoo still in the shower. The shampoo is a flowery, girlish scent, but it's better than sewage. I switch on the water and step inside, ready to get the funk of ditch water and ditch critters off me.

I've got to move fast if I'm going to pick up my daughter from Mom's without being too late. The last thing I need is any more surprises today.

Chapter 2

Cass

"**I** THINK IT'S A SIGN." LYING ON MY BACK ON THE CONCRETE DRIVE under Britt's orange Ford step-side, I grunt as I loosen the bolt holding the oil pan in place.

I've been helping my friends with auto maintenance ever since I took a shop class in high school. I was the only girl in the class, and the gym teacher who was stuck teaching thought it was funny. By contrast, I was very serious about being able to take care of my own vehicle in case of emergencies, and he was so impressed, he taught me all the basics. YouTube taught me the rest.

"They're all signs." Britt squats beside the wheel, watching as the oil drains from her dad's old vehicle she inherited after he died. "They've been going up all over town for a year."

"But it says, 'Follow your path.'" I position the bucket so it won't overflow, getting a splash of oil on my chest before scooting out from under the vehicle and placing my back to the tire. "I've got to follow my path."

My friend since middle school sits on the concrete beside me, her green eyes bright. "You've found something you love?"

My shoulders drop. "No, but it's time to get serious. I'm going to be thirty in a few months, and I have no purpose."

"Good lord, don't sail off that cliff. You have purpose." Britt bumps my shoulder with hers. "We just have to sort through all your *eras* and find the one that resonates with you the most. The one you keep wanting to go back to."

"Oh, sure, Taylor. It's just that simple."

"It's what I'd do!"

She's right, I guess.

Britt is so positive. Even when she's twisting her fingers with anxiety—a quirk that happens less and less now that Aiden is around to cover her small hands with his strong ones—she's able to look at problems as opportunities. I'd like to say it's because she had a better home life than I did growing up, but her family is even weirder than mine, consisting mostly of magicians and tarot readers and escape artists.

Maybe it's because of her job as a forensic photographer. She's forced to find meaning in terrible situations. I could never do what she does, but it led her to Aiden, the drop-dead gorgeous sheriff of our town.

Their relationship is enough to make me reconsider my permanent ban on men since Drake Redford announced I'd never get over his conceited ass. He had the nerve to say I'd be just like my mom, alone and aimless by the time I'm thirty.

I'd said he was jealous I actually had a life, but now that I'm twenty-nine and a half with no direction, no job, and no place to live, I'm getting nervous he might be right.

"Personally, I thought your pastry chef era was the best. I'm so happy you agreed to make your cinnamon-almond snickerdoodle cake for my wedding. I dreamed about it so long, I had to buy snickerdoodles to dunk in my morning coffee just to kill the cravings."

"First, I'm not a chef. I'd have to go to culinary school for that title." I bend my knee and rest my cheek on it. "Baking's okay, but it doesn't spark joy for me."

"Marie Kondo knows we can't have that," she teases. "What about your preschool dance teacher era?"

Studying my oil-blackened fingers, I can't help a smile. "I did love those squishy little baby arms and their sweet little faces when they were working so hard."

"They were so cuuute!"

"My favorite part was when I'd tell them to turn their toes out and they'd turn them in." I snort a laugh.

"Remember that one little girl who had her tongue out the whole time?" Britt joins me in giggling.

"She was so focused! I loved her!" Warmth fills my chest, and I feel like we're close to what I want. "But baby dance lessons don't pay enough to sustain a life."

The air fizzles out of my happiness balloon, and we both sigh. I glance over to see the oil has finished draining, and I lie back and scoot under her truck as she tilts her head to the side.

"You're really good with cars. I'd imagine owning your own garage would support a life."

"And go up against Bud?" I laugh loudly as I replace the bolt and unscrew the filter. "That would be a major town scandal, and to be honest, as fun as it is blowing the old guys' minds with my automotive skills, I'm not really interested in being a grease monkey for the rest of my life."

"Rude!" Britt cries, which only makes me laugh more.

Scooting back out from under the truck, I sit up again. "I'm a lost cause. I only love things that will leave me homeless."

"No negative talk!" She holds up a finger. "We've only just started our pro-con list. What about hairstylist?"

"It killed my lower back."

"Clean beauty?"

"Too much mess. Too many products. It took over my life."

"Pet groomer?"

"The last cat with mites cured me of that."

"Yick." Britt shudders. "I'm sure Mom would welcome you back at the Star Parlor. She always said you were a gifted empath."

"I made even less money as a psychic than I did as a baby dance teacher, and I don't know. It made me feel guilty. Was I really helping those people?"

"I'm sure you made them feel better. At least for that day."

My nose crinkles, and I shake my head. "I've done a lot of crazy shit through the years, haven't I?"

"And of all of them, the only one that makes you light up is working with little kids. Have you considered going back to college and getting certified to teach? You'd make a great kindergarten teacher."

Lifting the hood of the truck, I give her a worried glance. "I never went to college to start with." Turning the fresh carton of oil upright in the reservoir, I sigh. "I'd have to start from the beginning, and if I don't have enough money for rent, I definitely can't afford four years of college."

Britt crosses her arms, her brow furrowed. "There must be something you could do with little kids right now that doesn't require all that time and money."

I wrap an arm over her shoulders. "You are such a good friend worrying about this with me."

"Argh! Don't ruin my sweater!" She shoves me with her elbow. "You're covered in oil."

"I'm not covered in it!" Looking down, I notice the oil splatters on my overalls and white undershirt. "What can I say? It's a dirty job."

"Head up to my place and shower. The spare key is over the door of the Star Parlor, and I'm pretty sure I left some clothes behind. Heck, you can borrow some of Aiden's old things if you need to."

We're in the parking lot behind her mother's tarot reading studio, and I glance up at the loft apartment where Britt lived until she moved in with Aiden and Owen.

"Smart place to hide a key. I'd never look for it over the wrong door."

"It was Mom's idea."

Exhaling a shiver, I shake my head. "It's not just the money keeping me away from tarot. Every time I see your mom, I can't stop remembering the infamous afternoon of you and Aiden having sex upstairs. It kept getting louder, and there was nowhere to hide... I've never fled a building so fast in my life."

Her eyes roll. "Let it go. Ma knows Aiden and I have sex." We walk slowly to the back entrance. "Hell, with our wedding on the horizon, all anybody wants to know is how soon we're going to start having babies."

"I don't think I'll ever get used to them encouraging you to have sex. For so long they said *don't* do it. Now it's all go go go!"

"I think it's less about the physical act of love than it is about procreation. Old people love babies."

"I think you should enjoy being married first. I mean, as much as you can with Owen in the house." I slide my oil-stained hand down the front of my overalls before grabbing the door handle.

"Patricia has already offered to keep him every weekend with a wink and a nudge—and that's after keeping Pinky all week."

I laugh as I imagine Aiden's mom eagerly keeping her grandkids in the hopes of getting more. "Maybe that's my problem. I'm secretly an old lady obsessed with babies."

"You're an old soul. Now get cleaned up and meet me at the distillery. We need to curate the guest list. Oh! Wedding planner. We forgot to add that to your résumé!"

"*Wedding planner* does not go on my résumé. I'm only doing this for you because I love you, and I have no money to give you a real gift."

"Speaking of money, how much do I owe you for the oil change?"

"Are you kidding? You bought the oil. I'm not charging to

put it in your truck." I reach for the door just as she catches my arm.

"I love you, and I'm paying you for your service."

"We'll discuss it at the distillery. I can't stand here like this."

"That's why you don't have any money."

"One oil change isn't going to pay my bills, Britt."

She mutters something about being stubborn as I walk through the glass door behind the stores, and I shake my head, continuing up the short foyer to the tarot studio where I worked for six months last year.

It wasn't a bad job. Gwen gave me a short list of questions designed to uncover the heart of each client's problem—sort of like a therapist. Then she showed me how to give a reading that would comfort them. Every tarot card has at least five different meanings, so it was all about finding the combination that worked for that person.

Britt's right, I was able to make them happy. We never had an unsatisfied customer, which to Gwen meant I had a gift.

"I'm still not sure I agree with her," I mutter, sliding my fingers along the wooden molding above the door.

I take the key down, trotting up the stairs and inserting it into the doorknob. It turns easily, and I step inside the empty apartment, discarding my clothes in the small nook beside the washing machine just behind the refrigerator.

No direction, no job, no place to live…

Scrubbing my hand over my forehead, I push that thought away. "I'm not my mother." No matter what fucking Drake Redford said.

I can't listen to the rantings of a small-dicked, spoiled man-child trying to pressure me into marrying him—and utterly astonished someone had the nerve to tell him no.

Overalls off, undershirt off, I stomp to the bathroom in my black lace undies and no bra when the narrow door opens all by itself and a tall, dark figure emerges from the steamy room.

"Shit!" I start to scream, but the sound dies on my lips when Alex Stone materializes before me in all his naked glory.

Shiiit... My eyes bug as they flash from the tips of his damp, brown hair to his broad, muscled shoulders to the lines in his chest... I can't stop them moving lower... to the cut of his six-pack abs to the two, thrilling lines that form a V over his hips to the center of his pelvis.

"Holy shit." The breath leaves my body on a hot whisper, and my inner thighs tingle.

I'm frozen to the spot, gaping at the sight of his smooth, semi-erect, impressively large cock. It's thick and perfect with just enough veins and a mushroom cap that holds so much promise...

"See something you like?" His baritone voice snaps me out of my trance.

He doesn't move to cover himself, and I blink quickly from his dick to his hungry gaze, which is fixed on my bare breasts. His eyebrow arches, and he licks his lips.

He actually *licks his lips.*

It's when I remember I'm standing in front of him in only my black lace panties.

Slamming my arms over my chest, I stutter. "Wh-what are you doing here?"

"Aiden said I could use the shower to clean up." He gives me a wicked smile, putting a hand on his hip and not even trying to hide his mesmerizing physique. "Myrtle got loose, and we ended up in a ditch."

"Would you please?" I gesture towards his waist. "This isn't a men's locker room."

His hazel eyes squint, and his grin widens over straight, white teeth. "Sorry, I thought you were seeing something you liked."

"It's not… I can't…" Use your words, Cass. "I'm not used to seeing all that… out in the wild."

I wave my hand at his cock, which I'm pretty sure has grown thicker in the short time we've stood here facing each other half-naked.

Well, *I'm* half-naked. He's full monty.

"*That*, as in my dick?" Reaching inside the small bathroom, he's still not covering his junk, and my pussy is slippery and pulsing as fast as my heart.

I turn my back and take a few deep breaths to calm my volcanic hormones. How long has it been since I've had a nice, solid roll in the sack? *Too long!* my hormones answer, and never with someone so *endowed*.

Get a grip, Cass. It's freakin' Alex Stone. He's the most controlled, distant, reserved of the Stone brothers. We are nothing alike. We never share more than a few polite sentences when we're together, and for a long time, I was pretty sure he found me annoying, although I've never given him a reason.

"And I seem to remember you like wild things." A tease is in his tone, and the noise of drawers opening and closing sounds behind me, the rattle of clothes in a bag, and a thought tickles my brain.

"How could you possibly know something like that?"

"I've seen you skinny dipping."

"I haven't done that in fifteen years."

"Too bad. You can turn around now." He still has that tone, but I don't move.

I'm still standing here topless. "That's okay."

His low chuckle makes my stomach tighten. "Well, I'm heading out. The place is yours. See you around, Cass."

Nodding, I turn as he passes me and dash into the bathroom, closing the door and leaning my back against it. My heart hammers in my chest, and I glance at the removable showerhead.

Quickly stepping into the tub, I turn the water on warm and lower that nifty device between my thighs. Bracing my hand on the wall, I close my eyes and move it in slow circles over my pulsing clit.

It doesn't take long before my lips part, and a moan scrapes from my throat. I shudder through an intense orgasm as I imagine tracing my fingers over every line of muscle in his sexy body, leaning my head back as I ride it out on Alex Stone's massive cock.

Talk about a twist…

Chapter 3

Alex

I'VE CLOSED THE BAR EARLY, AND I'M STANDING BEHIND THE DARK-stained, reclaimed-wood barrier, polished to a high shine, cleaning a glass with my eyes fixed on my future sister-in-law and Cass Dixon leaning together and laughing softly as they peruse a list of names for the upcoming wedding.

Cass leans closer to her friend, and a glossy lock of dark, chestnut hair slides over her shoulder onto her breast. What happened in Britt's old apartment burns in my stomach. She's grown up, and her body has as well. She's softer, fuller, *mouthwatering...*

Tonight she's wearing a thin, white tank top and jean shorts. Her long arms and long legs are shapely like a dancer's, and her olive skin is warmed by the yellow lights. Britt is a drop of blonde sunshine, but Cass is something darker, more sensual.

It's been a long time since I've been with a woman, not that I was ever a fuck boy. I'm a patient guy, controlled, focused, willing to wait for the good things, but this afternoon in Britt's apartment, I was ready to go full caveman.

"Stop playing Mr. Aloof," Britt calls to me from her perch. "Get over here and weigh in on this."

Cass's gray-blue eyes meet mine briefly before blinking to the sheet in front of them. I don't miss the pink rising in her cheeks. It's an attractive hue that compliments her glossy, full lips.

Tossing the bar rag on the counter, I reach overhead and take down a bottle of our famous single-barrel, and walk slowly to where the women are sitting.

"What's so important you need my help?" I give Britt a pretend frown.

"Don't play grumpy with me. I know as well as you, your opinion is usually correct."

Britt's sunny, but not in an annoying way. She manages to walk that fine line between sweet and saccharine, and God knows she's made a world of difference in my brother's life. I hadn't seen him smile in seven years before she blasted back into town—nearly running him down with her old truck in the process.

The memory makes me chuckle. She got his ass back in the game fast.

"Between your mom's list and mine, we've got twenty too many people coming to the reception. Some of them have to go, or the fire marshal will be on our backs. And you know your law-abiding big brother won't let that happen."

"Let me see." I reach for the list, giving it a quick scan. Uncles, aunts, cousins… I don't land on a single name from our side I could cut without catching shit. That just leaves Britt's side. "You don't have twenty tight-rope walkers or poodle jugglers you could cut?"

"Very funny." Britt's eyes narrow, and she snatches the sheet from my hand. "I have more than circus freaks in my family, thank you very much."

"I'm just teasing." I nudge the side of her arm before taking down three tumblers and pouring us each a finger of our best bourbon. "We could open the back doors and extend the space onto the patio. Maybe string some lights in the trees and add a few picnic tables. What do you think, Cass? Would it work?"

She blinks away from me, turning to face the large, metal garage doors we usually keep closed and locked at the back of the room. "As long as the weather holds, it would certainly be enough space for twenty people. Possibly more."

"Problem solved." I lift my tumbler.

"I knew you could help us." Britt smiles, lifting her glass to clink against mine.

Cass raises her tumbler as well, but she still doesn't make direct eye contact with me. Her gaze lingers on the amber liquid in our glasses. We say a cheers, and sip the warm liquid. It's a drink to be savored, not shot.

"Mm," Britt tilts her head to the side, thoughtfully. "Smoky, smooth… oak with a hint of vanilla?"

"You got it." I nod. "Not as much caramel in this batch. I hope that's okay."

"It's amazing. You're really a genius when it comes to this stuff. Aiden has taught me the flavor notes to look for, but it's still pretty cool how you're able to coax so much from simple mash."

"Time, patience… My grandfather kept good notes, and he shared everything he knew with me."

"Weren't you only fifteen when he died?" Cass's eyes finally land on mine, and a charge resonates between us.

I was fifteen that day so long ago when I ran away from his funeral and found her. It was the first time I saw her naked. A smile curls my lips, and she quickly blinks away to her glass.

"I was younger than that when he started teaching me his technique, but he only let me taste it, hold the flavor on my tongue, then spit it out, which is how wine makers work."

"I'm sure your dad would've had a fit." Britt's nose wrinkles.

"The Stone family were never fans of my mother's boot-legger heritage, but I loved it." I look away, remembering the old man who took me fishing, talked to me about people and life. "Pop had a lot of wisdom. He taught me to wait, and good things would come when the time was right."

The words feel weighted, and my gaze moves to Cass again. My instinct rises, telling me to stop acting like a teenager. I put away my childish infatuation with her years ago when it was clear she only wanted to be friends. One renewed peek at her body isn't going to bring all that nonsense out of retirement.

Or is it…

The girls return to their prior conversation, and I don't interrupt. Instead, I make like a good bartender and pour us all another finger of bourbon.

"You're still left without a place to live. Just take my old loft," Britt says.

"I can't live there for free, and your mom will just try and get me to work at the Star Parlor again. You know I can't say no to her. She's very persuasive."

"So what will you do? Go back to Carol's?"

"Aunt Carol would be happy for me to live with her for the rest of my life, but I hate going backwards. I have to find my own way. Follow my path."

"You can't follow any path if you refuse to let people pay you for your work. Now let me pay you for the oil change."

"I'm not taking your money." Cass blocks Britt's hand, which is advancing with several bills folded together. "I changed your oil because it's easy, and there's no reason to pay for something that simple."

"It's skilled labor, and Bud would've charged me at least seventy-five dollars."

"Seventy-five dollars!" Cass gasps. "That's highway robbery! I can't believe he can look at himself in the mirror and charge you that much for a simple oil change on a twenty-year-old Ford. It's not like it's a BMW or a Porsche."

"He says it's twenty bucks for the oil, then labor charges—"

"Bud Dewey is full of shit, and I'm going to stop by his

garage tomorrow and give him a piece of my mind. The most he should dare charge you is thirty bucks."

"Okay… thirty, it is!" Britt peels two twenties off her wad of bills. "Here you go, and a ten-dollar tip because I love you."

"Britt Bailey, are you trying to trick me?"

I can't help a laugh. "What's this all about?" My deep voice contrasts with their light banter.

"Cass is broke, yet she does all these things for me *for free*—she changes the oil in my truck, plans my whole wedding, makes the wedding cake, flea-dips my dog, and she won't let me pay her a red cent!"

"You flea-dipped Edward?" I'm impressed by such a feat. Britt's bloodhound must weigh at least eighty pounds. "How do you lift him?"

"Oh, please. Edward is the sweetest dog on the planet. I tell him to get in the tub and sit, and he steps right in and sits. Done." Squinting one eye, she points at Britt. "That's the only reason I still do it for you. It would be different if he was an out-of-control mutt like some of the other pets I've had to wrestle to the ground—or if he were a cat who tried to maul me to death. Like I said, that era has ended. Full stop."

"Okay, okay!" Britt holds up her hands, and I'm fully invested.

I need more information. "What's this about *eras*?"

"Of the avalanche of jobs my beautiful friend is proficient at, she still hasn't found one she loves—"

"I haven't found the one that will pay my bills and keep me out of Aunt Carol's house. I know the ones I've loved."

"Which are?" I lean on my elbow, hungry to know more about the beauty who haunted my teenage dreams for too long.

"Babies." Britt leans forward on the bar a little too fast.

It catches me completely off guard, and I huff a laugh as I straighten. "I'm sorry… What?"

"Good lord, Britt." Another flush of pink stains Cass's soft cheeks. Shaking her head, she holds up a hand. "What she means is, I've loved the jobs when I'm working with children the most. I'm just not certified to teach, and baby dance classes don't pay the bills."

"Ah, that's right, you taught my daughter ballet lessons. Was that two years ago?" Damn, my head was so far up my ass in those days.

If we're talking eras, I was in my "success only comes before work in the dictionary" era, and I busted my ass twenty-four seven.

My primary focus was on breaking Stone Cold into the high-class world of premium spirits, and if it weren't for Mom's help, I'm not sure how I would've done it with Pinky only two and a half years old.

As it is, the distillery broke through, and now we're all doing very well.

"She was adorable, and a natural little dancer, too." Cass's eyes are warm, and the genuine affection in her tone hits me unexpectedly.

Shit, maybe my teenage infatuation isn't as dead as I'd like it to be.

"If I remember correctly, she really liked your classes. She talked about you nonstop." My eyes trace her hair as I remember my little girl saying Wonder Woman taught her class.

"Where is she now?"

"Sleepover at a friend's. They're doing a little spa birthday party or something."

"Say less!" Britt cries. "I want to have a little girl so much."

"They sent us pictures." I turn my phone so they can see my curly-haired cherub lying on her back on a palette surrounded by other little girls doing the same. Her stuffed piglet doll is under her arm.

"She's adorable!" Cass coos.

"Where are Piglet's cucumbers?" Britt teases.

"He probably ate them." Cass laughs, and our eyes connect once more, holding a moment longer.

I don't know if my vision is still clouded by our afternoon encounter or if it's the sweet things she's saying about my daughter, but it feels different, unique in a way that makes me hesitate. It makes me run my eyes over her hair and her cheekbones, the tip of her nose and her lips.

I feel Britt looking back and forth between us, and I shut it down, tucking my phone in my pocket. "I think it's time to call it a night, yes?"

The last thing I need is my tipsy sister-in-law picking up on any nascent chemistry between Cass and me.

"Morning does come early." Britt slides off her stool, and her shift in tone eases the concern in my chest. "I've got to be at the courthouse bright and early with the sheriff, aka, my future husband."

She trills out the last bit, and Cass slides off her stool with a grin, taking her friend's arm. "Any hot cases you can share with us?"

"Not really." Britt shrugs. "It's pretty quiet, other than the mysterious sign poster. I think it's all pretty harmless, but after what happened last year, Aiden wants to get to the bottom of who's doing it."

"He's not planning to press charges, is he?"

"I don't think so…" Britt tilts her head to the side. "I hope not!"

I'm walking behind them, my blazer over my arm as I hit the lights on the way out, and I don't miss a wobble in their step. "How are you two getting home?"

"I rode my bike," Britt announces brightly. "Your mom said I could have it now that I'm days away from being a member of the family."

She's already family in my mind, and I catch her arm. "It's too late for bike riding. I'm giving you both a ride home. Aiden would have my hide if I didn't, and I'd let him."

They don't argue—Britt even giggles something like consent, and we walk to my burgundy Tesla parked in a reserved space. With a touch we're on the road, and it only takes five minutes before I'm pulling into Aiden's driveway.

Britt gives my arm a squeeze before hopping out of the passenger's side. "Thanks for the ride, *Bubba*. See you tomorrow, Cass!"

"Owen hates that nickname." I exhale a laugh, glancing over my shoulder, but Cass is behind me in the dark backseat, almost like she's hiding. "Want to climb up front? You'll be more comfortable."

She hesitates a moment before sliding over and stepping out of the open door and climbing into the front. The door closes with a solid thump, and she pulls the seatbelt across her shoulder as I back out of the driveway.

"I've always wanted to ride in one of these." Her voice is quiet, her eyes tracing the console. "This is where my expertise ends. I know nothing about electric cars."

"Good news—you don't have to know much. There are no oil changes or fuel filters, and the only wear and tear is on the brake pads. Even that's reduced by regenerative braking."

"Impressive." She lifts her chin. "And they send you wireless upgrades? *Very* Big Brother."

I don't miss her tone. "It's one less thing to worry about in my opinion." My eyes drift to her smooth legs, her slim hands clasped in her lap. *Is she nervous?* I try to find a more neutral subject. "I heard you're looking for a place to live?"

"Do you know of anything?"

"Not at the moment—just wondering where I'm taking you tonight."

"Oh, sorry, I'm back at Carol's, I guess." She sighs heavily, slumping back in her seat.

"I thought you got along with your aunt?" I cast another glance at her face.

Her lips pull into a frown. "I do, I guess. She's always taken care of me, made sure I had a roof over my head and clothes to wear, food to eat…"

"But?"

She presses her head against the headrest, pinching the bridge of her nose. "It sounds so childish and selfish."

"Consider me forewarned."

More hesitation, and I feel her gray-blue eyes sizing me up before she continues. "If you must know, she says I'm just like my mother. And the truth is, I'm afraid she might be right. I never went to college. I chase dreams that don't pay anything and get me nowhere… My mother was broke and alone by the time she was thirty. The farthest she ever got was a small-town gig in a main-street honkey tonk."

"I never met your mother, but as far as I can tell, you're far from alone." Easing my foot off the gas, I do my best to prolong the drive across our town of only four stoplights. "You have a beautiful voice. It's been a while since I've heard it, but I remember."

A tenuous silence falls between us, and I wonder if we're finally going to address the elephant in the room.

"That would've been the first time you saw me naked."

Yep, we're going there.

"It was your voice that caught my attention. I had no idea you were skinny dipping."

"You expect me to believe you were entranced by my voice and not my prepubescent nipples?"

"They were pubescent." A tightness is in my lower stomach. "And I saw more than your nipples."

"You don't sound any more sorry now than you did then."

"I wasn't sorry, but it *was* an accident, a lot like what happened this afternoon when you walked in on me."

Silence falls between us, and she exhales a short laugh as I pull into her aunt's driveway. "I guess that makes us even."

"I wasn't keeping score."

"Me either." A tentative smile curls her lips, and she reaches for the door.

I wonder if she remembers kissing me that day. On that,

I am keeping score, and I'd like to make us even—right now would be nice.

I catch her forearm before she steps out of my car. "It's going to work out for you, Cass."

"How can you say that? You don't know anything about my situation."

"I know enough, and I'm always right. Ask Britt."

Her eyes move from my hand on her arm to my face. A smile lifts the corner of her lips, and her head tilts to the side. "You're a lot different with your clothes on."

"How so?"

She leans in, putting her lips dangerously close to mine, and whispers. "You're a lot cockier when you're naked."

My dick tightens, and I'm ready to catch her by the jaw and claim her mouth with mine.

Instead I arch an eyebrow. "Or is it just more cock?"

Her eyes widen, and she falls back against the seat covering her laugh with her hand. It's incredibly sexy, and it makes me smile.

Just as fast, she sits forward, lifting her chin and placing her hand on my cheek. "Thanks, Alex. I really needed to hear that tonight."

Her thumb moves over my lips, and her eyes follow. I'm ready to say fuck it and pull her to me when she quickly exits the vehicle. For a brief moment, I want to go after her, but I don't.

I have no reason to hold her, and I don't want to be her friend. I never have.

I want so much more.

For now, I'll let her go, but something's coming. I can feel it. I don't know why, but a series of events was set in motion this afternoon in Britt's old apartment

And I've learned to get the best, sometimes you have to be patient.

Chapter 4

Cass

"**A**NOTHER BOX ARRIVED!" MY AUNT CALLS FROM THE KITCHEN, and my head shoots up from the pillow as she continues muttering. "They just keep on coming."

"Fuck! I overslept." It's 7 a.m., the day before Britt's wedding, and I've got to get to the distillery.

The last few weeks have absolutely flown, and my stomach is in knots from needing everything to arrive on time, be set up properly, nothing broken, and all smooth sailing for the big day.

My top priority today is the cake, and I've brought everything to the industrial-sized kitchen at the distillery for it. I can put it all together and store it in the massive refrigerator for tomorrow.

Britt has always been such a good friend, and she's marrying the man of her dreams—her years and years of dreams, I happen to know. Planning this event is the only gift I have to give her, and I want it to be perfect.

"I'll get it," I yell, hopping around my room, pulling on black leggings and a white cotton tank top.

I yank an oversized sweater over my head, and it falls off one shoulder as I dash into the kitchen, whipping my hair into a ponytail on top of my head. "I'll be at the distillery all day, then I'm spending the night with Britt and Piper tonight. Bachelorette."

"Will you be drinking?" My aunt's eyebrow arches, and I fight my eye roll as I snatch the box off the counter.

"Yes, we'll be drinking. It's a celebration."

"I hope you don't plan to drive anywhere."

Everywhere in Eureka is walkable, but I don't bother pointing out the obvious. "We're staying at the apartment above the Star Parlor. All night."

"Bachelorette party." She shakes her gray head in a disapproving manner. "I'm sure you'll be doing things I don't want to know about."

I can't resist. "Yep, it'll be dildos and penis pops all night."

"Cassidy Dixon! I did not raise you to speak that way in my house…"

I don't have time to engage with her. I was thirteen when I came to her house, as grown as I would ever be. I simply call out a goodbye as I continue out the door to the strains of her speech about common decency and foul language.

Luckily, I haven't been around much this month to hear all her judgments and disapproving opinions on Britt moving in with Aiden before the wedding and "living in sin." I have no idea what I'll do after tomorrow.

Of course, my job hunt has been on hold as I've spent the bulk of this month planning the wedding. Alex said I could use his business account to order all the tables and place settings and plants and lights and everything. It's ultimately all the property of Stone Cold anyway, and it'll be packed up and stored on-site for the next event when we're done.

Five minutes later, I'm driving on the narrow, two-lane highway a mile outside of town where the distillery sits on ten acres of undeveloped country. It's a really beautiful drive, with the tall grass blowing in the sea breeze, the bright sun climbing higher in a baby-blue sky.

We're close enough to the coast, between Kiawah Island and Hilton Head, and tourists who know anything about bourbon often make a special trip to sample the famous, Stone Cold single-barrel reserve. I've been impressed by how many visitors a week they get.

I've also been impressed by how hard Alex works. He's either meeting with advertisers and liquor influencers, which is a thing—*who knew?*—or crunching numbers or checking batches or talking to suppliers or greeting guests and serving as bartender while he explains the process.

I really had no idea how much work went into making something like this successful. I always thought it was just alcohol. How hard do you have to sell it? Apparently, the answer is pretty hard if you want to be the very best on the market.

His Tesla is in his reserved spot, and my stomach tightens when I see it. As much as I've tried, I haven't been able to forget the night he drove me home, touching his face, looking into his smoky hazel eyes.

It was the second time that day he'd looked at me like he wanted to devour me. The first was in Britt's apartment when I caught him fresh out of the shower, and I couldn't deny the blaze of desire it sent racing to my toes.

It's going to work out for you, Cass. The slight rasp in his low voice made me want to kiss him. The unspoken invitation in his gaze made me want to straddle his lap and indulge my fantasy from earlier in the day.

Somehow, I managed to walk away. The last time I was in a similar situation with him, sixteen years ago, I didn't walk away. He was the cutest boy in town, and I'd noticed him my first day here, standing in the Pack-n-Save, holding an Icee. It made me think living with my aunt might not be so bad after all.

He'd watched me, and I might have added a little extra swish in my step for his benefit. Then after that day at the beach, he completely turned on me. A wall came down between us, and he acted like nothing had even happened, like I hadn't even kissed him.

Worse, he acted like we weren't even friends.

I decided that's what I got for giving away free kisses, and he'd be waiting a long time before he got another one, no matter how supportive he might sound. *Fool me once…*

Shaking these silly, childish thoughts aside, I leave the box on my passenger's seat—it's for tonight anyway—and hop out of my old gray Subaru Outback, Roger. Best car for the money, and also the easiest to work on, not that it ever needs it.

Alex is around here somewhere, but I head straight for the kitchen. I've got a cake to bake and decorate, sixty place settings to arrange, since we didn't cut the twenty extra guests, and assembly workers to direct this afternoon setting up the stages and the lights and the sound system.

That'll just leave the flower delivery in the morning, and we'll be all set to roll. My breath tightens in my lungs. We're so close. It's going to be so beautiful, but now I have to calm down and focus on the cake.

Stepping into the huge, walk-in storage closet, I find the giant canister of cake flour I carried over earlier this week. Baking powder and baking soda up next, butter, cinnamon, dark brown sugar, cream cheese, buttermilk, and a carton of eggs.

Setting my portable Bluetooth speaker on the metal counter, I pull up my favorite Haim playlist and start dragging out the measuring cups, parchment paper, cake stand, and bowls to the opening drum beats of "The Steps." The guitar chords ring out, and my hips start to sway along with my ponytail.

My sweater is off, and I'm up to my elbows in cake flour belting out the words to the song as I beat in the eggs. Shimmying my shoulders, I toss my ponytail as I prep the magic—my special snickerdoodle filling.

I don't know how much time has passed. I'm singing along with Haim's first hit "Forever," when I feel a presence behind me. I've never really been mystical like Britt's family, but it's like I have some sort of sixth sense for him.

Glancing over my shoulder, I bite my bottom lip instinctively when I see Alex Stone leaning against the door frame watching me. He's casual today in jeans and a dark-green Henley that hugs his broad shoulders and muscled arms, which are crossed over his defined chest. The dark scruff on his cheeks is a little thicker, and a smile lifts the corner of his sexy mouth.

Jeez Louise. I turn back quickly to what I'm doing, so I don't blush like an idiot, managing a casual, "Hey, there!"

"She sings, she bakes..." His low voice is fire in my veins as he walks into the kitchen. "*And* she dances."

"You were spying on me again." My voice is calm, playful even.

"You were singing again." He stands on the opposite side of the large, metal table where I'm combining brown sugar, flour, and cinnamon for the swirl. "Not Broadway this time, but I like it."

"It's impossible not to like Haim." I give the filling a final stir, and it's ready to be added to the batter.

"Who's Haim?" He walks around the table separating us to the long one behind me where the six pans holding the cake batter are waiting.

"A sister group out of Los Angeles. They open for Taylor Swift sometimes on the West Coast." He looks at me blankly, and I exhale a little laugh. "They're amazing."

"You're amazing."

Don't blush. Don't blush. Don't blush. His low voice is so certain, like it's an indisputable fact, and I wish it didn't completely throw me off balance.

I clear my throat and answer with a soft, "Thank you," focusing on the bowl in front of me and not the heat of his body so close to mine.

"You've done a lot of work these last few weeks. I'm eager to see it all come together tomorrow. I lined up a photographer to take some marketing photos…" He glances from what I'm mixing to the waiting pans behind me. "Cinnamon roll cake?"

"Close. It's my famous snickerdoodle cake." I take a small spoon and dip it into the filling I've just finished and hold it out for him to taste.

Hazel eyes meet mine as he places his full lips on the spoon, and my stomach dives. We've drifted past each other so long, like two stars in space, and now with Britt's wedding, we've been pushed closer together. Our attraction is elemental, like the pull of gravity…

And I'm acting dickmatized. Alex Stone has never shown any interest in me—other than for a free peep show. I'm not throwing myself at him again. I have some pride, after all.

His eyebrows rise, and he blinks a few times. "That's fucking delicious."

Not gonna lie. My pride loves hearing that. "Wait til I put it in the cake."

"This is *your* recipe? As in, you made it up?"

"It's not that hard." I shrug. "I'd been baking for a while, so I was used to how the flavors combined and the behavior of the ingredients. I just started experimenting with tastes I loved or other people loved. This one's based on a cinnamon sugar Pop-Tart. Britt loved those when we were in high school, and after I made it, it was her favorite cake."

"You're a cake artist."

"More like I know what works together, and I'm not afraid to try new things." I glance up at him, thinking we have something in common. "It's like your bourbon. It's your grandfather's recipe, but I'm sure you take a few liberties to make it yours."

"Not with the single barrel. With the special reserve, I take liberties. But the original is all Thomas Woolsen."

"Was that his name? Thomas Woolsen?" Leaning my hip against the counter, I'm so curious. I don't know anything about the old man whose death brought us together all those years ago.

"Yeah, I'm named for him."

"Alexander Thomas Stone." I say the words slowly, like I'm tasting them for the first time, and when I look up, he's studying my lips like he wants to taste me.

My stomach tightens, and my tongue slips out to wet my bottom lip.

He flinches before darting to meet my gaze again. "What will you do now?"

I blink, and it takes me a second to realize he means with the cinnamon filling.

"Oh," I breathe a laugh and snap out of my daydream, taking the bowl to where the pans of batter are waiting. "I add small spoonfuls to each of these."

He watches as I add the little dollops throughout the layers then spread them with a knife. As soon as I finish, he helps me slide the six pans into the waiting, industrial-sized double oven.

Then he picks up the bowl that held the cinnamon mixture and slides his finger over the side, taking another taste. "I'm already addicted."

"Just wait til you get a piece of the cake. That filling makes a sticky, chewy ribbon of cinnamon sugar in every bite."

"I'm with Britt. I think your baking era might be my favorite if this is what comes of it."

"If I had a kitchen this size with this much storage, it's possible baking might not be such a bad way to spend my time." Carrying the dirty pans to the sink, I switch on the hot water and grab the dish soap. "The problem is once you start doing something you love for money, the love fades, and it turns into just another job."

Alex grabs a towel and takes the clean pan from me to dry. We're standing side by side in front of the sink, and his warmth, his interest is all new and attractive to me. He's so easy to talk to, and it's cool to discover we have things in common.

After three years of high school in which we never

interacted, he went away to the naval academy, then into the military.

He's been back five years. What have I been doing for five years? Wasting half of them on Drake Redford, the conceited dick.

"Except babies." His voice is thoughtful.

"What?"

"Britt said working with kids is something you love."

"Oh…" I exhale a laugh. "It's that little hit of dopamine. Kids are the one job that hugs you back.

The last bowl is washed, and I turn my back to the sink as I watch him dry it. His hands are large and strong with nice, long fingers and neat, clean nails. His sleeves are pushed up to reveal muscular forearms with a few veins, and a heavy, stainless-steel watch is on his wrist along with a dark leather bracelet. My eyes flicker to his waist, and I have to suppress the memory of what's hiding in his pants.

"If they like you." He tosses the towel over his broad shoulder, smiling and looking too good.

These feelings are all fresh and unexpected—and motivated by seeing him naked, of course. Brilliantly, unbelievably naked.

And I've got work to do.

Grabbing the large metal bowl off the standing mixer, I start on the cinnamon buttercream frosting. "That's why I made the distinction. *Little* kids. Once they hit puberty, it all gets tricky."

Brown sugar, butter, cream cheese, vanilla extract, and a pinch of salt all gradually make their way into the mixer. Alex continues hanging out at the counter beside me, being far too distracting and not leaving.

I arch an eyebrow at him. "Don't you have somewhere to be?"

That makes him laugh. "Are you trying to get rid of me?"

"I'm worried about my frosting. You're watching it like a hungry predator about to pounce."

"What makes you think I'm watching your frosting?"

My jaw drops, and I swear, this man. "Are you sexually harassing me, Mr. Stone?"

"I'm not your boss, and it's Alex to you." The tease in his tone is fucking hot, but he takes a little turn. "Actually, I was thinking about how I've gotten used to you being here this past month. After tomorrow, it all comes to an end."

It's the same feeling I had this morning, and I'm surprised to hear him say it out loud.

"Are you going to miss me?" Giving him a little wink, I wonder if he might ask me on a date.

"I haven't seen you enough to miss you." That flat response, pops that bubble. "But I like what you've done with the event space. You're really good at this job you say you don't want. Maybe you could train someone to do what you've done here?"

Placing my hand on my hip, I face him. "You are the most unpredictable man. One minute it feels like you're encouraging me, then the next you're not, then you spin it again."

"I don't understand." His dark brow furrows over those gorgeous hazel eyes. "Is that a yes?"

"I'm doing all this for Britt. I'm doing my very best work because she's my very best friend. It doesn't change the fact that I'm almost thirty with no job, no money, and back to living with my super judgy aunt who drives me completely batshit crazy."

"Is *that* a yes?"

"Yes, it's a yes. Of course I'll train someone."

Alex nods. "Okay, then."

His jaw is set, and he seems to have made a decision. Only, I'm not sure it's the decision I'd hoped he'd make, and I'm cringing at my oversharing gaffe. TMI, Cass, jeez.

When he gets to the door he pauses. "I think you have

to do things you're not passionate about until you're able to do the thing you are. It's how we learn to appreciate our accomplishments."

"Is that your experience?" Frustration mingles with my embarrassment.

I'm sure it's easy to say when you're Alex fucking Stone, Mr. I'm Sure All the Time. He's never been in my shoes, and his job isn't a chore. He seems to really like it.

"Yeah." He gives me one last look, up and down. "I'll be in touch."

"Love can be fun!" Britt sings at the top of her lungs, dancing around the tiny living room of her old loft apartment.

She's belting out her favorite Shania Twain song, the song that saved her life last year, and Edward the bloodhound sits up on the couch and begins to howl at the top of his lungs.

"Sing it, Edward!" Piper calls from the kitchen, where she's mixing up watermelon margaritas.

We've recreated our favorite girls' night: movies, margaritas, Shania, and a box of bachelorette-party accessories I ordered online from Booty's Bachelorette Loot. Britt's wearing a headband with *Bride* in big pink letters above her head and a sash that reads *Same penis forever*. She's fanning herself with a big face on a stick, featuring Aiden's big face, of course.

Piper and I are wearing headbands that read *Let's go girls* and necklaces that say, *Drunk AF*. Britt's necklace reads *Engaged AF*.

"These watermelon margaritas go down too easy!" Britt shouts from where she's standing by the Bluetooth speaker, shaking her butt as she sips.

Nodding, I take a sip of my third, as I skip over to join her. "They're delicious!" My voice is too loud, and I put on the Shania classic, point to my headband, and yell, "Let's go, girls!"

She cranks the music, and we bump hips. I'm doing my best to drown my frustrating life and turn up the party.

"Why aren't we using these?" Piper skips over with her drink in one hand, dropping penis straws in each of our glasses. "Suck it!"

We all take sips, and Britt holds up her phone to take a selfie of the three of us with tiny penises clutched between our lips.

"Aiden's going to love this." She cackles, hitting send before skipping to the kitchen for a refill.

"I think we've made it to the bottom." I slide my fingers around the empty cardboard box, and all that's left is a receipt and a bumper sticker that reads *I got my BBL at Booty's.*

"What's that?" Piper takes it from me, then snorts a laugh.

"What's a BBL?" Britt's nose wrinkles.

"Seriously?" I cry. "You didn't know what vabbing was, and now you don't know what a BBL is?"

"Sorry I have a job, and I can't hang out on social media all day!"

"Rude!" I throw the penis-shaped stress ball at her, and she catches it. "BBL is Brazilian Butt Lift. It's when they take the fat from your thighs or your stomach or your arms or wherever, and they inject it into your butt to make it fuller."

Her brow furrows, and she looks over her shoulder. "Does it work?"

"Millions of Kardashians can't be wrong," Piper deadpans.

"Why can't we simply love the body we're in?" Britt complains. "There's so much pressure on women to look a certain way. It's ridiculous in this day and age…"

"Movie time!" I stand, cutting off her lecture and waving the remote to her flatscreen television. "What do we want? *Magic Mike XXL* or *Steel Magnolias*?"

They both look at me like *seriously?*

Once again, Piper deadpans, "Read the room, Cass."

"Yeah, read the room!" Britt throws the penis stress ball at me, and it bounces off my head.

"Hey! Don't throw penii at me!" I look all around my feet, but the little bugger seems to have disappeared. "Is it penii or penises?"

"Penises." Naturally, Piper as editor and publisher of the *Eureka Gazette* knows.

Edward puts his head on his paws, and we climb onto the sofa to watch some hot male bods. It's not long before we're squealing at Joe's naked butt tackling Channing into the pool to the tune of "Crazy Train."

Britt puts her head on my shoulder, and I feel her phone vibrate in her hip pocket. She fishes it out and laughs softly as she reads the screen.

"What?" I gently give her a nudge.

"Aiden says the guys are not having half as much fun as we are."

"What are they doing?"

"Alex closed the distillery, so they're hanging there. It's pretty low-key."

"I guess we're not really party animals."

"It's kind of hard to be a party animal in Eureka, South Carolina." Piper sighs, and a fresh wave of panic twists in my chest.

"Am I letting you down? Should I have booked a trip to New Orleans?" My temple throbs, but Britt grabs my hand, hopping onto her knees.

"You have done so much for me! I'm so happy to be right here in this loft for the first time in months with my best friends and my dog watching silly movies and wearing penises and drinking watermelon margaritas!" She squeezes me harder, reaching out to grab Piper's shoulder and pull her close. "I couldn't be happier if I lived in Las Vegas and we were all out on the strip sweating our asses off!"

"We can sweat our asses off right here!" Piper cries, and tears heat my eyes as I start to laugh.

"Promise?" I wipe my nose with the back of my hand.

"We might not get to do this again for a while." Britt hugs me one more time before flopping onto her butt and propping her feet on the narrow coffee table. "Now sit down here, and let's watch this movie before we fall asleep all over each other in that bed."

"I call the couch!" Piper yells.

I push her with my foot. "You always do."

"If I learned anything from my mom, it's to be prepared."

That makes us all laugh, since Piper's mom, Martha, is a doomsday prepper. I settle down between my two besties with Edward breathing his doggy breath over all of us sipping my watermelon margarita and feeling pretty content.

I might not have a job. I might not have any money or prospects, and my aunt might drive me crazy. But these two ladies always have my back.

Chapter 5

Alex

"To the man who gave up on faith, love, and all the rest of it." I hold up my tumbler of single-barrel, and our youngest brother, Adam, laughs.

"Dude, you did not go there."

"It's okay, I can take it." Aiden clinks his tumbler against both of ours. "It's true. I'd given up on pretty much everything after Annemarie. It's no secret."

I closed the bar in Stone Cold early, quite the feat for a Friday night, not that Eureka has a burgeoning nightlife. Just the opposite, in fact. Now the three of us are here giving our big brother a low-key bachelor send-off that suits him as sheriff, oldest, and a father.

It's the three of us giving each other shit, occasionally sharing what's on our minds, being together. After losing Pop then Dad a year later then five years later getting hit again, first by Adam's best friend Rex then Aiden's first wife Annemarie, we've developed the habit of coming to each other when life overwhelms us.

Adam and Aiden possibly more than me.

"Britt was always something special." Adam smiles, and mischief is in his eyes. "Hell, I thought about asking her out a few times myself."

Our youngest brother's announcement has the desired effect. Aiden's nostrils flare, and his chest puffs larger.

"Those days are over." A little growl is in his voice.

Adam holds up both hands, winking at me. "Pump the brakes, big guy. I'm just yanking your chain."

"Little shit," I chuckle, pouring Adam a finger of bourbon. "You can't resist."

"It's too easy." Adam lifts his tumbler. "All jokes aside, it's been inspiring to watch Britt Bailey melt your cold, cold heart. I thought you were a lost cause."

"Just because I wasn't interested in all your self-help nonsense?"

"There's a lot to be said for forgiveness and not holding grudges. That's how you get cancer."

Aiden turned dark after his wife was hit by a car walking home one evening. Then he found out she'd been having an affair right up to her death, and he went even darker.

For a long, long time he was so fiercely angry, even I wasn't sure he'd ever find his way back to the light. Until Britt drove back into town in a beat-up Ford pickup with bad brakes.

"May we all be so lucky as to be nearly run over by a truck." I can't resist, now that Aiden's actually smiling at people again.

"Don't get too cocky." He levels his gaze on me. "You're up next."

"Not me." I shake my head. "Love is not on my agenda."

"That's what I said."

"I'm not you."

"No, you're not." Aiden squints one eye at me. "You'll probably pine after some girl for years instead of taking your shot."

"I like how you make me sound like an asshole." My sarcasm hides my surprise. *What the fuck is he, a psychic?* "I prefer not to rush into things. I take my time with relationships, just like I take my time with whiskey."

"Women are not whiskey."

"You said a mouthful there, brother." Adam shoves his light brown hair away from his blue eyes.

Aiden holds his tumbler, pointing at both of us. "I'm picking up on a lot of unspoken shit right now. What are you two not saying?"

Luckily his phone buzzes, and he finishes his drink before checking the message.

"You're off duty tonight, Sheriff." I pour him another finger of single barrel.

I add more to Adam's and my glasses as well when I glance up and see a light in Aiden's blue eyes. A smile breaks across his face, and I know it's a text from Britt. She's the one person besides his son who can make him smile that way.

"What is it?" I ask, nodding at the device.

She's with Cass and Piper tonight, and I haven't been able to get Cass Dixon off my mind since our encounter in Britt's apartment. Watching her today in the kitchen swaying her cute little ass while she made the most delicious cake I've ever tasted didn't help matters.

Then she said my name that way, Alexander Thomas Stone. I'm not pining for her, and I'm not blowing my shot, despite what my oldest brother might say. Cass has been a variable I've never had time to solve for, and now that my life is somewhat calm, perhaps I can start.

"Bachelorette party." Aiden turns the phone so Adam and I can see the photo, and I almost choke on my drink.

Britt's in the middle with her two friends on each side of her, and they all have their full lips pursed around tiny dicks. It's silly, but damn, the image it conjures hits me directly below the belt.

The thought of Cass on her knees, looking up at me that way with my dick in my mouth… A sheen of sweat forms on the back of my neck, and I feel myself looking at it too long. Apparently, I'm not the only one.

Aiden whips his phone away, and now it's his turn to hassle us. "What the fuck were those looks about? Adam, you'd better not be thinking of Britt, or I'll punch your microdick."

"Microdick, my ass." He adjusts his crotch. "I wasn't looking at Britt."

My eyes cut to our youngest brother. He'd better not be thinking of Cass the same way I was, or we're going to have a problem.

"You're still hung up on that promise you made about Piper?" Aiden puts his phone face down on the bar, and my eyes linger on it.

"That was between us." Adam's voice changes in a way that pulls my attention to him.

His eyes are downcast, and he's sliding his thumb up and down the side of his glass.

"What's this about a promise?" I polish off my drink and lean my forearms on the bar. "Sounds more like you two are keeping secrets from me."

"It's nothing." He pushes the glass away.

"That look wasn't nothing."

With a heavy exhale, he explains. "The night of his accident, Rex made me promise to take care of Piper if anything happened to him."

"The same night?" He nods, and I'm quiet a moment, wondering if he has already had the thought I'm having. "Do you think it might not have been an accident?"

His best friend Rex died in a shocking, fiery accident after his motorcycle slammed into a light pole on the highway between Eureka and Hilton Head. State Troopers theorized he'd been clipped by a car, but it was impossible to know for sure from the wreckage.

Aiden's lips tighten, and he looks down.

Adam shakes his head, studying his glass. "I don't know."

"Did he know you had a thing for her?" Blue eyes cut to mine, and I hold up both hands. "Sorry, just asking. It's clear on your face you have feelings for her."

My youngest brother's jaw clenches, and guilt laces his response. "I don't know."

Reaching over, Aiden clasps his shoulder. "It's not a crime. It's been nine years. You should test those waters."

"Hell, yeah. You've already got a head start. Ryan adores you."

Piper's son is the same age as Owen, and they've been best friends since preschool.

"Piper can do so much better than me." Adam rests his elbow on the bar, pinching his lips between his fingers. "I was such a fuckup after all that happened, doing drugs, taking chances. I had to go away to try and get straight."

Adam did spiral after his friend died, but if you didn't know him, you'd think he was just a free-spirited surfer dude, living life on the edge, only caring about the moment, the rush. We knew him better. We knew he was hurting.

"Whatever happened to Rex, accident or otherwise, it's not your fault." Aiden's low voice is a comfort.

Their seven-year age difference made it easier for him to step into Dad's role for Adam, but we were too close in age. I had always gone to Pop when I needed someone to hear me, and I'd lost them both in the space of two years. It wasn't my style to spiral, but it's a time I hope never to relive.

Pushing off the bar, I grab the special reserve bourbon I'd been saving. "While I appreciate this moment of brotherly bonding, it's not the vibe we're going for tonight. It's your last night as a free man. We've got to liven this shit up."

"Hell, I haven't been a free man in a year." That light is still in my older brother's eyes.

"I got this." Adam hops off his barstool, pointing at me as he heads for the sleek jukebox in the back corner of the room.

I take down three fresh tumblers and pour us each two

fingers from the new bottle. "I've been saving this one. It's my newest batch. No one's tasted it yet, and I'm pretty sure it's going to knock that fucking Pappy Van Winkle off its perch."

Blink 182's "All the Small Things" blasts through the room, and while I'm not the biggest fan of Adam's LA surf punk, it definitely shifts the mood to something more bachelor-party oriented.

He joins us, and we sample my newest blend as our conversation shifts. Seeing Aiden embracing life again renews my sense of optimism that after a decade of heartache, maybe the three of us are moving into a new phase of our lives. One with more positive outcomes.

The song changes to the Red Hot Chili Peppers' version of "Higher Ground," and I concede. "Good one."

Aiden smiles in agreement before lifting his chin at me. "What are you going to do with Pinky next month?"

My brow furrows, and I glance up at him. "What do you mean?"

"Are you kidding?" Adam laughs. "Mom's been talking about her trip to Lake Como every Sunday for weeks."

I'm still frowning as Aiden explains. "She and Aunt Paige are taking Aunt Pearl to Italy to celebrate her 70th birthday. They rented a villa for the month."

"A month?" My throat tightens. "Why is this the first I'm hearing about it?"

"Because you don't pay attention? They're leaving right after the wedding."

"What the fuck?" My voice rises. "You'd think she'd have warned me."

Adam leans on the bar, chuckling. "It's almost like she expects you to pay attention when she speaks."

"I pay attention, but things have changed a lot in the last year." Since Britt and Aiden got engaged, Britt's mother Gwen and grandmother Edna have joined the Sunday lunch crew, and occasionally Cass and Piper show up. "It's not as easy to keep up in the crowd."

"Because you like things quiet and sneak off before dessert is served."

I can't argue with Adam's observation. When the group grows bigger than twelve, plus Britt's bloodhound, it's when I miss my fishing trips with Pop the most. I like peace and quiet. So sue me.

"I'm not sure how anybody knows what's going on when you're all talking at the same time."

"We can trade off," Aiden volunteers. "Trust me, her absence puts a crimp in Britt's and my honeymoon period, too."

"I've got you both covered." Adam points to me. "I can help you with P until you find a sitter, and Owen and Ryan are easy to watch. They keep each other entertained."

"Thanks, bro, but I'm going to need more than a sitter." Scrubbing my forehead, I try to think. For weeks, I've talked about finding a full-time nanny for my daughter, but there wasn't a sense of urgency.

Not to mention, no one has floated down on an umbrella ready to fill the position.

Unless…

Cass jumps to the forefront of my mind. She's looking for a place to live, a job working with kids, and I'd pay her well. It feels like a solution.

It also feels risky.

While Aiden and Adam are making plans for the boys, I'm wondering if it's possible to have a woman I'm lusting after under my roof full time without blurring the line between employee and employer.

The problem is I want to blur the line, and I'm running out of patience.

Chapter 6

Cass

SUNLIGHT BURNS ACROSS MY CLOSED EYES, AND MY HEAD JUMPS OFF the pillow. "Ohh… shit." The pain of a hangover slams me down again. "Too many watermelon margaritas!"

Last night, when we finally crashed, I made Piper give me the couch, since I have to get to the distillery to meet the florist first thing. Across from me Britt is on her back in the queen-sized bed, eye mask securely in place, making puppy-dog snores. Edward is at her feet, and Piper is beside her with her head under the pillow.

I try one more time to get up, grasping assorted pieces of furniture for balance as I take the ten steps to the small bathroom. Running cold water over a washcloth, I hold it to the back of my neck while I inspect the damage in the mirror.

Mascara is smeared under my eyes, and I vaguely remember us sitting on the rug, holding hands as we belted out "Wildest Dreams" by Taylor Swift and crying like a bunch of drunk dorks. I'm pretty sure Edward was howling along with us.

"I'm never drinking again." Grabbing a face wipe, I scrub

the makeup off my eyes and quickly apply tinted moisturizer and a fresh coat of mascara.

My hair is a wreck, but I don't have time. I whip it up into a ponytail, and once the flowers are in place, I'll cut out early to shower and repair the damage. I grab the bottle of ibuprofen out of the medicine cabinet and swallow two pills with a handful of water from the sink.

Stepping out of the bathroom, the sound of Britt's tiny snores makes me grin, and I study my two best friends, plus Edward the dog. I wouldn't trade last night for anything, even if it does mean I have the hangover from hell.

The big day is finally here. I've been busting my ass for a month, and it's going to be the very model of a modern *Town & Country* wedding.

It's been a lot of work, but it's all been pretty straightforward and drama-free. I'm so thankful Britt's not one of *those* brides. She's always been more traditional than her nutty family, but she's no bridezilla.

I'm sure wanting such a traditional ceremony has more to do with Aiden's family than hers. Britt's family would fit right in at the Elvis Chapel in Vegas, but she wants the fairytale. Hungover or not, I'm making sure she gets it today.

Pulling my faded denim overalls over my hips, I fasten one shoulder strap over my white tank and grab my phone.

"Ugh…" Piper groans softly from the bed, pulling her auburn head out from under the pillow. "You're actually moving? What are you? Immortal?"

"Hardly," I whisper, stepping into beige Birkenstocks. "I've got to get to the distillery to meet the florist. I'll see you two this afternoon."

"You're a machine. I'm going to die now." She shoves her head under the pillow again, and I exhale a laugh.

Her son Ryan spent last night with Owen at Aiden's mom's house. All three of the kids are in the wedding, and Patricia and

Gwen are in charge of getting them to the distillery on time, dressed and ready to perform.

My money's on Patricia for doing the lion's share of that job. Gwen is probably telling them supernatural stories and trying to feed them the dusty Fig Newtons she keeps in the pockets of her caftan. I have to hand it to her—it does keep them occupied when things get slow.

Owen is the ring bearer, Ryan is an usher, and Pinky is the petal girl. They're so cute, and they take their jobs very seriously, although I am a little worried about Pinky.

I had the florist make a special basket for her just in case she tripped over her floor-length dress. Alex's daughter is as serious about dropping petals as her father is about crafting bourbon, and remembering her little face at the rehearsal makes me smile as I drive out to the venue. I don't know her well, but at four and a half, she's a pistol.

Parking in the space beside Alex's empty reserved spot, I hop out just as the florist truck pulls into the lot.

"Perfect timing." I step out and wave at them, shouting over the noise of the truck while shading my eyes from the painful morning sun. "Pull around back."

I point to the loading area where the event space is located. God, I need coffee. It's an hour later and a million trips back and forth unloading flowers before I get a cup, thanks to Alex walking out to check on our progress.

"You're looking better than I expected after last night." He sizes me up from behind dark sunglasses.

"It's all an act." Lifting my chin, I nod towards the kitchen. "If I don't get a cup of coffee soon, I'm gonna…"

"Hold that thought." The smile curling his lips manages to do fuzzy things to my insides, despite my hungover state.

Get a grip, Cass. You've got work to do.

I return to helping the delivery guys arrange the small, floral centerpieces on each table. Men on ladders are wrapping twinkle lights around the rafters, and burly guys roll in

Ficus trees, paradise palms, and yuccas to fill in the gaps at the edges of the room and behind the stage.

"Here." Alex puts a cup of coffee in my hand, and I straighten from where I've just placed a centerpiece.

Sniffing the warm, dark liquid, I take a sip, and my whole body shudders. "Oh, that's so good." Alex chuckles softly beside me, and my eyes flutter open. "I owe you my life."

"We stayed up pretty late, too." He nods at the small table bouquet. "Hibiscus?"

"Hibiscus, zinnias, and daisies." I point to each bloom. "Britt said no matter what, *no lilies*, especially not stargazers. She made me swear."

"Stinkgazers," he says under his breath, and my ears quirk.

"Yeah, something like that. Aiden hates them?"

"We all do." He lifts a small glass bowl containing the arrangement. "We came off a series of bad years all punctuated by stargazer lilies. These are perfect."

He's so emphatic, it makes me laugh.

"Whatever you say." My eye catches on the clock over the door, and my heart drops. "Shit! It's already three? I've got to get out of here!"

I start to go when Alex catches my arm. "Wait, I need to talk to you about something... A job."

If this is about running his event planning, I might be a lot more open to the idea now that Britt's wedding is over, and I'm facing a long string of endless days of Aunt Carol's judgy lectures.

Still, I'm not going to make it if I don't go now.

Catching his hand, I meet his eyes. "I'm interested, but I've got to get ready. Let's talk after the wedding."

"Done." His voice is so empathic, I feel like we don't even need to talk later. It's decided.

We will talk, but for now, I've got to get ready.

"I now pronounce you Mr. and Mrs. Aiden Stone. You may kiss the bride." Old Reverend Shepherd holds out his hands, and for a split second, Aiden studies Britt's face.

She's absolutely stunning in a white sleeveless gown with a full, tulle skirt. Her blonde hair is arranged in loose waves down her back.

My heart squeezes in my chest, and Piper's chin drops. As Britt's only two bridesmaids, we're both dressed in tan satin slip-dresses. Mine is knee-length, while Piper's flows to the floor. Our hair is loose down our backs as well, with two little French braids on each side to hold it out of our eyes.

The guys are all in black, two-piece suits with ties that match our dresses, the only difference being Aiden's is a bow tie. I'm doing my best not to look at Alex every few seconds, but it's difficult.

He's the darkest of the three brothers, and the suit fits him perfectly. The light scruff of a beard is neat on his cheeks, and his dark, wavy hair is smoothed behind his ears. I fight my eyes dropping below his waist, and every time his hazel eyes meet mine, I'm sure he knows.

I don't want to talk to him about a job later. I want to talk to him about getting to know each other better, about continuing what we started this weekend.

My rebellious eyes slide to his again, and this time it's like a roll of thunder. A subtle smile curls his full lips, and heat rises in my cheeks. Imagining him looking at me the same way, thinking what I'm thinking, makes my pussy clench.

Aiden lifts Britt's veil for the kiss, and my gaze returns to them. The soft yellow lights behind them cast a glow, and I make a mental note to give this florist a rave review.

The full effect of the sparkling event space, the flowers on the backs of the chairs, the lights, the family, and the guys

standing at the front, smiling and waiting for us is perfectly gorgeous. It's sacred.

Aiden cups Britt's small face in his hands, smiling deeply into
her fast-blinking eyes, and the tears I was holding now spill onto
my cheeks. Piper presses the back of her hand to her lips, and a
few sniffles echo from the front row, where the moms are seated.

The love between Britt and Aiden is so pure and hard-won,
when their mouths unite, the room bursts into applause.

Britt's lips curl into a smile, and Aiden's do the same against
hers. One more longing look at each other, and they turn to their
friends and family as the recessional music begins.

I've never felt so surrounded by love—love flowing from
us to the audience and back again. I might have planned this
wedding, but I never could have conjured this atmosphere. It's
all for them.

Lifting the tissue I hid behind my bouquet, I dry my eyes
before nudging Piper. She takes it from me, and I gaze over the
crowd as they exit to the tasting room and the lawn while we
finish with photographs.

Happiness shines in my chest like the sun, until my eyes
land on the one gaze capable of ruining it all. It's like a shot of
lidocaine in the top of each of my cheeks.

My smile melts, and I cut my eyes at Piper. Only she's too
busy drying her tears and hugging Britt. I reach for her arm, but
the photographer appears and starts barking orders.

"We don't have much time before the guests return." The
young woman waves her hand, directing us to our positions.

"We might have to rethink this part for next time." Alex is
at my side, taking my arm. "If the weather's bad, we won't be
able to hustle the guests outside for twenty minutes."

"It's true." I'm distracted, scanning the faces of the guests
through the windows, but I don't see him.

"We only need a few shots of the entire party." The photographer orders us back to the places we held for the ceremony.

We hold as she takes several angles before moving through

the groups. She shoots the bridesmaids, the groomsmen, the mothers, the children, the happy couple. While we take photos, workmen break down the chairs and arrange the stage and the DJ booth.

It feels like an eternity passes of me chewing my nail before Britt grabs my hand. "Finally!" she hisses under her breath.

Aiden's finishing up with his brothers, as she hustles us to the doors leading to the tasting room. The little boys have ditched their suit jackets, and Pinky's running in circles, swinging her empty basket over her head and singing a made-up song about petal girls.

Britt throws open the doors and calls to the waiting crowd, "Time to party!"

Smiles and laughter greet us as they return to the event space. The bartenders take their stations, and the catering staff uncovers the large silver platters of food.

The DJ cranks up the music, and Britt loops her arms through Piper's and mine. Champagne flutes are placed in our hands, and we do a quick clink before drinking.

"You did it!" Piper smiles so big, and I hear a camera shutter click.

"Cass did it!" Britt clinks my glass again, and I take another sip, my eyes scanning the room for the face I saw earlier.

Maybe he was just here for the ceremony, and he's gone. Yes, I decide that must be what happened. The fist of nerves starts to unclench in my chest, when *fuck*.

"What's the matter?" Britt slides her arm around my waist. "Why are you frowning? It's all so beautiful!"

Turning my face to the side of her hair, I whisper, "Why is Drake Redford here? He wasn't on the guest list!"

"Oh." Her bottom lip slips between her teeth, and her nose wrinkles. "Aiden ran into him yesterday at the Pack-n-Save. He felt bad that Drake was in town for a visit, and he wasn't invited to the wedding. Everyone is here. Anyway, that's all ancient history, right?"

"Of course it is, but it's ancient history I never want to re-visit. Our breakup was not pretty. He told me I'd regret turning down his proposal, and I said I could do better. Now he'll see I *didn't* do better."

"But you *are* doing better! You're happy!"

"I can't even pay rent!" My fingernail is between my teeth again. "I hate being wrong."

"Were you wrong?"

"No..."

Still, I turned down the proposal of a millionaire real-estate developer, and now I'm unemployed with no job prospects and living at home again with Aunt Carol.

"Do you still have feelings for him?" Her whisper goes higher.

"No." Of that, I'm sure. "He was so annoying. He didn't like kissing with his tongue, he hated the sound of chewing..."

"If he didn't like tongue-kissing, I'm guessing he didn't like other tongue-things."

"You said it, sister. Not a single orgasm."

"So what's the big deal? Don't talk to him. Stay by me."

The DJ breaks through the music. "I need the bride and groom on the floor for their first dance together as husband and wife!"

Britt's lips twist, and I shake my head. "I can't dance with the two of you."

"You've got this. Drake Redford is the amoebas on fleas on rats."

Aiden steps up behind her, smile-frowning at her declaration. "Sorry, Cass, I need to borrow my wife."

"Sure." I shrug, waving my hand. "Take her away."

The opening monologue of Shania Twain's "From This Moment" whispers through the room, and Britt gives my hand a squeeze before Aiden sweeps her into his arms.

The melody begins, and the two of them sway slowly, gaz-ing into each other's eyes, dreamy smiles on their faces. A crowd forms at the edge of the dance floor to watch, and I scan the room for Piper.

When I find her, she's standing in the front row holding hands with Patricia and Gwen, and completely ignoring Owen and Ryan racing around the room like they've had ten sugary drinks each.

They probably have.

My eyes drift farther back, and I see Pinky holding Alex's hands as she stands on his feet, stepping side to side and twisting her hips so her full skirt swishes around her legs.

The sight makes my chest squeeze, and I want to linger and watch them. Instead, I take a step back… then another… and another…

I'm doing my best to fade into the crowd while slowly, unobtrusively making my way to the kitchen. I'm right there, all ready to slip through the door, when the unwelcome voice stops me.

"Here you are." The sound of his voice ignites irritation in my blood. "You're looking good."

It's not a compliment, more like surprise, as if I would've spiraled into hideousness without him.

Lifting my chin, I adopt the same tone of surprise. "You look well yourself."

Of course he does. Drake Redford comes from old Hilton Head family money. He's even wearing a beige linen suit and beige tie. His cheeks are burnished like he's been on his sailboat all day, and his longish, auburn-brown hair is stylishly messy around his collar.

So much wasted potential. I don't blame myself for falling for him, but I do blame myself for staying with him too long.

"What's new with you?" He tips his chin. "Or is it the same old thing?"

My lips tighten, but I hold my temper in check. "Well, for starters, I planned this wedding."

"You're in with the Stones?" He looks around, lifting an eyebrow. "Alex Stone is a bit of a wunderkind, taking his grandfather's business and turning it into a world-class brand before he was thirty. At this rate it'll be a billion-dollar label by the time he's thirty-five."

"He works his ass off. I can attest to that."

"You're together? Is it serious?" The arch in his eyebrow, the genuine astonishment in his voice, as if I could never appeal to someone like Alex Stone, fans an old anger in my chest.

"It's not really something we want to publicize. Tonight is all about the bride and groom."

"You and Alex Stone…" His eyes narrow, like he's calling my bluff. "I get why you'd latch onto him, but what does he see in you?"

"Everything he likes, I guess." I laugh, waving my hand so cavalier, so easy, *la-dee-dah*. "He especially loves my cake—*by the ocean*, if you know what I mean."

His brow lowers. "Is that so?"

I exhale a happy sigh. "He made saying *yes* so easy."

My brain is freaking out. *What the hell am I talking about?*

Luckily, the DJ rescues me from my big mouth. "Can I get the bridesmaids and the groomsmen on the floor for the friends and family dance?"

"Duty calls!" I smile, giving him a little wave. "Enjoy the party."

He watches me in a way that knots my stomach, but I fix my eyes on Alex, who's waiting on the dance floor, smiling.

He has no idea.

Chapter 7

Alex

CASS TAKES MY BREATH AWAY.

I know this night is all about my brother and Britt, but I can't take my eyes off her. I can't keep my thoughts from running down a rabbit hole of the two of us together. I could take her back to my office, sit her on the edge of my desk, run my hands under her silky skirt... higher up her smooth thighs, until I reach her center...

Even better, we could skip down to that little lagoon from years ago, strip off our clothes and slide our naked bodies together in the warm water.

The tan dress she's wearing hugs her curves in a way that ignites all my memories of her body like a centerfold, an image I've had the privilege of seeing twice. Her nipples pierce the thin fabric, and I instinctively swallow.

I want to roll those tight little peaks between my fingers. I want to lift her breasts in my hands and bury my face in her soft skin.

Getting through the ceremony without popping a boner

was a challenge. I tried not to stare at her the entire time, but every time our eyes met, it was a charge of electricity. Her cheeks warmed as if she knew what I was thinking, and I wondered if she might be thinking the same.

Now we're being called to dance together while Aiden dances with Mom and Britt dances with Owen. It's supposed to be very family-oriented and sweet, but the thoughts on my mind are as far from sweet as you can get.

The DJ cranks up an old Frank Sinatra hit about flying to the moon, and I'm ready to take her there.

She slips her slender hand in mine, and I pull her to my chest, speaking in her ear. "I can't get over how amazing everything turned out."

Her other hand is on my shoulder, and she leans back to meet my eyes. "It really came together well, didn't it?"

The yellow lights cast a soft glow over her skin, and for a moment, I'm that fifteen-year-old boy, struck by her beauty and at a loss for words.

"Only one thing is missing." My eyes trace the line of her cheek. "You didn't sing a song."

"Stop." A laugh whispers past her lips, and she leans forward. "You're embarrassing me."

"Why? You have a beautiful voice. I think it would've been the cherry on top."

"I think Britt has enough entertainment without me barging onto the stage."

"I don't think it would've gone that way."

"It's not happening."

Pressing my lips together, I trace a lock of hair behind her shoulder, and she shivers. It's fucking hot, but everyone is watching us.

"I only hope you can train someone to do half of what you've done here, and I can't wait for that cake."

"It's going to change your life." She gives me a teasing grin, her blue eyes shining.

"I believe it."

We're swaying side to side, and she feels so good in my arms. She smells like warm jasmine, and I want to taste her. I imagine nibbling her lips, teasing her slowly, building the pressure. The last thing I want to do is hire her, but I've run out of options.

I need help.

Her brow furrows, almost like she can sense my internal conflict. The song is on its last chorus, and I'm out of time.

"About that job I mentioned earlier, my mom is going to Italy for a month, and I have no one to help me with Penelope. I thought, since you like working with kids, you might consider being her nanny. Just until kindergarten starts in August?"

She blinks faster with every word, and when I finish, her lips part. "You want me to be your daughter's nanny?"

"For about three weeks—until school starts. Longer if you like doing it, of course. I have a garage apartment where you can stay, and all your meals would be included. If you want them. I'll pay you, of course."

Her eyes drift to where Pinky is standing on a chair in front of a baby in a carrier, arranging petals around its head, and her nose wrinkles with a smile. Not gonna lie, her reaction to my daughter is almost as captivating as the way she looked at me in Britt's apartment.

"Okay." Her eyes flicker to mine again. "I'll do it. When do you want me to start?"

"Is Monday too soon?"

The song ends, and an upbeat Bruno Mars tune brings the crowd onto the floor. I'm still holding Cass's hand, and I lead her off to where we can get a few drinks and finish our talk.

In my mind, I'm debating the ethics of being her employer while also wanting to sleep with her. It's completely unethical, which is why I'll encourage her to stop when Mom returns. Then when kindergarten starts, Cass will no longer work for me, and I can move to Plan B—getting her naked again.

The thought almost makes me chuckle, but a tall fellow I vaguely recognize steps in front of us, blocking our progress.

"Alex." He holds out a hand. "Drake Redford. It's been a long time."

"Ah, Drake." I shake his hand, and Cass stiffens at my side. "Good to see you again."

"I gotta say, you've impressed the hell out of me with this place." He claps me on the shoulder. "I've been tracking your success, and it's damn remarkable."

"Thank you."

Cass releases my hand and takes a subtle step behind me, almost as if she's trying to hide. Drake Redford is more Aiden's acquaintance. I've always thought he was something of a blowhard, and the way Cass is acting, as if she's trying to hide from him, makes me like him even less.

I'm about to make an excuse for us to leave when he continues. "What you've done here is a masterclass in brand development. You really should write a book. It would be a bestseller."

"I think I'll stick to making bourbon for now. Having a superior product is the real secret."

Sure, I bust my ass to get our single barrel in front of the people who matter, but Pop's original recipe is the true magic. I won't let him be left out of the equation.

"And I see you landed this pretty lady." He tips his head towards Cass, and her fingers tighten on my arm. "I'd be salty about it, but I guess you're the best man."

It's like he launched into speaking Russian. I don't understand a word he's saying. "I'm sorry, what? Aiden didn't actually have a best man..."

He steps forward, putting his arm over my shoulder and looking around like we're sharing a secret. "Cass told me you're keeping your engagement on the DL because of the wedding, but let me be the first to congratulate you."

A little yipping noise comes from behind me, and the skin on the back of my neck tightens. I step out of his embrace, glancing at Cass, whose face is tight. She told Drake Redford we're engaged?

I mean, naturally, I'm flattered. I like the idea of her thinking of me if she's in need of a romantic partner. On the other hand, *What the fuck?*

"I…" Hesitating, I study her pleading eyes and decide to play along for now. "I didn't realize you two were so close. Honey, you told him?"

"I'm sorry." Cass's voice is a little too high, her laugh a little too giggly. "But you know Drake. He just weaseled it out of me. He's such a rat."

"Yeah." I look from her to him and back again. "I can tell that about him."

"I'm trying not to get my feelings hurt by all these compliments." Drake laughs, pressing his palm to his chest. "I'll be honest, I didn't believe her at first. Speaking in the vernacular, I don't see no ring."

"It's being sized," I answer quickly, moving her hand into mine and lacing our fingers. "Now, if you'll excuse us. We were just on our way to my office."

"Slipping out for a *tête-à-tête*?" He gives me a smarmy grin. "I won't tell a soul."

He looks like he's on the verge of messaging Deux Moi the second we're gone, but I don't break character. "Thanks for not ruining our surprise."

He makes a comment as we leave about secrets being safe with him, but I'm still trying to get my head around the idea that Cass told him we're engaged. Why would she do that?

Instead of going to the bar as I'd originally intended, I take a detour through the tasting room all the way back to my office. Her hand is still clasped in mine, and her heels click on the wood floors as she trots to keep up with me.

When we reach our destination, I release her, flicking on the light and shutting the heavy wooden door. I press my back to it, and she walks to the opposite side of the room, turning her back to the bookshelves and facing me with wide eyes. Her chest moves up and down quickly with her breathing, and her nipples continue teasing me through the thin fabric of her dress.

My office is a large, elegant space with bookshelves and two leather armchairs across from a dark mahogany desk. A green banker's lamp is on the corner, but the center is wide open with only a leather blotting pad covering the shiny wood.

My fantasy of bringing her here earlier presses against my temples, and her breathless voice only fuels the fire. "I'm so sorry, Alex. I don't know how he got the idea we're engaged."

"You didn't tell him?" I slide my jacket off my shoulders, draping it over the arm of a leather chair. Next, I reach up and loosen my tie, lifting it over my head and unbuttoning my top two buttons.

"He came up to me before our dance, and he was being such an arrogant asshole to me—like always." She shakes her head, and my dislike of Drake Redford intensifies.

"In what way was he being an asshole to you?" I'm ready to find his ass again and make him apologize.

"He's just… I don't know." She shoves her hair behind her ears. "When we broke up, he said I'd regret it. He said I'd never be anything but an out-of-work hippie, then when he showed up and started asking me questions, I couldn't let him be right."

"So you told him we were together?"

"Sort of." Her eyes drop to the floor again. "He was going on and on about the distillery and your brand, and I said I could vouch for how hard you work. Then he asked if we were involved, and I didn't exactly say no… but I didn't say we were engaged."

"But you didn't correct him."

"No." Her tone is guilty.

I study her, wondering what to do with this information. She used me to protect her from her asshole ex. She told him we were together, and she made enough of a case that he got the idea I asked her to marry me.

My eyes narrow, and the more I think about it, the more I like it. I'd like to build on this foundation.

Closing the space between us, I reach out to lift her chin gently with my finger. "It's okay. I'm not mad."

"You're not?" Wide blue eyes meet mine, and damn, the truth hits me right in the chest.

Aiden was fucking right. I've been pining for this woman since I was a teenager, and I've never wanted to admit it. I've done other things, pursued other interests, went away for years…

And now I'm back.

And I'm not a boy anymore.

"Drake Redford's a prick. If it helps you save face with him, I can play along for a night."

"Oh my god, are you serious? You'd do that for me?"

"I can't see how it would hurt anything. Provided he *does* keep it a secret."

She skips forward, throwing her arms around my neck before stepping back quickly and holding out her hands. "Just til he leaves, and I'm so sorry again for dragging you into my mess."

"Stuff happens." I smile, leaning closer and speaking conspiratorially. "We'll lay it on thick. Make him sorry he… broke up with you?"

"Lord no, I broke up with him the night he proposed."

"Ouch!" I almost laugh. "He proposed, and you said no?"

"I should've done it long before then." Her annoyance starts to rise. "He was so lazy. It's like he didn't care if I was happy or satisfied. He just figured all his money would make up for it."

"I take it all his money did *not* make up for it?"

"It did not."

I'm glad to hear it. I'm glad she didn't settle for a big bank account instead of something more. I've got a bigger bank account, and I can give her a hell of a lot more.

"Live and learn." I hold out my hand. "Shall we return to the party? I think we've been back here long enough for his imagination to fill in the blanks."

She bypasses my hand, hugging my arm against her chest and rising up to kiss my cheek. "Thank you for this. You really are a good friend."

My insides recoil at her trying to friend-zone me, but I swallow back my impulse to shut it down. Instead, I have a better idea.

"Before we go, we need to do something."

"What's that?"

"Do you trust me?"

She nods in a sweet, obedient way that makes my dick hard and gives me all sorts of dirty thoughts. Setting my eyes on hers, I take her by the waist and pull her firmly against my chest. She inhales sharply, but I'm moving with purpose.

I cup the side of her cheek with one hand, threading my fingers in her silky, dark hair and giving it a gentle pull.

Before she can say another word, I cover her mouth with mine.

Chapter 8

Cass

MY HEAD SPINS, MY PANTIES IGNITE, AND THE EARTH DISAPPEARS from beneath my feet.

Alex Stone is kissing me.

No, he's not just kissing me, he's making love to my mouth.

His lips slide across mine, then he nips my upper one lightly with his teeth before tracing my bottom one with his tongue. He's tasting me, sampling me, and my pussy squeezes with need.

He smells like soap and spice and warm woods, and he feels like strength and domination and ownership. My eyes close, and my fingers curl against his hard biceps.

His arm circles my waist, and our mouths open. Tongues curl, and he tastes like fine bourbon and cinnamon. He tastes like all my desires.

I exhale a broken whimper. I'm hot and slick, and my hands move higher to his broad shoulders, holding tight so I don't melt to the ground. I press my body against his, and he growls low in response. My nipples tighten, and I want *more*.

I want him to slide his hands down to my ass. I want him

to gather my skirt in his fingers and rip my thong away. I want him to spin me around and bend me over his desk. I want him to take out his thick cock and drive it deep and hard, over and over.

It's pressing against my stomach, and I've been dreaming of him fucking me since the day I saw him nude in Britt's apartment. I'm not thinking about humiliating Drake anymore. I'm not thinking about our conversation on the dance floor.

The only thing on my mind is Alex Stone standing in front of me naked, water running down the lines of his muscles, hazel eyes focused on mine like a predator, cock hardening and lifting with need for my body.

His head moves, and I chase his lips with mine. I'm acting on pure instinct now, needing more of this drug he's allowed me to sample.

I'm already addicted.

But his hand loosens on the side of my head. He slides his thumb down my cheek, and his kisses go from deep and consuming to light and withdrawing.

I almost cry out, *No…* as he steps back, bracing me against the bookcase.

Blinking slowly, I look up into his eyes, and he quirks a grin. "You okay?"

Nodding, it takes me a minute to find my voice. "Yeah…"

"Good." He turns, sweeping his jacket off the chair and pulling it over his still-unbuttoned shirt. "We can't act like we've never done that before if we're engaged."

I look down, giving my head a little shake to get my brain going again. I need a fresh pair of underwear. I need a moment alone to finish what he's started.

"Ready to head back to the party?" He's so casual.

Is he seriously unaffected by what just happened? I've never been kissed like that in my life, and I'm pretty sure I wasn't imagining the possession in his embrace. I definitely didn't imagine that growl or the curl of his fingers against my scalp.

He straightens his collar and reaches for my hand, pulling

it into the crook of his arm. Then he opens the door, and we're walking down the narrow hall, past the enormous wooden barrels of whiskey, to the event space where the sounds of the "Cha-Cha Slide" echo.

"Not sorry we missed that one." He exhales a laugh, nodding at the bartender serving a pair of guests leaning against the tasting bar.

"Hey, where have you been?" I recognize Piper's voice and realize the couple at the bar is Piper and Adam.

Alex straightens beside me. "What are you two doing out here?"

"We had to get out of there." Piper waves her hands towards the event space. "If I'm forced to do the Cha Cha Slide one more time… It's bad enough they do it at every single school function."

"I asked Sam to open the tasting bar for us." Adam motions to the stocky guy behind the bar, who gives Alex a nod.

"Can I pour you something, Mr. Stone?"

"Sure, give us two?" He glances at me, and I nod. "Two special reserves."

He's so confident, like the earth didn't completely move just now in his office.

By contrast, I can't meet his eyes without blushing—and it's the last thing I need Piper and her inquiring mind to see. She'll be on us like a duck on a june bug.

"What's the Charlie Brown anyway?" Piper's still fussing about the music.

"It's a little back and forth donkey move." I show her, and she snorts a laugh.

"How do you know that?"

"Preschool dance classes."

The song starts to fade, and the "Cupid Shuffle" kicks off, mixing into the beat.

"Somebody needs to unplug that DJ," Piper groans. "Excuse

me, Miss Wedding Planner, did you know he was going to play these songs?"

"Britt asked for them! She said the kids will love it, and they're easy for the older people who don't know how to dance that well."

"I do not call following orders dancing."

"When are they cutting the cake?" Alex touches my arm. "I can't wait to taste it."

The rumble in his voice sends my mind to the very naughty place I described to Drake. I'd be happy for Alex to taste my *cake by the ocean*, but I distract myself before my face bursts into flames.

I nod at the antique clock above the glass double doors of the main entrance to the brewery. "It should be getting close. It's after eight."

"Shit! We'd better get back there before Britt comes looking for us." Piper puts her glass down and loops her hand in Adam's arm. "Ready to move to the right, to the right, and kick three times?"

"I'm a pro when it comes to the 'Cupid Shuffle.'" Adam smiles at her like he wants to do a little cake-eating of his own.

Piper doesn't seem to notice.

"Maybe they'll do the 'Cotton Eyed Joe' next," Alex taunts.

"Don't even say it. That song makes me stabby."

"It reminds me of a video game," I laugh, and Piper's green-hazel eyes zoom in on my hand gripping Alex's arm.

"You never told me where you two were just now."

She's a bloodhound, but Alex is prepared. "Cass has officially agreed to be Penelope's new nanny. We were working out the details."

"Oh, that's fun." Piper loops her arm in mine, leaning forward to meet Alex's eyes. "She is *great* with kids."

"So I've heard. I'm looking forward to having her at our house." He's so easy and complimentary, and it's doing funny things to my insides.

It's like he's staked a claim on me with that kiss, and I'm strangely drawn to his side.

Which is ridiculous, because I'm not engaged to him. I'm working for him. It's a completely normal arrangement—not the harebrained scheme I dragged him into for tonight.

"Good work, bro." Adam nods at him over our heads. "Does that mean I'm off the hook for Monday?"

"Yeah… I think?" Alex looks at me.

"Yes! Definitely. I can move my stuff in tomorrow, and you can show me the ropes."

"I'm so glad." Piper gives me a squeeze. "Now I don't have to save space on the front page for when you murder your aunt."

Alex gives me a nudge. "You can use it to write up this reception at Stone Cold distillery's newest event space. Executed by the brilliant Cassidy Dixon."

Another stomach flip at him calling me brilliant. My fingers tighten on his sleeve, and I want to kiss his scruffy cheek.

Britt waves frantically as we enter the venue, and we make our way to where she's standing with Aiden by the cake. "Where have you guys been? I thought we were going to have to play 'The Hustle' next!"

Piper tilts her head to the side. "Now, that one, I actually like."

The music fades out quickly, since it's time to cut the cake. A long, ribboned knife is on the table, and we all gather behind the newlyweds as they hold it in both their hands for the first slice. Phone flashes and camera shutters go off all around us, and Aiden holds up the piece for Britt to bite. She does the same for him, letting out a squeal when it hits her tongue.

"Do we have to share it?" she asks me, covering her mouth with her hand.

I shrug. "It's your wedding reception."

Waving me away, she passes the knife to her mother, who

starts slicing, and I grab two plates, catching Alex's arm and pulling him to where Pinky is bouncing on her toes at the edge of the dance floor.

I motion for her to join us, and her bright blue eyes light when she sees cake.

"Miss Cass!" She runs, sliding to a stop in front of me. "Can I have a piece of cake, too?"

"You can have this piece of cake. I got it just for you."

Alex pulls out two chairs, and we sit beside a small, white table. Pinky puts her hands on my knees, watching as I cut a bite for her to eat. Her strawberry-blonde curls are in perfect ringlets around her ears, and they're held back with small, ribbon barrettes.

She has little rosebud lips and a dimple in her chin, and she reminds me of a baby Disney princess in her floor-length tulle dress. A tan, satin ribbon is tied in a bow around her waist, and she's the cutest thing.

I hold out the fork with the cake on it, and she rises onto her tiptoes to take a bite. At the same time, she and her dad burst into noises of approval.

Pinky waves her hands over her head and bounces around in a circle in front of me singing, "I love this cake! I love this cake!"

I start to laugh, and Alex slides his hand over my forearm. The affectionate gesture warms my insides.

"It's delicious." His voice is butter.

"Well, thank you both. I'm so glad you like it."

"You made this cake?" Pinky's blue eyes are wide.

"I sure did, and your dad helped me."

"Daddy says he only makes adult beverages and reheats the food Gram brings us."

My eyebrow arches, and I glance at him.

He grins. "I might have oversold the meals-included part of the job. You're welcome to use the kitchen, though."

"In the hopes I might make enough for three?"

Tilting his head to the side, he starts a comeback when another voice interrupts us.

"This is a cozy group." Drake stands beside Pinky holding a plate of cake and a flute of champagne. "Ready-made family, Cass?"

"Ahh…" I'm completely startled.

"Something like that." Alex smiles confidently.

Pinky holds my knees, bouncing on her toes with her mouth open like a little bird.

"Here you go." My voice is quiet as I feed her another piece, and she breaks into another round of circle-hopping and chanting.

I imagine she'll crash hard after this day.

Or she'll be up all night.

In two days, I'll be living with them, and I'll know. My chest squeezes at the thought, and I sneak a glance at Alex. His square jaw is set, and his protective side is so sexy. I want to curl my fingers in his hair and rest my head on his shoulder like he really is my future husband.

"I'd like to run something past you, Stone." He glances at me feeding cake to Alex's energetic little girl. "I wonder if you might have some time to meet on Monday?"

I freeze, flashing worried eyes to Alex. He gives me a little wink, and while I'm sure it's all part of the fake engagement act, I feel it all the way to my toes.

Tearing my eyes from his, I glance up at our unwelcome visitor. "Britt said you were only in town for the weekend."

Drake's eyes narrow, and it's so obvious he's sizing us up. "I decided to stick around a few days to pursue some of my personal interests."

"What might those be?" Alex leans back, draping his arm across the back of my chair.

"I'll discuss it with you on Monday. I don't want to spoil this festive occasion with business talk."

He strides away into the crowd, and I turn worried eyes on Alex. "What do we do?"

"Don't worry about it." He traces his fingers lightly on my back, satisfaction in his gaze. "You'll move your things into my place tomorrow, and I'll meet with him on Monday."

He smiles, and my eyes catch on his full lips, remembering our kiss.

Alex Stone has succeeded at everything he's ever set out to do. I'm sure he can handle this little mess I created. He asked me if I trusted him, but the real question is do I trust myself?

Chapter 9

Alex

"THAT ONE'S TOO BIG." PINKY'S VOICE IS QUIETLY SERIOUS AS SHE points her little finger at the small pancake I've just dropped onto the hot frying pan. "It can be yours."

"Thanks," I laugh, dipping another, smaller scoop and dropping it in.

She lifts her chin. "That one's better. Do more like that one."

It's possible my little perfectionist apple didn't fall too far from the tree... if that's how the saying goes.

We're observing our Sunday morning tradition—penny cakes with butter, powdered sugar, and real maple syrup. Penny cakes are the one thing I can cook, according to her, only now that she's old enough to supervise, she likes her penny cakes no bigger than a quarter and not too brown.

After shutting down the reception last night, I carried this sleeping nugget out to my car with Cass following us, holding my hand because Drake Redford stayed until the very end. I got the feeling he was watching us the entire time, hoping to catch us lying.

Joke's on him. I actually enjoyed holding Cass's hand and spending the evening with her and my daughter. I like watching them getting to know each other.

I've always had the lingering fear I'm letting Pinky down somehow. I'm a single dad who grew up with two brothers. I don't know the first thing about what a little girl needs.

Mom's been a great help, and she reassures me all the time I'm doing a good job. Still, Cass seems to have that girly vibe on lock. I'm looking forward to her taking the reins and answering all of Pinky's questions.

"Did Gram tell you she's going to Italy with her sisters?" I flip the tiny pancakes as Pinky watches me for any sign of error.

Her curly head nods, her small voice focused. "She's going to stay in a house on Lake Coco, and they're going to drink lemon cellos because it's Aunt Pearl's favorite."

"It's Lake Como, and they'll drink limoncello."

Her tiny brow furrows, and she looks up at me. "That's what I said, Daddy."

"Anyway, she's going to be gone until school starts, so I asked someone to come and stay with us to keep you company."

Pinky's lips press together, and a flash of worry crosses her face. "You're not going to stay with me?"

That's a punch of guilt straight to the gut.

"I have to work, Baby, but remember Miss Cass from last night?" She nods slowly. "I asked her to come and stay with us. Is that okay?"

Her little eyes widen, and she sits up straight on the bar across from me. "Miss Cass, my dance teacher? Will she make us a delicious cake?"

I exhale a sigh of relief and scoop the final penny cakes onto a small plate. "Maybe. If we ask nicely."

"I can ask really, really nice. Gram taught me. Want to hear?"

"Sure. Sit in the stool."

She climbs into the barstool, and I put the plate in front of her with a ramekin of maple syrup.

She squares her little shoulders, puts her hands in her lap, and blinks up at me with round eyes. "Daddy, would you please pass me the powdered sugar?"

Her expression is so serious, I can't help a laugh, which makes her frown immediately.

"Why are you laughing? I asked real nice like Gram said."

Biting back my grin, I nod. "Sorry, Sweet P, you asked very nicely. That was very good." Grabbing the glass bottle of powdered sugar, I hand it to her. "Not too much, now."

She turns it over, giving the bottle a hard shake, and I take the stool beside her with my cup of coffee. For a moment, I watch her dancing in her chair side to side as she swirls her tiny pancakes in the syrup and eats them.

I managed to get her hair back in one of those little scrunchies so she doesn't get it all sticky. I'm always amazed how my mom can just walk up and with one hand, whip it out of her face in two seconds flat. It takes me two minutes, two hands, and *much* whining from my daughter.

Today's ponytail isn't straight or neat, but it's doing its job.

"When Miss Cass gets here, I need you to be a good helper for her. Can you do that?"

She finishes her bite, nodding vigorously as she continues rocking side to side in her chair. "Miss Murphy said I'm the best helper. She let me move my monkey all the way to the finish line for helping."

I'm not sure what any of that means, but I'll go with it. "That's very good. Miss Cass won't know where we keep all our stuff or what you do every day. I'll tell her, but will you help her remember if she forgets?"

Her eyes widen, and she nods. "I'll tell her *everything*."

"That's my girl."

She spears another penny cake, looking up at me. "But it's summertime now. Gram says in summertime, we do whatever we want."

"That's true, but we still have things we do everyday."

Rocking back and forth in her chair, she nods. "Like bath time."

"Right. Like bath time and meals and whatever else you do."

"In the summer we swim in Gram's pool."

"There you go."

Nodding, she shoves her last penny cake into her little mouth. "I can do that."

"Don't talk with your mouth full." Reaching out with a napkin, I wipe the syrup off her chin as she wiggles. "Finish your milk and brush your teeth."

"Ew! Daddy, that's gross." Her nose wrinkles, and she hops off the stool, carrying her plate to the sink.

At least she's mastered cleaning up her place. I'm not a total failure. Unless Mom taught her that. Still, brushing teeth is something I can control.

"It's not as gross as cavities and bad breath." I stab three penny cakes at a time, and shove them in my mouth before carrying my plate to the sink.

"Gram lets me wait until after *Nemo* to brush my teeth. That way it doesn't taste yucky."

Hesitating at the cooktop, I watch as she pulls up the animated movie on the streaming service.

"Okay." I set the timer on my phone. "When this dings, that means pause the movie and brush your teeth."

The orchestral music begins, and I quickly load the dishwasher and head back to my master suite on the first floor.

All the other bedrooms, including my daughter's, are on the second floor with connecting bathrooms. I would offer to let Cass take one of them, but she might prefer having more personal space.

And after that kiss last night, it might be a good idea to give us some boundaries. When she pressed her body to mine, her soft curves melting into my arms, I almost lost control. I almost yanked her skirt up and drove my cock home.

The fantasy has a semi rising in my pants.

Fuck, she's so sexy. Keeping her in the garage apartment is the right idea. Otherwise, I don't think I'd make it through the month without testing her willingness to push some boundaries.

That settles it. The day kindergarten starts, she is no longer my employee. It's the day I can bring what I've been thinking about into the realm of possibility. Until then…

A banging noise comes from the garage, and my stomach tightens. She's here.

My pulse ticks faster, and I give the house a quick survey. The pine floors are warm and inviting, and the vaulted, exposed pine ceilings make the living room appear larger than it is. Harriet came on Friday, so the rugs are vacuumed and the furniture is dusted.

Pinky is on the couch happily watching her fish movie. Reaching down, I slide the messy ponytail I did out of her hair, and her shiny pink curls fall around her little shoulders. That's better.

Returning to the kitchen, I drop the band in a drawer, giving that space a cursory glance. Our breakfast dishes are in the sink, but the room is otherwise spotless. A vase of Gerber daisies is on the reclaimed wood bar, again, thanks to Harriet the maid, and the sun shines through the windows, giving the place a happy morning vibe.

It's an inviting workspace, I think.

Stopping in front of the large mirror in the foyer, I rake my fingers through my dark hair. Overnight, it seems, my hair has gotten too long. It'll have to do. Glancing down at my jeans and white linen button-up shirt, I roll the sleeves to look less formal.

Welcoming. I'm going for welcoming.

Clearing my throat, I trot down the short flight of steps to the garage, hitting the button on the way down. The metal double-door rises, and I watch as her sexy legs are exposed first, followed by the cutoff denim overalls she's always wearing, with a strap over one shoulder so her white tank top is exposed along with her smooth shoulders.

The baggy overalls completely hide her body, which I know from twice exposure is as hot as fuck.

"Hey!" Her voice is a little breathy, but optimistic.

"Hey." I close the space between us, stopping in front of her older Subaru. "Welcome. Mi casa es su casa."

"Really?" Her nose wrinkles, and I shrug.

"Sort of. Your apartment is up these stairs." I gesture to the staircase. "I'll help you carry your stuff."

Stepping around to the open hatchback of her car, I grab a large suitcase out of the back. Crates of toiletries and assorted accessories are stacked beside it.

"Oh! You don't have to—"

"You can't carry all this up those stairs, and even if you could, my mom would never forgive me if I let you."

A shaky laugh slips through her lips, and she picks up a crate, her eyes flickering to mine and back again. "Perks of living in the South?"

"Make the most of it."

She seems a little nervous, which makes me want to put her at ease. I want her to know this arrangement doesn't have to be so formal.

I walk up the stairs with her large, heavy suitcase, stopping at the door and inserting the key. "You'll have the only set of these."

"That's a terrible idea." She steps up behind me with the crate in her hand. "We should figure out a good hiding place for at least one. In the drawer at the bottom of the stairs?"

"Too obvious." I unlock the door, and the musty smell of unused air hits me. "I need to open a window and turn on the air conditioner."

Why didn't I do that first thing?

"You forget I've lived in Eureka since I was thirteen." She pushes past me, depositing the crate on the floor inside. "I know all about hot, humid weather and unoccupied houses."

"It's a good place." I don't want her to think I've relegated her to a moldy shit hole. "I wasn't thinking."

"After last night, I'm surprised either of us is up and moving around this morning."

Last night has been on my mind all morning. We probably should make a plan for Drake and what's happening with our fake engagement. Instead, we continue unloading her car until my phone goes off, and I remember the little princess I left in front of the TV.

"Time to brush our teeth."

Cass's eyebrows curve. "Is it a group activity?"

"For Penelope, I mean. She wanted to drink her milk and watch *Finding Nemo*."

"Oh, I love *Finding Nemo*! I'll go with you." Cass puts the box on the floor. "I can finish later, after she's asleep. I don't want to miss anything."

"You sure?"

"Lead the way!"

We jog down the stairs and into the house, where Pinky is lying on her side, clutching Piglet and watching the orange fish talking to a turtle.

"Oh, it's Crush—my favorite part!" Cass skips forward and sits by my daughter on the couch, giving her a little bump. "Hey, dude!"

"Dude! You're here!" Pinky sits up as soon as Cass joins her, and the two of them smile at each other.

"This is the best part of the movie." Cass bounces slightly on the cushion.

The fish and the turtles shoot through the water, and Pinky hugs her stuffed pig tightly, climbing onto her knees and putting her hand on Cass's shoulder.

Cass gives her waist a reassuring squeeze. "They're shooting the curl."

"Like Uncle Adam! Sweet." She sounds like one of the little turtles.

"He's got some serious thrill issues, Dude," Cass says, and Pinky beams at her.

I cross my arms, leaning my shoulder against the wall and smiling at the two of them quoting lines together.

"Dad said you're going to stay with me until kindergarten!" P's voice is high and excited.

"Yep, and we're going to have so. Much. Fun!" Cass boops her little nose with every word.

My daughter's eyes widen with her smile, and I can tell she's as taken with her new nanny as I am.

She holds out the floppy, faded-pink stuffed animal. "This is my friend Piglet. He's been with me since I was born."

Cass makes an impressed face and shakes the stuffed animal's foot. "How do you do, Piglet? I can tell you're a well-loved pig."

"Miss Holly says pigs are as smart as dogs." Pinky settles her stuffed friend at her side. "But Daddy said Piglet can't go with me to school, and he had to stay home and nap during the wedding. He could get lost, and he can't find his way home like Myrtle can."

"Your dad is right. We don't want to lose Piglet."

They return to watching the movie and quoting lines. Dory spies something orange and white, and it's Marlin. She does it again, and it's still Marlin—and the two of them look at each other and laugh.

Then Cass taps Pinky's shoulder, and her voice turns into a long, deep, sing-song. "Let's take a breaaaak and brush our teeeeth!"

My chin pulls back, and I'm not sure what's happening right now. At the same time, the blue fish in the movie starts doing the same thing. Apparently they're speaking whale.

Pinky doesn't miss a beat. "Ooooh-kaaay!"

Cass snorts a laugh, and Pinky hops off the couch, grabbing Cass's hand and shouting. "I'll show you my room!"

This is working out too well.

Cass glances back at me. "If there's anything you need to do today, I've got things covered here."

"Yes, you do." I smile like I've made some big discovery, but the truth is everyone, including Cass, told me she was great with kids. "It's Sunday. We're usually at Mom's for lunch."

"Gram said today is special because of the wedding. We're going to have desserts tonight instead of lunch."

"She wants to tell the kids good-bye before she leaves tomorrow."

"Ah," Cass's chin lifts. "I'll finish unpacking while you go."

In the meantime, I guess I've got the afternoon to myself.

For the first time in a long time, I could actually go fishing, but what I really want to do is watch my fake fiancée fitting seamlessly into my little family.

Chapter 10

Cass

PENELOPE STONE IS A LITTLE GIRL AFTER MY OWN HEART. BY suppertime, we've finished *Nemo*, and she's shown me all the dolls in her room. Her favorite stuffed princess doll is Ariel, because she lives at the beach like we do, but her daddy said she can never trade any of her body parts for a boy, which she thinks is silly. She would never do something like that.

She likes Eric's dog way better.

And Sebastian.

Alex has been drifting around watching us most of the day, and I can't tell if he's checking on us or if he doesn't know what to do with his free time.

The stacked boxes of my belongings in the garage apartment are on my mind, and I consider letting him take over while I unpack. I don't, because the truth is, I like spending time with Pinky. She's cute and funny, and she's teaching me a lot about her dad.

It's a complete contrast to the controlled, all-business side he projects in his element at the distillery. He's never unsure or at a loss there.

Even last night at the reception, the way he took charge, putting his arm around me and holding my hand as if daring Drake to challenge us. It's hot.

When I return to the kitchen, he has three plates of roast chicken and scalloped potatoes, shrimp and grits, and assorted rolls prepared for dinner.

"I'm impressed." I can't help teasing him.

"Like I said, I'm an excellent re-heater," he teases right back, placing one plate in the microwave and hitting the start button. "Mom made us all plates from the reception last night. She asked us to have the kids over at seven."

"I'll unpack while you're gone. When you get back, do you want me to bathe her? Get her ready for bed?"

"We usually read a book together at bedtime." A small dimple I've never noticed appears in his cheek when he smiles. "She really likes you. Maybe you could take over bath time, and I'll keep the book?"

"Sounds like a plan!"

"Then we need to talk." The shift in his tone tenses my stomach.

I'm sure he means we need to talk about the fake engagement I've roped him into, and standing here in front of him, in broad daylight with no alcohol or adrenaline mixing in my veins, I want to crawl under a rock and hide. How could I do that to him? He must think I'm completely insane.

Embarrassment burns in my cheeks, and I'm not so hungry anymore. "I'll go ahead and start unpacking. Just let me know when you're back."

The garage apartment is the same style as the house, with smooth pine floors and ceilings. It reminds me of a mountain cottage, and it smells like wood and books and crisp air-conditioned air.

Walking to the small bookcase, I peruse the titles. He has

two biographies of Alexander Hamilton, one of John Adams, *The Road* by Cormac McCarthy, *The Human Stain* by Phillip Roth, and one lone title by Barbara Kingsolver, *Prodigal Summer*.

"Hello, how did you get here?" I pull the lush green hardback from the shelf, turning it in my hands.

I prefer romance and happily ever afters—the spicier the better. Still, it's nice to see he's a bit well-rounded.

A queen-sized bed is across the room against the wall, and beside it, a door leads to a large, full bathroom. Flipping on the light, I exhale a happy sigh when I see a garden tub situated in the corner.

I'm already planning long soaks with fizzies and candles—after Penelope is tucked in for the night, of course. Opening the music app on my phone, I cue up the soundtrack for *Mamma Mia, Here We Go Again* and get to work unpacking my few belongings to the sounds of Cher singing "Fernando."

I've moved so many times, I've become a pro at fitting all my things in one suitcase and a few collapsible crates. It doesn't take long for me to arrange my clothes in the closet, my personal belongings on the shelves, my Kindle on the nightstand, and my toiletries in the bathroom.

I go ahead and take a quick shower while I'm waiting for Alex and Pinky to return, and I slip into black yoga pants and black sports bra with a long-sleeved, tan sweater on top. I've just finished brushing my hair when I hear the sound of the garage closing below.

Damn electric cars. I'll never get used to how quiet they are.

I step into a pair of black Birkenstock sandals before heading out the door and trotting down the stairs. He stands out of the car, and his full lips twitch with a near-smile when he sees me. One eyebrow rises, and a thrill flashes to my toes.

It's the same look as when he kissed me, and I kind of hate working for him now. I'd like to trot down the stairs, walk straight to him and put my arms around his neck. I'd like another of his underwear-igniting kisses. I'd like his hands under my sweater, sliding across my skin. I'd like to touch the thick cock he's hiding in his pants…

He hesitates, his eyes never leaving me, and my skin heats as I wonder if he can read my mind, if he's thinking the same thing as me.

"*Daa-daay!*" Pinky shouts from the backseat, breaking the spell.

I snort a laugh, and he grins, turning to open the door as I continue down the stairs.

He lifts the little princess out of her booster seat, and I stand back, waiting. "I'm going to have to get used to your silent car."

"Did we sneak up on you?" He lifts Penelope in an arc before placing her on her feet in front of me.

"The garage door gave you away." I reach out, and she grabs my hand, skipping beside me. "How was your dessert?"

"We had your cake again, and I ate two pieces!" She holds up two fingers, and my eyebrows rise.

"Wow! I hope they were little pieces."

"They were not." Alex's voice is almost a growl, and I press my lips together.

"Daddy says I'm going to be up all night on a sugar high. Is that like up in a balloon? I want to be high like a balloon!" She jumps up and down pumping one little fist over her head like a cheerleader.

"It's not really like a balloon." I glance at him over my shoulder, and he shakes his head.

"But I want to go up in a balloon! Can we do that while you're here?"

"I know something even better. It'll help you relax, and you can dream about riding in a balloon. Sound good?" She nods her red head vigorously. "I'll grab it from my room and meet you in your bathroom."

Minutes later, I'm upstairs in the main house running a large tub of warm water and adding soothing essential oils and bubbles, nothing too irritating for her delicate skin.

She bounces into the bathroom in her birthday suit, and I laugh. "You're naked as a jaybird!"

That makes her jump more, pumping her elbows like wings as her strawberry curls fly all around her shoulders. I see the reason for Alex's frustration. She's a live wire.

Grabbing a scrunchie, I swoop her hair up on top of her head before helping her into the bath. "Did you have fun at your gram's house?"

She nods, looking down at the thin layer of bubbles floating on the top of the water. "She gave me all the cake."

"Your gram loves you very much." I take a large, natural sponge with lavender soap and rub it gently in large circles over her back.

"She's going to be gone a long time." Her little voice goes quiet, and I bend down to check her expression.

"But she'll be back soon, and while she's gone, I'll be here to play with you."

"Gram is Daddy's mom, but she's not my mom."

I dip the sponge in the warm water and rub it slowly down her little arms, thinking about this. "She's your grandmother, which is a very special kind of mom. She loves you very much, and so does your dad."

Her little chin bobs, but she studies her fingers in the suds. "I know. He loves me twice as much, because I don't have a mom, like Nemo. None of the princesses have mommies."

I'm not sure if it's the calming lavender bringing her down or if it's this turn in the conversation. I haven't talked to Alex about what to say if her mother comes up, and I'm at a total loss, looking for any way to give her comfort.

"I grew up without a mom, too."

Her blue eyes fly to mine. "You did?"

"Yep." I rub the sponge over her back again, slower. "I moved here to live with my aunt when I was thirteen."

"Did she die?" She blinks round eyes at me.

"No. She couldn't take care of me, so my aunt took over.

I didn't understand it at the time, but it makes more sense to me now."

Her eyes return to her fingers in the bubbles. "My mom can't take care of me either. Daddy said she's working far, far away in Africa, so I can't ever talk to her." Her voice is so serious, and I put the sponge aside. "Gram said I should talk to her whenever I need to talk to my mom, but now she's gone, too."

I'm sitting on the bathroom floor, resting my chin on my hand. Her little expression is so sad, and I trace my finger along a curl that's slipped out of the scrunchie, moving it behind her ear.

"Your gram will be back in a few weeks." My voice is gentle. "I know that feels like a long time, but it'll pass so fast. And while she's gone, maybe you can talk to me if you want to talk to your gram or your mom? I'm not a gram or a mom, but I know things."

Her rosebud lips press together, and she blinks a few times at the bubbles.

Lifting her chin, our eyes meet again, and it's clear she's thinking about it. "You know all the Dory parts in *Nemo*."

"I do." I give her an easy smile. "Remember what Dory says when life gets you down?"

I sing the words to "Just keep swimming" softly, and her eyes blink a few times as her expression starts to relax. A hint of a smile lifts her lips, and we sing the words together, finishing the song.

She puts her hand on mine. "I can talk to you."

"And I'll do my very best to be a good listener." I kiss her little forehead as I push myself to stand, grabbing a fluffy purple towel off the rack. "Now you need to get out of this tub and get ready for bed. The water's all cold."

She stands, and I hold out my hands for her to jump onto the bathmat where I quickly rub the towel all over her little body. "Ready to snuggle in your bed and dream about going up in a beautiful balloon?"

"Yes!" She holds my shoulders as she steps into her underwear. "My bath smells like Gram's yard."

"It's called lavender." I drop her Ariel nightgown over her head before taking her hand as we walk into the bedroom where her dad is sitting on the foot of her bed holding a thin book.

Our eyes meet, and his are so full, my stomach tightens. I can only imagine he heard our conversation, and I hope I didn't overstep or say the wrong thing.

I help Pinky onto her pillow, settle Piglet at her side and kiss the top of her head. "I'll see you in the morning, okay?"

She nods, and Alex moves to sit beside her, holding the book so she can see the pictures. Her little head is snug against his side, and I slip out of the room, going down to the kitchen to wait for him to finish.

Chapter 11

Alex

CASS IS A FUCKING NATURAL WHEN IT COMES TO KIDS. NO WONDER Britt said she should be a teacher.

Listening to them talking in the bathroom, P telling her about her mom and Cass sharing her own story, was a simultaneous punch to the gut and a soothing caress.

Why didn't I consider that Penelope might misinterpret my mother's trip to Italy as another abandonment? Of course she did, but Cass handled it beautifully.

So beautifully I want to give her a raise.

Not only did she navigate those waters, she managed to calm my little sugar fiend so well, she was asleep before I even made it halfway through the book, and it's her favorite, a dog-eared copy of *Dogzilla*, passed down through the grandkids since it belonged to Adam.

Hustling down the stairs, I find Cass leaning on the bar studying her phone. I pause a moment to take in her long frame. Her hair hangs in loose waves down her back, and she's wearing black yoga pants and another one of those sweaters that falls off one shoulder like a tease.

I imagine sliding the other one down, and the entire garment dropping to the floor. It's an image that makes my dick hard, knowing what's hidden beneath—her perfect breasts, her flat stomach, her round hips.

I want to taste her…

She hears me and stands quickly, shoving the phone into a pocket on the side of her pants. Her expression is worried, and she's talking fast.

"I'm sorry I keep screwing everything up." Her chin drops, and she shoves a shiny lock of dark hair behind her ear. "I didn't know what to say when Penelope brought up her mom just now. I should've just listened to her and waited to ask you what to do. I shouldn't have assumed or tried to—"

"Stop apologizing." It comes out as more of an order than I intend, and she stops short. I walk over to the cabinet and take down a bottle of the single-barrel reserve I keep at the house. "Want a drink?"

She nods, and I take two tumblers from the cabinet and pour each of us a glass.

"I'm not angry at all. I've never heard Penelope talk to anyone the way she talks to you, outside of family, and I thought you handled it very well, considering she caught you off guard."

"Thank you." Her voice is soft, and she studies the glass of whiskey. "She has all your expressions. It's so funny to see her little face so serious, so like you. Only the color's wrong."

"She gets that from Jessica." I take a small sip, savoring the rich, smoky flavor.

"Was that your wife?"

"We were never married."

"Oh, I thought…"

"Everyone did. But we were no more married than you and I are engaged."

Her cheeks flush, and she shakes her head, taking a sip of whiskey. We're quiet a moment, until she asks. "Why not?"

I think about those months, Jessica being pregnant, the conversations we had, the deals and negotiations between us.

"We were never in love." Confusion lines her eyes, and I explain. "You know those stories about one-night stands that turn into love? We didn't have that. We were too different. She wanted to travel to war zones, document what was happening, live her life on the edge of death all the time."

"It sounds exciting."

"Maybe. For some." I take another sip of whiskey. "I wanted a family. I wanted Pinky, and she wanted freedom."

"Wow. That's tough."

Shaking my head, I exhale a laugh. "It's not as dramatic as you think. It was actually pretty simple. We shook hands and walked away. We both got what we wanted."

"She gets a life of adventure, and you get a funny little girl who eats too much cake on a Sunday night?"

"I'll take my side of the bargain any day." I clink her glass softly. "By the way, whatever you did at bath time worked. She was asleep after three pages."

"Just good old-fashioned lavender, cedar, and ylang-ylang."

"I have no idea what that is, but I liked getting to hear you sing again."

Her cheeks flush, and I watch as she sips the whiskey.

"Everyone was right," I continue. "You're very good with children."

Setting her glass down, she frowns thoughtfully. "Kids are easy. Whatever they're thinking comes right out of their mouths. I appreciate that level of honesty. A child would never ghost you."

Leaning on my elbow I study her, liking what I see more and more with each passing minute. "It helps they have no phones or social media."

"I still don't think they would. Kids are too real. They don't hide their feelings the way adults do. They don't lie or play politics."

"I've never liked politicians either." I finish my glass, feeling more relaxed myself.

She tilts her head to the side. "You do have to play politics to sell your brand. You have to talk to people you don't know and convince them to try your product."

"That's different." I take a step closer. "I'd never ghost you."

Exhaling a laugh, she drops her chin. "I believe you. You have no problems being direct, and it seems you always know what you want."

She has no idea.

"Speaking of what I want, about this engagement…"

"Oh, God," she groans, dropping her face into her hands. "What a mess."

Reaching into my pocket, I remove a black velvet pouch I retrieved from my room before coming down. "This is for you."

Her hand lowers, and she takes the pouch from me. "What is it?"

She loosens the knot and takes out a delicate gold ring with a large diamond swaddled in two angel's wings.

"Oh…" It comes out as a gasp. "It's so beautiful. I've never seen anything like it."

"Try it on."

Blue eyes fly to mine. "You're giving this to me?"

She slips it on her finger, and I notice it fits perfectly.

"Since Drake is hanging around a few more days, you can use it when you need to. Or, hell, wear it all the time. Whatever makes sense."

Her lips are parted, and I remember kissing her, slipping my tongue between those soft pillows, tasting her sweetness. I remember her beautiful voice singing in the ocean so long ago, *I believe in angels…*

"Did you buy it for her?" Her question pulls me from my fantasy.

"What?" My brow furrows. "For who?"

"Penelope's mom. Was this for her?"

I almost laugh. "No." The thought of giving this ring to Jessica is ludicrous. "I saw it in a jewelry store in Hawaii, and I bought it."

"I love it, but it's not for me." She shakes her head, looking down at the ring.

"Why not?" A touch of amusement is in my tone.

"I'm no angel. I'm a mess. I have no direction, I've had a million jobs, I still don't know who I want to be, and I'm practically thirty."

She has no idea how wrong she is.

Lifting my hand, I trace a lock of dark hair behind her ear. "I think you're smart and curious. You're a little wild, but what's wrong with that? Even the angels take their share of bourbon."

"What does that mean?"

"The angel's share is the amount of bourbon that evaporates during aging."

"Bourbon-drinking angels." Shaking her head, she turns away. "That's not me. I'm just like my mother—ask Drake."

Anger tightens my stomach. "Drake is a douche, and I'd never agree with his sour-grapes opinion of you. I've never met your mother, so I can't know if you're like her, unless she's kind and supportive of her friends."

"When I was a child, I'd lie and tell people my mother was a Broadway singer so I didn't have to tell them the truth." Her voice is quiet. "The truth is she was a failed Branson climber, who never came back for me."

Our glasses are empty, and I study the hurt in her eyes. "Then I'd say you're nothing like her. After hearing you with my daughter, I can't imagine you leaving a child behind."

"Drake also said I was a gold digger."

The anger in my stomach moves to my fist, and I expect I'll have to pop that guy in the mouth one of these days. "If that were true, you'd still be with him."

"I suppose." Her eyes meet mine now. "You know what I'd really like? I'd like to find something that makes me happy, and then just do it forever—be very boring and predictable for the rest of my life."

A laugh slips through my lips. "I can't think of anything worse."

"You're one to talk. You measure every action, plan every step, control every outcome…"

"I wouldn't be a single dad if that were true."

"But it worked out for you, and you're doing what you love and being predictable." Her pretty eyes return to her empty glass. "I'm like a dandelion puff blowing in the wind."

I trace the line of her profile, her upturned nose, her full lips. I remember how lost I felt in San Diego after Pinky was born and Jessica left. I spent a lot of time thinking about what I wanted. I thought about the past and the things I left behind, and I booked the next plane home.

This beautiful girl was only a memory then. Now she's standing right in front of me. "You're so much more than that."

"You don't know anything about me."

"I know enough. I've known you since we were kids, and we have a month to get to know each other as adults. Maybe after that, you'll see yourself the way I do."

"You see me as wild. I think you're being generous. Messy, yes, but wild?" Her dark head shakes, and I'm ready to pull her to me.

"You're not afraid to try new things. You're not afraid of bullies… And you like to swim naked in the ocean."

"That doesn't make me wild. That makes me impulsive."

"We have a whole month to see who's right."

Her eyes slant, and she takes a step closer. "I spent all last month at the distillery, and I barely saw you. Why should this month be any different?"

I take a step closer, like a magnet drawn to metal. "I was focused on the new line last month. Now that it's launched…"

Her eyebrow arches, and she lifts her chin. "You'll be focused on me?"

The prospect of this fans the heat smoldering in my bloodstream. "Do you trust me?"

It's the second time I've asked her this question, and that pinpoint dimple appears at the corner of her mouth when she smiles. "I've already told you I do."

I lift her left hand, loving her openness, loving how nicely my ring fits her finger, loving the idea that after all these years, our time has come.

"Maybe we can start by having some fun."

Chapter 12

Cass

HIS NEARNESS IS OVERWHELMING. HE'S SO INTENSE, AND I'VE NEVER been the focus of all that attention. Now he's looking at me like a meal, and I'm having a hard time staying on my feet. I want what he's suggesting, although I'm not really sure what he means by having fun.

I think I know, but he hasn't said it in so many words.

Hazel eyes trace my face, and I do the same, studying his dark hair that curls in soft waves around his ears. I want to slide the loose lock off his forehead. I want to scratch my nails through his beard and kiss him. I want to touch him like he's mine.

"I like having fun." I wish I didn't sound like a child when I said it.

I'm sure he's used to confident women who know what they want out of life. Women who don't question everything, who are as focused and sure as he always is. Women like Jessica, whom I'm trying not to hate for being so bold and adventurous and living her life on the edge in Africa…

Although, she did leave her daughter behind, which is something I would never do.

And Alex doesn't seem to miss her at all.

So maybe *hate* is too strong a word, but I don't like her very much.

He lifts my hand, grinning as he studies the gorgeous ring on my finger. "Good. We can start with this engagement…"

A cringe tingles at the back of my neck. "Apologies all around."

"I don't accept them." His voice is firm. "I like that you reached for me… for what? Protection?"

"More like validation."

"How so?"

"Oh… He's so impressed by you." Scrubbing my fingers over my cringey skin, I try to find the words. "I've never seen him impressed by anyone other than himself, and he always made me feel so worthless. I've always been so ashamed of my situation, my mom, and my life… When he just assumed we were together, I let him. Being with you gave me value." My voice goes quiet. "And I never should have taken advantage of your friendship that way—"

"I'm *not* your friend." He's stern, and shame grips my throat.

I bared my soul to him, and this is how he treats me?

"Right. I forgot you were always too good to be friends with me." I start to turn away, to storm out of the kitchen when he catches me by the upper arm, pulling me to him.

His eyes flash with fire, and my heart beats faster. The hairs on my arms rise. He's possessive and predatory, and I remember he knows what I look like naked.

"No, Cass…" He draws closer, forcing my head to tilt back to look up at him. Our lips are so close, his warm breath skates across my cheek. "I'm not your friend, because when it comes to us, the *friend zone* is not my lane."

I swallow and my voice is breathy. "What is your lane?"

His hand slides up my waist, under my sweater, and his

thumb circles my nipple through my sports bra. It hardens at once, and I exhale a little whimper.

My tongue slips out to wet my lips, and his darkening eyes move to them. I can't breathe. He continues circling, watching my lips part, making my pussy wetter as his mouth drifts lower.

Placing my hands on his chest, I rise onto my toes. My eyes flutter closed, and I press my lips to his just like I did so long ago when he was a sad, handsome boy who'd lost his grandfather.

When he told me I was pretty, and my entire body came to life.

His full lips are soft and warm, and as soon as they touch mine, his hand tightens on my waist, pulling my pelvis flush against his.

His erection is against my belly. A low growl rumbles in his throat, and he takes control.

The kiss turns possessive, demanding. The hand on my breast moves into the side of my hair as he opens my mouth with his.

Again, I whimper when his tongue slides against mine, curling and coaxing, and my hands rise higher, tracing my nails along his square jaw. I hold his scruffy cheeks like he's mine, like we're in this for real.

Images of his naked body flood my memory, and I want him against me, inside me. No one has ever kissed me this way, like he's staking his claim, and he'll never let me leave him.

"This is my lane, Cass." His voice is rough, and his lips move to my ear. "It's always been my lane. Understand?"

My eyes are closed, and I'm nodding before he finishes speaking. "Yes…"

He grips my chin in his fingers. "Look at me." My eyes flutter open, and the raw hunger in his is a strike of electricity through my core. "Don't ever mistake me as a friend again. I want more than that."

"Okay…" I'm still processing when a noise behind us breaks the scene.

It's a little-girl sniffle that parts us at once. I'm breathing fast when I turn, rushing to where Pinky stands at the entrance to the kitchen rubbing her eyes. I can't tell if she's fully awake, and I don't know if she saw us kissing. I only know Alex isn't in a position to help her.

I lower to a squat in front of her. "Are you okay, sweetie?"

Her bottom lip is pushed out slightly, and she puts her hand on my shoulder, whimpering. "My balloon popped and it made a loud noise and I fell out of the sky and now my tummy hurts."

"Oh, no!" I pull her into a hug, and both her arms go around my neck. "Dream balloons shouldn't pop. Let's go back and see if we can dream up a better balloon, one of the shiny kinds that never pop."

She tucks her head into my neck, and I look back at Alex, who's standing behind the bar watching me with a mixture of frustration and gratitude in his eyes.

I walk slowly up the stairs, humming a song from *Nemo* as we go higher, and she's asleep by the time we get to her bedroom. I tuck her in with Piglet and switch on the pale, blue-moon nightlight before closing the door.

Jogging down the stairs, the mood in the kitchen has changed. The lights seem brighter, and Alex has put away the whiskey and is washing the glasses at the sink.

I stop by the door leading out to the garage, wondering what to do. When I left things were heating up. Now it seems the moment has passed, but I don't want to misread the situation, not after that kiss.

"I'm pretty sure she was sleepwalking." My voice is lighter. "I doubt she saw us."

He switches off the water, turning slowly to face me. "Good. I wasn't thinking just now. Whatever I do, I can't forget she's a part of this. I can't let her be confused or hurt."

"Of course." It feels like a dismissal, and I take another step towards the door, clearing my throat and pulling my sweater onto my shoulder again. "You don't have to explain. I completely understand. I'll see you in the morning."

He dries his hands with the towel, his dark brow furrowed. I take one last look at his handsome frame before I go. It would be so decadent to forget everything, to ask him to come with me and blur all the lines, take what we want.

It would be so hot, but it's not him. I'm not even sure it's me. At least not on my first night in his home, as his employee.

My hand is on the doorknob, when his voice stops me. "I leave for work at eight. Pinky's usually up by then, so that can be your start time."

A shadow of regret flickers in his eyes, but just as quickly he's back to business.

I'm more disappointed than surprised. The real surprise was the kiss. Alex Stone does nothing without thorough examination.

Maintaining the brightness in my voice, I manage a smile. "I'll be here at eight, then."

"Thank you." He's not looking at me, and I steal one last look at his face before I disappear out the side door.

It's an expression I've seen before when he's sampling a new blend or thinking about adding a service. Problem solving.

Only, I don't want to be a problem for him, even if I seem to keep creating them, from being his fake fiancée to being the nanny he wants to kiss... and hopefully do so much more with.

Climbing the stairs to my garage apartment, I study the diamond on my hand surrounded by angel's wings. In all the years of circling him, I never dreamed I'd be this close to him. I never let the thought enter my mind, because it seemed impossible.

I always tried to be his friend, and now I finally understand why we never were. I turn over everything he said to me. I'm smart and curious and a little wild, and he seems to dislike Drake Redford as much as me.

A month of fun with a man I've seen naked and who doesn't want to be friends. Pressing my lips together, I swallow the bubble of excitement rising in my stomach. What kind of twist is this?

"Daddy told you a secret last night." Pinky sits at the bar eating toast spread with almond butter and strawberry preserves.

My stomach tenses, and I'm not sure what to say.

It's just the two of us. Alex and I exchanged a brief, professional good morning when I arrived five minutes ago. He was gorgeous as always in jeans that hugged his ass perfectly and a long-sleeved, maroon Henley. His dark hair grazed his collar, and he said something about needing a haircut before letting us know he'd be home by five.

Now he's gone, and I'm holding a cup of coffee facing his adorable mini-me, who's waiting for a response and wearing the exact same expression I left him with last night: Problem-solving.

Clearly, she was not sleepwalking last night, and she did see us in a clutch. "What makes you think that?"

"He was talking in your ear." Her serious expression is too cute. "Was it something about me?"

"No, um… he was actually telling me a joke."

She takes a big bite of toast and nods knowingly. "That's why you didn't laugh. Uncle Adam says Daddy has no sense of humor. He's like Marlin."

Pressing my lips together, I almost laugh. "Don't talk with your mouth full, okay?"

She takes another big bite of toast, and I'm not sure Alex needs to be funny. He's sexy as sin, which more than makes up for a lack of comedic skills in my book.

"I need to run a few errands today. Want to brush your teeth so you can go with me?"

"Yes!" She drops the toast at once and hops off the stool, running towards the stairs. "We can watch *Nemo* later!"

Something tells me I might have that movie memorized by

the end of this job—more so than I already do. After a quick clean-up, I head upstairs to look through her drawers and familiarize myself with her closet.

At four and a half, she's old enough to pick out her clothes and make her bed, so when she races into the room from brushing her teeth, I stop her.

"Let's make this bed, okay?" Her little shoulders fall, but I'm no pushover. "Come on."

Together we make the bed and straighten her toys. Then I let her pick out her outfit for the day. Not too bad. She pulls on a white sleeveless dress with little blue flowers all over it.

"Let's do your hair." I sit her on her bed and French-braid the front of her hair out of her eyes. The rest I don't touch, and her perfect spirals hang in shiny sausages.

"I like your hair!" She spins fast with her curls flying around her shoulders, threading her fingers in my long ponytail.

"Thanks! I like your hair."

Smiling like we're the best of friends, she takes my hand and grabs Piglet as we head out the door.

Coffee in hand, and Pinky in her booster seat, we make the drive to Britt's old apartment. Alex's massive home is on the outskirts of town, closer to the beach, so it takes a few minutes to get there. "Paper Rings" by Taylor Swift plays on my phone, and Pinky sings right along with me at the top of her lungs.

"We're lucky!" I cry as we pull into an empty parking space close to the courthouse before crossing the street.

She points at the purple neon sign for the Star Parlor. "Ryan says they do magic in there, but Bubba says they only do card tricks."

I grab the key from above the door as I consider her statement. Aiden was very hostile towards Britt's family's business when they first got together. I have no idea how Alex feels about tarot and magic, or the fact that I used to do it as well.

We really should have a conversation about all these

landmines, but how can I possibly anticipate what a four-year-old will say?

"They definitely have fancy cards in there." It's a good, safe reply, and I catch her hand. "Let's see what's up here, okay?"

Piper said they packed up everything after the party, so there's no danger of Pinky seeing anything inappropriate. I just have to get the box and figure out where it's going to live until the next bachelorette.

Unlocking the door, I'm still humming "Paper Rings" when my eye catches the angel ring still on my finger. I forgot to take it off, and a tickle fills my stomach. I like shiny things… but I have to remind myself it's not real. We're just pretending while Drake is in town.

The brown box sits on the coffee table, and I walk over to grab it as Pinky runs to look out the window. That *BBL* bumper sticker falls to the floor, and I scoop it up, stuffing it in my pocket.

Pinky calls, "Daddy's here!"

"What?" I walk over to where she's looking at the town square below.

Alex's car is parked in Aiden's reserved spot.

"I wonder what he's up to." My voice is quiet, but I have a wild hair. "Come on, we have to take this box to my car. Then who wants to go for a swim?"

"Me! Me! Me!" Pinky jumps around waving her arms.

"Maybe we'll swing by and pick up your cousin." Adam probably needs a break.

She holds my pocket as we return to my car, and I put the box in my trunk before buckling her into the booster seat. We're about to head out when I make a quick stop by Alex's car.

Let the games begin…

Chapter 13

Alex

"**D**ID YOU SEE ME DOING THE CUPID SHUFFLE?" DEPUTY DOUG flaps his arms like a bird as he slides to the right in front of Holly's desk. "I haven't danced that much since Julia graduated college. I didn't see you dancing, Al. Don't you like to dance?"

"I saw him dancing with Cass Dixon, and I had to grab a fan." Holly gives me a wink. "The chemistry was real."

My eyes narrow, and I wonder if anyone else noticed.

"Oh, yeah, she's a looker." Doug waggles his eyebrows at me as he swipes a Krispy Kreme donut from the open box on Holly's desk. "You think they did more than dance?"

The two of them titter conspiratorially, and it's like I'm not even in the room. I'm certainly not needed in the conversation.

Shaking my head, I look around the open space. "If you'll just show me which desk is Britt's?"

Aiden asked me to stop by the office and pick up his wife's laptop, even though they're supposed to be taking a few days off for their honeymoon while Adam keeps Owen.

I'd hoped to be in and out, but one of the quirks of small-town life is it always takes thirty minutes longer to run any errand, especially when people you've known most of your life are involved.

Some would call it charming.

"Right this way, boss." Doug does a little shoulder jostle before leading me to a small desk across the open room. "Although I guess I'm the boss when Aiden's on vacation. Let's hope no major crimes occur."

"I'll second that every day," Holly calls from her desk.

Doug's been the deputy sheriff since my dad was alive, and as easygoing and helpful as he is, I agree with Holly. I'm glad we're never in danger of him running things.

"Speaking of, that sure was a weird crime spree we had last year." He chatters as I take the laptop and cord off the wooden desk.

Beside it is a stack of pictures of the small wooden signs that appear sporadically around town with little sayings or affirmations painted on them.

"Still no idea who's doing these?" I hold one up.

"No clue." Doug's voice is thoughtful.

The sign reads *Open your heart*, and I quip, "Maybe it's Madonna."

Doug's silent laugh shakes his whole body. "Wouldn't that be something? Or her number one fan."

It was a pretty lame joke, and I've got what I need. "Any messages for Aiden?"

He polishes off the donut, licking his thumb and index finger. "Just keep enjoying married life. It's going to be fun having them two working here together. Like one of those old TV shows, *Moonlighting* or something."

"Tell him we want more babies!" Holly yells from her desk.

I'll leave that message for her to deliver. Waving, I head out the door. I've already been here too long, and I'm supposed to be meeting with that prick Drake Redford in fifteen minutes.

I can't imagine what's on his mind, but if he plans to suggest we work together in some way, he's got another thing coming. Cass has told me enough to want to call off this morning's meeting, but it would be unprofessional at this late hour. I'll deal with him in other ways.

I leave Britt's laptop on the porch swing and text my brother. I don't have time to chat. By the time I'm at the distillery, Drake is already there, sitting in his Range Rover and looking at his phone.

Quickly parking in my reserved space, I hit the lock button and step out. "Sorry I'm late. Had to run an errand for my brother."

"No worries, man." He steps out of the vehicle and reaches for my hand.

Hesitating, I study his palm before giving him a brief shake. "We should have the place to ourselves. Did you want a tour? A peek at the honey barrel?"

"I'll save that for next time. Walk with me." He smiles that obnoxious grin. "It's better if I show you what's on my mind. Help you catch the vision."

As if I'm interested in his vision. Still, I follow him as he walks across the parking lot, out to the pea-gravel drive, and towards the road. He's wearing a brown suit and leather loafers, so I'm guessing we're not going far.

At the beginning of the road, he stops. "Take a look around. What do you see?"

My brow quirks, and I'm not sure what he's getting at. "I see my family's land."

"And I see opportunity!" He spreads his arm across the quiet green fields like he's in the opening number of a Broadway musical. "Picture it. A resort hotel with a golf course, a splash pad for the kids, and all the customers you could want right here in your own backyard."

It actually *is* my own backyard, and I can't think of anything worse than plugging up the beautiful scenery with high rises and traffic and noise and litter.

Exhaling a brief laugh, I shake my head. "We're not interested in selling."

"Are you kidding me?" His brows rise, and he pauses for a moment. "You haven't heard my offer yet."

"We don't need the money." I'm returning to the distillery, and he's right behind me. "Let the golfers go to Kiawah, and the beachcombers can go to Hilton Head."

"What about the foodies? The bourbon enthusiasts?"

"I don't need a bunch of taters ruining the scenery."

"Now you're just being a snob." He laughs. "I think Eureka is ripe for development. It's my job to spot these things. I'm offering to let you in on the ground floor of something big."

"I've already got my big thing." I stop when we reach the cars. "I appreciate you stopping by. If that's all you wanted to say, I've got work to do."

"And I thought you were a visionary. Guess I was wrong."

His words don't bother me if that's his goal. "Eureka's not interested in being developed. We like things the way they are."

"Sounds like that's your opinion, man. I'd like to take it to the people, see what they have to say. Maybe this won't be the spot, but you'll regret missing the opportunity."

"Suit yourself. I'm only trying to save you some time." I leave him standing beside my car, but I'm halfway to the door when a loud burst of laughter stops me.

Turning back, I frown at him. "What's so funny?"

"Sorry." He makes a big show of clearing his throat, putting his hand on his chest. "Let me be the first to say it. Nice ass."

Now I'm really frowning. "What?"

He barks a laugh, rapping his knuckles on the back-door

window of my car. "Tell your fiancée I said hey. I'll be seeing you two around town."

He climbs into his Range Rover still laughing, and I wonder if the real problem Cass had with Drake was because he might be gay. Whatever. I'm no judge.

Turning, I head inside. I need to see how well the cleaning crew did and get ready to be open for business tomorrow.

Chapter 14

Cass

"**W**HAT ARE YOU DOING HERE?" PIPER GREETS ME AT THE DOOR of Adam's place, and Pinky races through it, yelling for Bubba and Ryan.

"I figured Owen could use some company." I follow my friend inside, to where Adam's standing at the bar in his kitchen.

"Looks like we shared a brain today."

"Hey, girl." He walks over to give me a hug. "How's the pink cyclone treating you?"

"She's not a cyclone." I cross my arms, lifting my chin. "She's a princess, and she's really sweet."

"I see you haven't crossed her yet." Adam snorts, going to the coffeepot. "Coffee?"

"Please." I'm about to follow him when what feels like pincers clip me by the third finger of my left hand.

"What. The frick?" Piper's eyes are wide.

Shit. I forgot to take off that fucking ring. Adam's back is turned, and I'm spiraling. How do I keep getting into these situations?

I'm about to answer her when my phone buzzes in my hand, and I look down to see it's a text from Alex. "Hold that thought. This might be important."

Holding up my finger, I dash out the door again to read it.

Everything good? is all he wrote, and my shoulders drop.

Scrubbing my fingers over my forehead, I confess. *Dropped by Adam's to take Owen swimming, and Piper saw the ring. What do I say?*

Gray dots appear then stop.

Then they start again, and they stop.

I'm chewing on my thumbnail, dying of suspense mixed with dread, when he finally responds. *Met with Drake. He's planning to stay. Has a development idea.*

"Shit," I hiss under my breath, my thumbs moving quickly over my phone face.

I guess we have to confess. The thought makes me sick to my stomach.

Drake is going to be such an asshole when I come clean. He'll make some major case about it, and I'll have to leave town until he goes away. Alex will be embarrassed, and I'll look like a fool. Why did I pull Alex into this?

I know why. I told him why. Alex Stone makes me feel like I'm not a fuck up. He doesn't judge me, and being with him makes me feel like I have value.

Clearly I need therapy. I'm aware my sense of worth should come from within, but it doesn't. My phone buzzes, and I jump when I read his text.

I'm willing to keep going if you are.

My eyes widen as I stare at his words. My fingers tremble as I text, *You are?*

Yes.

What does that mean?

I'm chewing my thumb as the gray dots float. *It means I'll be damned if I let that dickhead shame you.*

I can't text anymore. I hit the call button on my phone.

He answers before the first ring. "You have a problem with that?" It's his all-business, take-no-excuses tone, and my stomach tightens.

"You'd do that for me?" My voice is soft, and stupidly, I want to cry.

"Yes."

"But what about our friends? Piper's not going to believe this ring is just a gift."

He's quiet a moment, and I imagine that problem-solving expression on his face. "Let them think what they will, and when he leaves, we can come up with some excuse to break it off. You think I work too much, or you don't like the way I chew my food."

I don't say I could never imagine breaking up with him if he were truly my fiancé. Instead, I go with, "What about Pinky?"

"She doesn't have to know."

"I think she'll find out if everyone's talking about it."

"Tell Piper we're keeping it a secret from her until we set a date. She'll respect our wishes."

Inhaling slowly, I try to dismiss the feeling of dread at this arrangement. He asked me if I trusted him *twice*, and I said yes both times. Still, this is playing with fire.

"Are you with me, Cass?" I like the way he says my name.

I like the idea of him wanting to protect me. I remember his words last night, *I like you coming to me for protection…* I like the idea of being with him, like we're on a team, like we're a real family. Something I've never had.

"I'm with you." I wish my voice didn't tremble when I said it.

"You can fill me in on how it goes tonight."

We say goodbye and disconnect the phone, and I wrap my arms around my waist a moment. Piper's face appears in the window, and when she sees I'm off the phone, she steps outside.

"Did you two get your stories straight?"

I've never lied to my friends, and I'm not sure how good of an actress I can be.

Straightening my shoulders, I channel Idina Menzel, who played Elphaba in *Wicked* on Broadway… and Elsa in *Frozen*.

I push back my hair and smile. "Alex and I are engaged."

"What?" Piper's voice goes so high, if Edward were here, he'd howl. "It happened at the wedding reception, didn't it? I knew you weren't just talking in his office. And what's this nanny thing? A cover?"

"Shh!" I put my hand up in front of her mouth. "We haven't told Pinky. We don't want her to be hurt if anything… changes."

It comes out so smoothly, I'm clearly a natural-born liar.

"What the hell would change? Alex is hot as fuck, and while I wouldn't have immediately put the two of you together, it makes perfect sense if you think about it."

"It does?" I'm desperate to hear more.

"Of course! He's so serious and professional and working all the time, and you're…" My eyes narrow, and she links our arms. "You're easygoing and fun and empathetic and hot. I'm glad to know he's not blind. Plus you're great with kids. When did this happen? While you were planning the wedding? Did you catch wedding fever?"

I'm not a fan of the comparison chart she just drew, and I'm onto her not-so-smooth redirection. But I can't argue. I am a mess.

"Sort of." I try to imagine how we might've decided to get married in a month. "We just sort of hit it off, and when he gave me the ring it was more of a promise of something more."

She clasps her hands, blinking happily. "That's so adorably old-fashioned—and so Alex. I'm sure that's the spark. You're both old souls. What's his star sign?"

"Capricorn."

"Ooh… Pisces and Capricorn. That's a good match." She smiles at me in a knowing way. "So I take it you're not really his nanny?"

"No, I am. I mean, that's the story we're telling Pinky." I feel like my actorly talents are faltering. "Just until we're 100 percent sure this is going to work. Will you help me keep it a secret?"

"We have to tell Britt. She'll never forgive us if we keep it from her."

"No!" The pressure starts to build in my chest, and I wish Alex were here to jump in and help. Piper's expression is total confusion, and I'm thinking fast. "I mean, if we tell Britt, we'll have to tell Aiden, and then Owen will find out, and he might tell Pinky."

Jesus, talk about weaving a tangled web!

My friend presses her lips together, then nods. "Okay. But we can't keep it from her for too long or she'll be pissed at us."

"Just for now, and I'll be sure she isn't pissed at you." I start to take the ring off my finger, but she stops me, tilting my hand side to side.

"It's so beautiful!" Her voice thickens. "First Britt, now you. I'm going to be all alone before it's over."

"What? No, you're not!" I throw my arms around her, pulling her into a hug. "I would never let you be alone."

"Me and Ma and her ridiculous doomsday cellar." She laughs, wiping a tear off her cheek.

It's a punch to the gut.

I'm lying my ass off, and she's getting a hundred percent emotionally invested.

I'm going to hell.

"Stop it, and stop crying! Nothing's going to change." My arm is around her shoulder, and her arm is around my waist as I turn us towards the house. "We're going to take these kids swimming, and we're not going to say a word about this to Adam or anybody. Okay?"

"Okay…" She exhales heavily. "But it's going to be hard."

"That's what she said," I quip, pulling the ring off my finger and shoving it into my pocket. "Now dry your eyes. We'll tell everyone at the right time. Trust me."

I wish I sounded as confident as Alex does when he says those words to me, but in reality, I've never pulled a stunt like this, and I'm scared as shit over how it's going to play out.

It's after five when we finally return to the house. I invite Adam and Owen to join us for supper because Adam is an incredible cook, and Alex and I have already copped to being expert re-heaters. I'm not sure how that's going to play out.

Parking the car, I let Pinky out before going to the trunk to remove the box of bachelorette supplies. "Would you mind taking Pinky inside? I've just got to carry this upstairs."

Owen takes his little cousin's hand, but Adam walks straight to where I'm holding the enormous box.

"Give me that." He lifts it out of my hands. "You're in the garage apartment?"

"It's not that heavy." I step back crossing my arms. "I could've taken it up there myself."

"I'll meet you inside."

He enters the garage, and I follow the kids around to the side door. Alex is standing at the bar in the kitchen in those ass-hugging jeans and that muscled-chest-and-biceps-hugging Henley. His hair is perfectly messy, and when they enter, Pinky lets out a loud, "Daddy!"

I pause a moment to watch him scoop up his little redhead and give her a hug, and it's so adorable, I'm pretty sure I ovulate. He's such a good daddy.

"I've got the latest *Fortnite* on the Xbox," he tells Owen, who lets out a little hoot and gives him a high-five before taking off to the living room.

Pinky starts squirming to get down, and the minute her feet hit the floor, she runs after her cousin.

Alex looks up, and our eyes meet through the glass door. It's a silent earthquake. His smile is warm liquid in my veins, and I want to walk straight into his arms, kiss his lips, and tuck my nose in his neck, inhaling his warm cedar and soap scent.

He walks over to open the door for me, hazel eyes roaming my body. "Hey." It's a low vibration in the charged air around us.

"Hey." My reply is higher, softer.

"Everything go okay today?"

I nod, stepping closer so I can put my hand on his forearm as he leads me into the house. "I did just what you said. I told Piper we were keeping it quiet for now. We didn't even tell Adam."

Not that it was hard. Adam's eyes followed my friend like she was a mountain begging to be climbed, which she didn't even seem to notice.

When Piper said she had to check in at the paper, Adam said he had to pick up donations for the church's food bank. Ryan stayed with us, and I spent the afternoon teaching Pinky a kid-friendly dance routine to "Fergalicious" while the boys threw a baseball back and forth.

"Tell me what?" Adam's voice elicits a little yelp from me.

We both turn to face him, and he starts to laugh. "You two couldn't look any more guilty if you tried. What are you hiding?"

"Nothing!" My voice is too high, and my brain is spinning. "We, ah, we were…"

Alex steps in and finishes my sentence. "We were going to offer to keep Owen for you the rest of the week. To give you a break."

He shakes his head like he doesn't buy it, but he plays along. "Nah, I told Owen he could help me in the community garden tomorrow. I like him working with me."

He continues past us, and I put my hands on my face, peeping through my fingers at Alex. He winks and hooks a finger through mine in response, pulling me into the house. The familiar move makes my insides all squishy and warm.

Like Piper, I never considered him a possibility before. He was always so smart and fine and distant. Now I'm practically obsessed with him.

"Let me help you with that." He goes to where Adam is dragging leftover reception food out of the refrigerator.

"I'll chop up some fresh veggies and sauté them together…" Adam is already spinning his culinary magic when I go to where Pinky is hanging on her cousin in front of the television.

Owen keeps rolling his shoulder and telling her to get off him, and I'm not sure Fortnight is the best game for a four-year-old to watch.

"Let's get the chlorine out of your hair, Pink!" I call brightly.

"Noo!" She falls back on the couch with a loud wail. "I'm helping Bubba kill the bad guys."

"No, you're not!" Owen snaps. "Stop calling me Bubba and go wash your hair!"

His response only makes her dig in her heels harder. Her little back arches off the couch, and I know two things—she's tired, and she's hungry. I also remember what Adam said about not crossing the pink cyclone.

Chewing my lip, I don't want to seem like I can't handle Alex's daughter, even when she's being a pill. Looking around, my eyes land on Piglet.

"I think all that shooting scares Piglet." My head tilts to the side, and I lift the stuffed pig, stroking his head. "It's okay, Piglet, I'll take you upstairs so you don't have to be alone."

Pinky stills on the couch, her little face turning serious as she watches me cradling her bestie.

I lay it on thick. "You're a good little pig, you know? I'll let you use my special shampoo and conditioner to get the chlorine out of your fur. And maybe we can paint your toenails when we're done."

She's off the couch in a jump. "Piglet doesn't have toenails! He can't wear polish!"

"Huh." Twisting my lips, I examine his stuffed hooves. "That's too bad. I was in the mood to give someone a pedicure."

Sliding her little hand in my arm, she reassures me. "It's okay. You can give me a pedicure!"

Narrowing my eyes, I pretend to consider this alternative. "You'll have to wash your hair first, and we can't take too long because Uncle Adam is making a delicious dinner."

She bypasses me, running up the stairs faster than I can catch her. "I'll be so fast!"

"Let me help you rinse your hair!" I climb the stairs after her feeling pretty good about my mastery of preschooler manipulation.

When we return to the kitchen, a gorgeous platter of snapped green beans, yellow squash, and grilled tomatoes sits beside grilled chicken breasts and crescent rolls in the middle of the table. Pinky's toes are painted with Esse's Ballet Slipper, which is the palest shade of pink available—another thing I didn't ask Alex about first.

I've got to do better.

The kids are ravenous after our day of activity. I'm pretty ravenous myself, and we don't talk much during the meal. Alex and Adam, by contrast, chat nonstop about Drake the Douche's plan to turn Eureka into the newest high-end resort location on the Carolina coast.

"We're not even that close to the beach." Adam's tone is logical.

Alex is a bit fiercer. "He's like every developer I've ever met. He can't see a beautiful, undisturbed patch of nature without wanting to muck it up with hotels and parking lots."

His brother laughs. "I had no idea you were such a conservationist."

"I'm not a conservationist. I just don't want him screwing with Eureka."

"I think everyone will agree with that."

The kids hop down and return to the living room, and I collect our plates, carrying them to the sink.

The men have fallen silent until Adam lifts his wine glass as if to toast. "I've been meaning to tell you, Bro, nice ass."

Alex coughs on his sip, setting his glass down a little too hard. "What the fuck?"

"Language, please." Adam glances over his shoulder to where the kids aren't listening, barely containing his laughter.

My eyes widen, and I turn to the sink fast, rinsing the plates and trying not to snort.

"It's all good," Adam continues. "I don't think they heard you."

"Why did you say that to me?" Alex actually looks over his shoulder and down his back, and I can't hold back.

A laugh hiccups in my throat.

"Although, I've heard it's a painful procedure." His brother continues. "Where did they find fat on *your* body?"

"What the hell are you talking about?" Alex is so confused, and I'm about to pee holding in my laughter.

"Don't worry—your secret's safe with me." He pats Alex on the shoulder on his way to the living room. "Owen, we gotta get home little man. Morning comes early."

Owen exhales a half-hearted protest, and Pinky's eyes are heavy as she lies on the couch behind him. Aiden's son gives us all hugs before following his uncle to the door.

"Night, babe." Adam kisses my cheek, calling back as he leaves. "Better watch your car. Somebody's pranking you."

Alex goes to the door leading to the garage, and I skip into the living room, scooping a sleeping little girl off the couch. I carry her up the stairs, and she doesn't even open her eyes as I help her brush her teeth then exchange her dress for her nightgown.

Her daddy is waiting in the bedroom when we return, and he leans down to kiss her forehead as she snuggles with Piglet.

Our eyes meet, and I can see I'm in trouble now.

Chapter 15

Alex

GOT MY *BBL* FROM BOOTY'S! THE BRIGHT YELLOW BUMPER STICKER announces in red lettering from the passenger's side rear window of my car.

Right where I'd never see it.

Scraping my thumbnail over the vinyl, I try to get it off, but I can't. How long has this been here? My jaw tightens when I remember Drake complimenting my ass, and I rub a hand over my mouth trying to think.

It wasn't there after the wedding. I loaded and unloaded Pinky and all the leftovers Mom sent home with us. I'd have seen it then, or my mom definitely would have. I can only imagine how that would've gone down.

Actually, I'm pretty sure she doesn't know what a Brazilian Butt Lift is, so probably nothing would've gone down besides confusion. The name *Booty's* is vaguely familiar, and I stand, doing my best to place where I've heard it before.

My eyes drift to the stairs, and I think about Cass's suspicious retreat to the kitchen when Adam brought it up. I've only been around one other person since Saturday.

Standing there in the garage, staring at the garish bumper sticker, I start to laugh. "Fuck, she got me," I mutter to myself.

The irritation simmering in my stomach turns to an amusing urge for payback, and I head into the house. She wants to play games? She has no idea who she's up against.

I hear noises upstairs, and I slowly climb to where she's guiding my daughter through brushing her teeth. Pinky's eyes are closed through the entire process, and I don't think she'll be up for a story tonight.

No worries, because I have other plans.

Cass's eyes flicker to mine where I'm waiting in the doorway, and she blinks away quickly. *That's right, you're busted.*

Biting the inside of my lip, I don't smile. I'll use her thinking I'm pissed to my advantage.

Then she hits me with her secret weapon. Sitting on the side of Pinky's bed, she strokes her hand over my daughter's head as she softly sings a lullaby about a castle on a cloud.

It's a melancholy little song, but fuck, her voice is so beautiful. It changes the burn in my stomach to something deeper, something urgent.

She whispers the last words about how crying is not allowed, and I'm ready to pull her to me and make sure she never sheds another tear as long as she lives.

Pinky is long gone in dreamland when Cass stands and tiptoes in my direction. We step out of the room, and she closes the door silently before looking up at me.

I'm standing in front of her trying to remember how I managed to speak the last time I heard her sing. I was stronger than I thought at fifteen, because I'd also just seen her naked body for the first time—pert little tits, flat stomach…

She was my teenage wet dream, a fucking siren from the sea, and still I spoke to her that day.

"You said your mother was a singer?"

She nods. "She wanted to be the next Stevie Nicks. She loved her songs and her witchy style, but she never got anywhere with it."

"What happened to her?"

A little sigh slips from her lips. "She died in a hotel on St Louis Street."

"Jesus, I'm so sorry."

"It wasn't your fault." Her chin lifts in a defensive way, and her narrow shoulders shrug. "She made her choices. They didn't include me… or any of us."

"Maybe she felt like she couldn't come back empty-handed?"

"Or the things she left behind didn't have value to her."

"Her choices are her mistakes. They have nothing to do with you." I want to touch her, help her see how much I see in her. "Your beautiful voice is your gift, like your future."

Smoky gray-blue eyes meet mine, and her lips slide into a half-smile. "I sing for fun. As for my future, I want something that will pay the bills and not break my heart."

"Sounds like everyone in the world."

"Not everyone."

Reaching out, I clasp her hand, threading our fingers and leading her downstairs with a gentle tug. I feel like I understand her more now than I've ever understood anyone in my life. I've been disappointed by that person. The only difference was, she wasn't my mother.

When we reach the first floor, I look down at the fingers of her left hand tangled in mine. I imagine our lives entwined. I imagine us married. A secure future for her, where no one is left behind and no hearts are broken.

My eyes meet hers, and she's so open. Everything I said last night about waiting is out the window. I want to lift her in my arms, carry her out the door and up the stairs to her apartment. I want to spend the night with her in my arms, but is it too much? Too fast?

She looks down at our hands. "I appreciate you wanting to shield me from Drake."

"He's a pompous asshole." I pull her closer.

As much as I want more, I'd settle for another kiss, even if it damn near kills me every time I have to pull away from her.

She doesn't resist. "I guess if we're going to be engaged, we should know more about each other."

"As much as makes sense for people in our position."

"What's our position?" Her dark head tilts to the side, and my fingers curl wanting to thread in her silky hair.

"We got engaged after only a month. Obviously, we have great sexual chemistry."

"Obviously?" Amusement lines her face in a way that has my dick hardening in my pants. "Is that the only reason people get engaged after a month?"

"The only one I can think of." My hand slides to her waist, pulling her to me. "Unless a green card is involved."

"We're both citizens..."

I love a woman who isn't afraid to play, and playing with her is the only thing on my mind right now. "Everyone's going to assume we have crazy sex."

"Do we?" It's a hot exhale on her lips, and fuck me, I'm gone.

I gaze intently into her eyes. I don't ever want to do anything with her unless she's 100 percent onboard. No teasing. No games.

"Want to find out?"

Say yes. Say yes.

Instead, she hesitates, and her teeth press against her bottom lip.

Grabbing the reins, I take a step back. "Too fast?"

"No..." She shakes her head. "I mean, I want to, but what happens in the end?"

Fuck whoever told her she wasn't smart. She's fucking brilliant, and she knows to protect herself.

I, by contrast, am completely off book. I'm so calculated and patient when it comes to everything. Except her.

She's my kryptonite.

"Why don't we worry about that when it happens." I don't recognize my voice.

Reaching for her cheek, I pull her mouth to mine. It's a different kiss from the ones we've shared before. I don't tease. I don't lick her lips and nibble. I seal my mouth over hers and consume.

A soft noise slips from her throat, and her fingers curl against my shoulders, pulling her body closer to mine.

"Come with me." Her hand is clasped firmly in mine, and I lead her down the short hall off the living room to where my bedroom is located.

Heat twists low in my pelvis as I pull her through the door. I've wanted this so long, and now it's happening. Facing the door, I take a breath as I turn the lock, then I look at her.

Her back is against the wall. She's breathing fast, and her hair hangs in messy waves around her face. Raking my eyes down her body, her breasts rise and fall rapidly, hard nipples piercing her white cotton tank.

She's not wearing a bra, and I groan audibly. "I have to have you."

My cock is an iron rod in my jeans as I close the space between us, grasping her waist. Our mouths collide again, tongues curling, and her body melts into me. She's fresh air and sunshine, and I kiss her face. I kiss her closed eyes. I can't get enough of her.

Moving my mouth to the side of her jaw, near her ear, she exhales another noise, and it stokes the fire in my belly. I'm ready to nail her against this wall.

"I love that sound." My hands move along her waist, tracing the soft skin of her torso, rising higher to the breasts I've dreamed of touching since I was fifteen.

Lifting her shirt, they spill out, and her back arches eagerly.

"Your body is so beautiful." I palm the sides of her breasts, sliding my thumbs back and forth over her hardened nipples.

I'm hypnotized, watching the way she responds to my touch.

She whispers urgently, "Kiss them."

Leaning forward, I cover her breast with my mouth, sucking and flicking my tongue back and forth over the hardened tips.

"Oh, fuck," she gasps, moving closer.

I trace my lips to the other side, repeating the process, loving the feel of her fingers in my hair, threading and pulling.

I lift my chin to take another hit of her luscious mouth. "I want to kiss every part of you."

Her hands are on my cheeks, and she's kissing me in a way she hasn't until now. Her lips pull mine, and her tongue chases mine as if something inside her has awakened. She's as hungry and eager as I am, and I love it.

Reaching behind her, I slide my hand down the back of her thigh, gathering her long skirt in my fist until I'm touching bare skin. Her body trembles as I trail my fingers higher, over her round ass, before catching the thin string of her thong and yanking it down.

"Rip it off me," she gasps at my ear, biting and kissing.

I'm not sure it'll tear without hurting her. "I have a better idea."

Dropping to one knee, I catch the elastic waist of her skirt, and pull it down her legs, taking that scrap of nylon along with it.

For a moment, I gaze up at her naked body, so fucking gorgeous it hurts. She's in only that white tank, her full lips parted, and her dark hair hanging around her cheeks.

"Fuck, Cass, look at you."

A wash of pink tints her pretty face, and her knee bends, crossing a thigh over her pussy. "Take off your shirt at least."

Sitting back on my heels, I grab the back of my Henley and rip it over my head. "Better?"

She exhales a short laugh, running her fingers through my hair and pushing it off my forehead. "Getting there."

I slide my hands up the outside of her thighs in a worshipful move, and I lean forward, tracing my nose along her skin, inhaling the scent of faded coconut sunscreen, chlorine, and something deeper, the hidden depths of the ocean.

My mouth waters, and I kiss her hip, tracing my lips lower, down her belly, feeling her muscles tremble at my touch. She moans, and her fingers curl in my hair as I part her legs, sliding my tongue up the slit of her pussy.

"Fuck!" she yelps, and I'm addicted to her taste, saltwater and sweetness.

I lap my tongue again and again over her rigid clit, and her knees bend. I catch one leg, putting it over my shoulder, and she moans louder as I focus all my attention on this magical place between her thighs.

Her legs begin to shake, and she pulls my hair, rocking her hips against my face and chanting words I don't understand. Reaching up, I sink my thumb into her, and she's so fucking wet. Her juices coat my palm, as I do it again and again.

"That's right," I groan. "Ride my hand. Come for me."

An animal noise grunts from her body and with another circle of my tongue over her clit, her hand flies to her mouth, muffling her scream as she comes hard, bucking against my nose. I smile, giving her another suck, but she pulls back.

"It's too much," she gasps. "I can't…"

"Sure you can." I kiss the side of her hip, moving my lips higher as I rise to my knees.

When I stand, I'm so close, her hardened nipples graze my bare chest through thin cotton. She leans forward, pressing her face against me and inhaling. Her small hands circle my waist, traveling higher up my back.

"You're so perfect," she murmurs, and I slide my palm along her cheek, lifting her face to mine.

"You're perfect." I capture her mouth, kissing her deeply.

She rises on her tiptoes, wrapping her arms around my neck as if she'll climb me.

I'd let her. I want her body all over mine.

Reaching down, I lift her legs around my waist and carry her to the bed. "I'm going to fuck you now. Hard."

"Oh, God." Her mouth covers mine again, pulling and tasting, and I'm glad she came as fully as she did because I'm about to lose it.

I quickly lay her on the bed and unfasten my jeans, shoving them down my legs and stepping out as I grab a condom from my nightstand drawer. It's been years, but thank fuck, I still have a few strays mixed in with the quarters and charging cords.

I tear it open, ready to roll it on fast, when I realize she's changed positions on the bed. Her head is at my hips, and I almost shoot when her warm tongue curls around the tip of my cock. It's a shot of electricity that nearly buckles my knees.

"Cass…" I grip the back of her head. "Fuck. I could fuck your brains out."

It's been so long since anything but my own fist has touched my dick, and it feels incredible.

She pulls me deeper into her throat, fingers lightly tracing my balls, and I fight the urge to thrust. It takes all my willpower to cup her shoulders and guide her back onto the bed.

Her brow furrows, and I shake my head. "I don't want to come down your throat the first time."

She exhales a soft laugh and lies back against the pillows, her beautiful body nude except for that thin tank, which has risen to expose the rounded bottoms of her breasts.

Condom on, I put a knee between her legs, leaning forward to kiss her again. Her hands cup my cheeks, and she rises to meet me, arching her back and pulling us closer.

Her arms wrap around me, and her lips are at my ear. "I want your body on mine. I want you in me, holding me down."

Each phrase is punctuated with a kiss, her mouth moving closer until it's over mine. My tongue finds hers as my cock sinks deep into her slippery core. She's so fucking tight and wet, I have to be still a moment. My eyes squeeze closed with a groan, and when I finally find control, I start to rock.

Her body moves with mine, up and down like the waves on the sea. Her knees rise, and I reach down to grip her ass as I drive deeper, faster. Her arms tighten, and she grinds against me, meeting me with every thrust.

We're hot and desperate, grabbing and pulling, and I'm not going to last. Her body trembles, and she whimpers in my ear as her pussy breaks into rhythmic spasms. It's too fucking much, and it's been too long.

My body tenses, and mind-blowing pleasure radiates through my cock. My ass tightens, and with a low, haggard groan I come hard, pulsing again and again.

Lowering my face, I hold as the aftershocks jerk through my muscles.

"Shit," I groan, kissing her neck.

My heart beats so hard, and my eyes are closed as I try to calm my breathing, as I hold onto her like the one thing keeping me on the planet.

She's amazing. She's everything, and at last, I have her.

What scares me is how easy it would be to never let her go.

Chapter 16

Cass

Alex Stone is perfect. His body is a Michelangelo, and his mouth is the stuff of dreams. I've never come twice in a row so fast without battery-operated assistance.

My mind is reeling. I've never had sex like this in my life. I'm not sure my legs even work anymore, and the space between my thighs is shimmering and vibrating like a New Year's Eve fireworks show.

And I'm freaking terrified.

The reality of what we're doing is just waiting to drop on me and crush my heart to powder. The fire I've been playing with is officially out of control.

Alex Stone is not my boyfriend, and as much as I love his beautiful ring, I'm *really* his employee. I'm really *not* his fiancée.

He told me he doesn't want to hurt Pinky, that we have to be careful, but sleeping with him is as far from careful as we can get. It's the last thing I should be doing, yet here I am, lying beneath his delicious weight, on the edge of falling in love with him.

With a deep groan, he moves to lie beside me on the bed. "Definitely crazy chemistry."

A lazy smile curls his lips, like we're playing a game, and I have to force myself to smile in response. "Yeah. Crazy."

I sound like a loon. *What am I doing?*

I've always found his control attractive. His ability to compartmentalize. Of course, he's in control in bed. He's in control of everything, including this fictitious engagement. I dragged him into it; now he's setting all the rules.

What did he say? We're getting to know each other as much as we can for two people who got engaged after only a month?

Only we're not engaged. It's all pretend.

And while I can pretend-kiss him, I can't pretend his touch doesn't affect me. I'm not like him. My emotions are always on my sleeve. The whole reason I was so good at tarot is because I'm too empathetic. Just ask Gwen.

Sitting up slowly, I rub my hands over my eyes as I try to put my brain back together. I seriously need a minute alone.

"At least that's one thing we don't have to lie about." I wonder if he hears the guilt in my tone.

Apparently not.

He climbs out of bed, and I watch his toned ass flex as he walks to his en suite bathroom. All jokes aside, there is *nothing* wrong with that ass.

I listen as he disposes of the condom and runs water in the sink. After a few moments, he returns wearing black boxer briefs that should be illegal and carrying a washcloth in his hand.

"For you." He holds it out, and I slide to the edge of the bed, taking it from him.

"Thanks." But I can't clean up here.

Instead, I step over to where my skirt lies in a puddle at his door. I don't see my thong anywhere, but I don't waste time searching. I'm more concerned with getting out of here and getting my head straight.

"I think I'll just take a shower at my place." I step into my skirt, quickly pulling it over my hips.

He closes the space between us, gently touching my upper arm. "Are we good?"

"Yeah…" I blink up at him, forcing a light laugh. "Yes!"

Too good, if you ask me.

"I think it's okay if you'd like to spend the night with me. Penelope's a sound sleeper. She rarely comes to my room at night, and we can lock the door just in case."

"Oh, no. I don't think that's a good idea." *For so many reasons.* "We have to follow our rules, don't we?"

"We have rules?" Disappointment quirks his brow, and my insides melt.

God, yes, I need rules if I'm going to play this way with him. He's too damn fine and too damn good in bed. *Focus, Cass.*

"We don't want to confuse her, remember? You don't want her to be hurt?"

"Right. Of course not." He nods, but he doesn't sound as firm as he did the other night.

Stepping forward, I kiss his cheek. I have to touch him one more time for my own mental health. Hesitating, I inhale his clean scent now tinged with sex and sweat. *Mouthwatering.*

He catches my hand before I leave, and looks directly into my eyes. "I think I'm going to enjoy getting to know you better."

My lips press together, and I nod. "Me, too."

It's the truest thing I've said all night.

I squeeze his hand, releasing it as I leave his bedroom, headed for my apartment above the garage. I've lost control of this situation, and I've got to find it again. If I don't I'm going to drown.

Ten minutes later, I'm soaking in my tub, turning over everything that happened, the way he kissed me, the way he told me I was beautiful. My chin rests on my knees, and I'm up to my armpits in scented, lavender-water and foamy bubbles.

We talked about my mom, which is something I never do.

He said I don't have to be defined by what she did, but I always have. I'm the orphaned daughter of a failed nightclub singer, whereas he's the scion of a close-knit, well-adjusted, by-the-book ideal.

I would watch him when I was younger, thinking how wonderful it would be to be a part of a family like that, to have that level of support and safety. Adam was a wild child, but even he didn't stray too far from the fold.

His dad was the freaking sheriff, after all. Until he died, I guess.

My lips puff out with a heavy exhale, and I need to talk to Britt. She always has a sensible approach to my self-inflicted problems, when all I can see is an irresponsible, anxious mess. The kind of woman Drake Redford says I am.

Only, if I talk to Britt, I'll have to tell her everything. Then I'd have to tell Piper as well, and I'm not sure I'm prepared for that level of honesty—or embarrassment.

Not after Alex said we're in this together.

"Oh, God." I lift my hands out of the water and run them over my face.

It felt so good when he said that. I want to be on his team.

I got everything I dreamed of tonight. I was in his bed, loving his body, feeling beautiful and cherished and soaking up all that delicious strength being with him promises...

And if I'd spent the night in his arms, I definitely would've fallen in love with him. Then what? The month ends, and we shake hands and walk away?

Thinking about it makes my stomach hurt.

I'm not made that way.

Standing, I grab a towel off the rack and dry off quickly, lifting the drain on the tub. I grab my fluffy purple robe off the hook and wrap it around my body, pacing the small apartment as I chew my thumb.

A glance at the clock tells me it's after ten. Maybe that's too late to call her on her honeymoon, but a text won't hurt, will it? Lifting my phone, I carefully weigh my words.

Hey, girl, hey! How's married life? I hit send and chew on the side of my thumb again.

They're probably having amazing sex, making perfect little babies, and I won't hear from her until tomorrow. Exhaling heavily, I'm about to toss my phone on the bed when it buzzes in my hand.

Divine… My brow quirks at her answer, but I wasn't expecting less, was I? Then she continues. *Honestly, not much different than it was before. What's up?*

My thumbs fly as I text. *Not much. Don't want to bother you on your honeymoon.*

Gray dots precede her reply. *Piper said you're Alex's nanny. How's that?*

Fun! Pinky is a hoot. So smart and funny, and Alex is… I'm not sure how to finish.

I almost type *determined, driven, wonderful.* I suppose those are all things a fiancée would say, but I don't want to lie again.

He can be intimidating, but don't sell yourself short. You're multi-talented! He wouldn't have hired you if he wasn't impressed.

Or if he wasn't tricked into it, I think, chewing my lip. Except, hadn't he mentioned the job before I said we were engaged?

I realize I've left Britt hanging, and I quickly text. *It's only a month. What then?*

Is he paying you well?

My fingers still. I never even asked how much he's paying me. I was too anxious to get out of Aunt Carol's house, and with everything else, it never came up.

She misinterprets my silence. *NVM—Mrs. Priddy is retiring, and everyone is moving up. They need a K teacher.*

My brow furrows, and while I like the idea… *I'm not certified.*

Do this. A link lights up on my phone for an accelerated certification program at the community college in Ridgeland.

I tap the link and quickly navigate to the tuition page. *It's still a lot of money.*

You might get a tuition waiver. Need-based, rural community...

You think?

I do, and you're great with kids.

My chest rises, and I feel more in control of my life already. I could actually do this. *Thanks, Britt.*

NP! I want you teaching my kids!

I imagine her smiling up at me like the bright blonde ray of sunshine she is, and a smile lifts my cheeks. My eyes heat with tears, like a sentimental goose, but I'm really fucking happy.

It's a real path that won't take a million years or cost a million dollars—and I like it a lot! Teaching kindergarten would be the sweetest thing. Of course, it would have its challenges like anything else, but it's just what I want.

Tapping on the link, I quickly fill out the application for enrollment. Then I open my email program and begin brainstorming a letter to the school. I'll get Britt to help me with it.

The end of the month doesn't feel so bleak anymore, and it's like a weight off my shoulders. I do a little dance around the apartment, Sir Mix-a-Lot's "Baby Got Back" playing in my head, before pulling on a sleep shirt.

Shuffling over to my desk, I plug the charging cord into my laptop, and my eyes fall on the angel ring sitting in a small dish. I scoop it up and slip it on my finger, holding out my hand to admire it on my finger before crawling into bed and tucking it under my chin.

A woman with a future doesn't need silly schemes to make herself valuable. But it doesn't mean I don't like wearing his ring.

A woman with a future can also be a little naughty, because nothing is sexier than a woman who knows what she wants.

Chapter 17

Alex

I F THERE'S ONE THING I KNOW, IT'S WOMEN ARE NOT LIKE DISTILLING the perfect bourbon. You can't simply do the steps, follow the established rules, and achieve the desired outcome.

For example, I got one of the worst night's sleep of my life last night worrying I'd made a critical error with Cass.

Granted, it's an error I'd like to make again and again, and she seemed very willing in the moment. Hell, she seemed to be enjoying herself as much as I was. I know for a fact she came twice—I was counting.

I wanted to do more, but the way she practically ran from my bedroom had my head spinning. What went wrong?

Consent is very important to me, and I asked her plainly if she wanted to do it. I don't know why she went from hot to cold so fast. Did I let her down somehow?

For the next seven hours, I tossed and turned rehashing every word I'd said and searching for my mistake. Not finding it, I spent the next hour preparing my apology.

Now, I'm here, all ready to fall on my sword when she

bounces into the kitchen smiling and even giving me a little wink as she pours her coffee.

"Morning, boss." The tease in her tone changes the whole vibe of the room.

My stomach unknots, and I lean closer to her ear. "I didn't expect to like the sound of that so much."

"Got any orders for me?" Her eyebrow arches, and she has no idea.

"For starters, have a fun, *busy* day and wear this little lady out again."

My daughter's at the bar singing as she eats her yogurt and strawberries. I hadn't been paying much attention, since I'd been worrying about Cass's appearance.

Now I realize she's chanting over and over, "T-A-S-T-E-Y, tasty!"

"That's not how you spell *tasty*."

Cass laughs. "It is if you're Fergalicious."

Pinky holds up her jelly toast with two fingers. "So delicious!"

I'm not following, but Cass is enjoying her performance. Her smile is a huge relief, and I've got to get to work. I've got a nine o'clock meeting with an old friend in the business, and then I've got payback to plan.

"See you two at five." My eyes slide over her body one last time.

Today she's in beige linen pants and a cropped top that shows off her stomach. It reminds me too much of sliding my hands under her shirt and devouring her breasts. I want to touch her again, so I'd better get out of here before I pop an inappropriate semi.

"We'll do something very active." She lifts her cup, and my ring is on her finger.

I don't expect my response to seeing her this way, in my kitchen wearing my ring. For a moment, it's like I'm looking ahead in time to an idealized version of the future.

I wish I'd gotten a better night's sleep. This is what happens when I don't trust my instincts. They've served me pretty damn well up to this point, and they're telling me this is the girl I'm going to marry.

"Damn, that is some good-ass whiskey." Willie "Bender" Cartwright exhales a throaty laugh as he rocks back in his chair at the tasting bar. "You definitely have the gift."

Satisfaction warms my chest, and I like to imagine Pop looking down on what I've done with the place. "You're the expert."

Even though he's twenty years older than me, I've been close to Bender since I was a kid, since he would stop by and shoot the shit with my dad over bottles of beer on the back porch.

Fast forward fifteen years, and he's my biggest fan and best promoter. A legend in the industry, Bender has called more unicorns than anyone can count. He's the original influencer, and tastemakers listen to what he says.

Brands are made on his approval alone.

He was the first one to pronounce our single barrel the best since Pappy van Winkle, and he started the hunt for Stone Cold when I needed all the help I could get. Needless to say, his rough-around-the-edges presence is welcome at our campfire any time, and when he says he's in town for a visit, I make room on my schedule.

He takes another sip, clearing his gravelly throat. "Yep. I think this is the best yet."

"I felt pretty confident when I tasted it, but your word seals the deal."

"I wouldn't say it if it weren't true." He chuckles, lighting a cigar. "Your pop was a genius and one of the few people who'd dump the whole batch in the ditch if he wasn't satisfied. Couldn't get him to give it to me."

He laughs more, and it's another reason I cherish Bender's friendship. So few people are left who remember Pop, and I gravitate to stories that reveal a side of him I never saw. As my grandfather he was wisdom and nostalgia, but with his friends, he was mischievous and fun.

"I want him to be remembered." I turn the bottle with his image on the label.

Bender exhales a thin stream of smoke. "He was proud of you as a kid, and he'd be proud of the man you've become."

"I appreciate that."

"It's true." He nods. "And how's that little spitfire daughter of yours? Last time I saw her, she called me a grumpy old billygoat."

My jaw clenches, and I give him a tight smile. "Sorry about that. I can't keep her away from Aiden's son and his friends."

His laugh is more of a bark, and he slaps a hand on the polished bar as he rises from his chair. "Don't apologize. She's not wrong, and I expect she'll get feistier as she gets older."

"She starts kindergarten in the fall. It feels like that time has flown, and yet it felt like it took forever."

"The days are long, but the years are fast. I don't know who said that." He polishes off the last of the bourbon. "What I do know is we've got another unicorn on our hands here. I'll let Chip know."

"Thanks, Ben."

Chip Rogers is the publisher of *Bourbon Standard*, which is the industry bible.

"Don't thank me. It's simply the truth."

I follow him past the large, oak barrels that line the interior of the tasting room out the glass doors leading to the porch. His pickup is parked next to my car, and I walk with him to the vehicle.

"Aiden married that little Bailey girl." He leans his arm on the door after he opens it. "That was something else about her daddy. I wouldn't have expected it to play out that way, but I'm glad justice was served. I know that case weighed heavy on Andrew."

"We were all pretty shocked, but Britt and her mom were glad to have answers. They're glad to put it all to rest."

"Yeah," He lifts his chin, looking towards the grassy field. "I was thinking about paying a visit to Gwen, seeing as I'm in the neighborhood and all."

My brow arches, and I scratch my jaw. "That's an interesting idea."

"Think so?" He puts a hand on his hip, turning to me. "There was a time not too long ago when it felt like something might happen between us. Wouldn't be surprised if that time has passed."

I confess, I'm having a hard time picturing Gypsy Gwen with Grumpy Billy Goat Bender. Still, I'm not one to crush anybody's dream.

"It might not've passed. Being alone gets old after a while."

He exhales, nodding. "You talking from experience?"

"Maybe." Sleeping with Cass woke me up to how long it's been.

"What about that?" He angles his cigar at me. "You're a good-looking man. I'm sure you could find a lady pretty easy."

I almost laugh at him turning the tables on me. Instead, I answer honestly. "There might be something in the works. It's too soon to tell, but it's promising."

"Good." He climbs into the truck. "You're too young to put out to pasture."

He slams the door, and I shake my head at his ability to

fish information right out of me like a still pond on a cloudy day.

It's been a while since I've been fishing.

Making a mental note, I head back to my office to see what I can do about this gauntlet that's been thrown. Brazilian Butt Lift, my ass. That girl is asking for it.

Hopping on Amazon, I spend several minutes searching, until I find the perfect thing. Clicking on expedited shipping, it should be here tonight.

I lean back in my chair, satisfied when my phone buzzes on the desk. Aiden is texting our brothers group chat.

What's this bullshit about developing the land around Stone Cold?

I tap a quick reply. *You're supposed to be on your honeymoon.*

Adam is right behind me. *Get back to your wife. Nothing's going to change in a week.*

I am with my wife. Aiden's surly tone comes through even in text form. *We're at the courthouse, and Drake Redford is canvassing town square.*

Leaning forward, I run my hand over my mouth. *How so?*

Collecting signatures, Aiden replies. *He can drag it to the town council, but we're not fucking with that land. Go to the Disney resort in Hilton Head, asshole.*

I couldn't agree more. *They can't force anything.*

Gray dots float, and I wait to see who has something to say. I don't know if it'll be Adam or Aiden, but I know if the three of us are in agreement, nothing's going to change.

Britt says he makes a good case. Aiden's reply pulls me up short. *Says if it'll help us, if they keep it small, it could work.*

Fuck me. Let's talk about this in person.

It's as far as I'll go.

If the impetus is to capitalize on the brand of Stone Cold distillery, we don't need it. Hell, I can barely keep up with demand as it is. I'm adding barrels every day, and it'll still take at least four years to cross the country.

Once Ben talks to Chip, the demand will get even more punishing. We could be looking at prices approaching several hundreds for a bottle, simply because we can't make it fast enough.

However, if Britt thinks it could help the town, I'd be willing to hear her thought process. If it were me, I'd say no. Hilton Head and Kiawah are practically unlivable at peak times of the year, and I don't want that here.

It's very *Not in my backyard*, and I don't care. Sue me.

Adam? I send the text mostly to take the temperature of the room.

I'm pretty confident I'm right, but I don't like to presuppose.

Your daughter's a scratch baseball player, he replies.

Frowning at my phone, my thumbs move quickly. **What are you talking about?**

Come to the ball field and you'll see.

Pocketing my phone, I wave at the bartenders opening the tasting room on my way out the door. At four and a half, Pinky's old enough for T-ball, but she does like to keep up with her cousin.

By the time I make it into town, a cluster of older residents has formed around the gazebo in the square in front of the courthouse. I park in an empty space across from the Star Parlor, just as Gwen walks out in her usual tarot-reading attire.

Today she's in a floor-length, black, white, and pink caftan with gold bracelets down her long arms and a scarf tied around her billowy blonde hair. Hesitating, I try to picture her with my wizened old friend with his cowboy boots and cigars.

Her first husband was an escape artist, and as far as I know, Bender's only talent is spotting a good bourbon, which I care about greatly. Not so sure he's exciting enough for her.

"My daughter is supposed to be on her honeymoon."
Gwen crosses the street to where I'm standing, surrounding
me in the scent of patchouli.

"Looks like they got cabin fever."

We walk to the gazebo where Aiden is standing with his
hands on his hips and a scowl on his face behind Britt. She's at
the head of the small group of residents, and she's interrogat-
ing Drake like it's headline news.

I glance around, and of course, Piper is right beside her,
recording it all on her phone.

"How would a development like this affect property val-
ues?" Britt sounds pretty informed.

"I expect they'd go up as the location becomes more de-
sirable." Drake is ready.

"Which means taxes would go up as well," she finishes,
and the small group emits a collective groan.

Good one, Britt. I don't say it out loud, because I'm not
sure where she's going with this.

"South Carolina still has some of the lowest property
taxes in the nation," Drake counters. "And any increase would
support the schools."

My eyes narrow. Drake Redford doesn't live in Eureka,
he's not married, and he doesn't have any kids. Like he cares
about the schools.

I'm about to say as much when Gwen holds up her hand
like she's in class. Her bracelets fall down her arm with a
clink. "How much would it increase traffic on Main Street?"

Again, I frown, considering her business is located on
Main Street, and it's possible an increase in traffic might be
good for her. Not that she needs it from what I understand.

"We could build access roads around the town square out
to the resort. Tourists would be encouraged to walk or bike
here and not destroy the existing atmosphere."

"In this heat?" Terra Belle's shriekey voice pipes up from
behind the gazebo, and I see her approaching with her sister

Liberty. "Nobody's going to walk from that distillery to town. It's two miles!"

"How much is it going to increase crime in Eureka?" Liberty is as fussy as her sister, and I exhale a laugh.

Those two will shut Drake down pretty fast. Aiden catches my eye, and I lift my chin, pointing across the street in the direction of the ball field. He nods in response, and I leave him to it.

I'm ready to see my daughter and my future wife. Even if it is fake, I like the sound of it. Strolling up to the field, I notice a small, white board attached to the chain-link fence reading, *Dreams do come true.*

Interesting choice for a baseball field.

"Welp, they're at it again." Doug strolls up beside me, nodding at the small sign.

"Looks like I was wrong about it being Madonna. I guess it's Kevin Costner."

He wheezes another laugh, slapping the top of his leg. "Wouldn't that be something?"

"Yes." I shake my head at how much he likes that joke. "Still, it's a good clue. Whoever it is loves the 1980s. Maybe he or she is somebody your age."

"Maybe it's Drake Reynolds." Doug nods towards the dispersing crowd. "There's a *Field of Dreams* bourbon, and Drake wants to build that big resort to attract all the fans of Stone Cold."

"I never saw that movie, and the signs predate his plan."

"Just ruling out possibilities." Doug shrugs. "What are these little guys doing?"

"Batter... batter, batter..." Owen's voice rings out from the first base line, and I scan the mostly empty field.

Ryan stands where the pitcher would be, and Adam is covering third base. A little girl about my daughter's age stands with a bat, in front of a tee with a ball on top.

"We want a pitcher, not a belly itcher!" Pinky's voice taunts from the dugout across the field under the trees.

My stomach tightens when I spot Cass outside the fence on the opposite side of the field chatting with Julia Belle.

"You got this, Crimson!" Julia calls, clapping her hands.

Julia and her mother Liberty moved in with Terra after Christmas. I don't know why or what happened, but I'm pretty sure the little batter is Julia's daughter.

She pulls the bat back, and when she swings it forward, I notice her eyes are closed. Miraculously, she still hits the ball, but she doesn't stop there. She does a full twirl all the way around before staggering a few steps, almost falling.

"Run, Crimey, run!" Pinky is on her feet, yelling at the top of her lungs.

Owen dashes forward to scoop the ball off the ground, and he charges at the surprised four-year-old. Her brown eyes widen as she drops her helmet, and she turns and starts running to her mother.

"Wrong way, Crimey!" Pinky is jumping up and down, screaming so loud I'm afraid she'll go hoarse. "Run to first base! Run to first!"

It's too late. Owen tags her, and Adam walks forward to try and comfort the now-crying child. Julia goes to them and picks up her daughter. Crimson puts her head on her mom's shoulder, sucking her fingers, and the two return to the dugout.

"There's no crying in baseball," Owen grumbles, kicking dirt as he returns to his spot at first base.

"Good play, Owen!" Doug calls, clapping, but I'm not getting pulled into this little-league drama.

I'm not even sure if this is a real game, and I'm willing to bet my brother is forcing him to play with the girls.

Instead, I hustle over to where my daughter is pulling on a helmet, grabbing a bat, and striding onto the field with purpose. Cass's eyes light when she sees me, and she jogs to meet me halfway.

"Hey." I fight the sudden urge to pull her in for a kiss.

She's so pretty with her hair up in a ponytail, the ends bouncing around her smooth shoulders. Her stomach is exposed by her crop top, and she's a little breathless.

"You're not going to believe how well she can hit the ball!" Her cheeks are flushed. "She didn't want to use the tee, so Adam is doing coach's pitch."

Glancing up, I notice the boys in the field are backing up. Pinky is at the plate, and she lines herself up like a pro, lifting the bat and squinting one eye. She even has a little ball of something in her cheek.

"Is my daughter chewing tobacco?"

"Big League Chew." Cass snorts a laugh. "I have no idea where Adam found it, but he gave it to all the kids. He said it's what the real players like."

Ryan is covering third now, and my brother stands midway between the pitcher's mound and home plate, holding up the ball. "You ready, P?"

"I was born ready!" she yells.

Cass turns wide eyes on me, and I look down, covering my laugh with my hand. Bender was right, she's only getting feistier as she gets older.

A boy in a catcher's mask squats behind her, and I nod in his direction. "Who's the little guy catching?"

"One of Owen's classmates."

Adam holds up the ball and gently tosses it underhand to my frowning daughter. I hold my breath as she swings hard. Her eyes don't close, but she also doesn't make contact. It goes straight into the little guy's mitt.

"Strrriike!" The catcher growls like a real umpire. "You got lucky, kid. You couldn't hit the ground if you fell off a ladder."

"I can to hit!" Pinky shouts at him. "I'll hit you!"

"Look at me, P!" Adam calls, breaking up the scuffle. "Ready? Keep your eye on the ball."

She nods, pushing her helmet up her forehead, and my brother pulls back for another easy pitch. Pinky's elbows rise, and she winds up, lifting her little leg as she swings with all her might. Her lips push out, and the bat makes contact with a loud crack.

"Holy shit!" My jaw drops, and the ball shoots past Adam, almost hitting him in a line drive.

He's not wearing a glove, and he dodges just in time. Pinky's running hard, rounding first base on her way to second. Owen is chasing the ball into center field, and Ryan's on third yelling for him to throw it. When he does, it goes past Ryan's glove. My daughter keeps going, pumping her little legs as fast as she can, and now I'm yelling.

"Run, Pinky, run!" Cass is screaming the same thing as me, and jumping up and down beside me as she grips the fence.

"Throw it, Ryan!" the catcher yells from home, and Adam is behind him now.

My throat is tight, and I'm gripping the fence in both hands as my daughter drops to one leg.

"Holy shit!" I say again as her little body slides between the kid's legs seconds before the ball hits his glove.

"Safe!" Adam yells, and I launch over the fence, running to where she's jumping up and down, pumping her fists over her head as she cheers.

Scooping her up in my arms, I put her on my shoulder, holding her hand as we jump around home plate. "You hit a home run, P!"

"I did!" she yells, smiling so big.

"She hit a homer!" Cass cries as she dashes through the opening in the fence to where we're cheering.

Adam, Julia, and Crimson are with us, dancing all around,

and Owen, Ryan, and their friend are standing with their arms crossed watching us.

"Come on, boys." Adam motions to them. "That was a great play."

Owen shakes his head, but he walks to where we're standing. "Good job, P."

Pinky wiggles on my shoulder, and I set her on her feet. She immediately runs to Owen, throwing her arms around his waist and hugging him.

"Thanks, Bubba! I couldn't have done it without you!"

Cass and I exchange a worried glance, and Cass quickly kneels beside the two. "You did show her how to lift her leg to get more force. Remember?"

"Oh, yeah." Owen nods, patting her little arms half-heart-edly. "You learn fast."

My daughter turns to Cass and hugs her. "I love baseball! I love you, Cass!"

Sliding my hand over the ache in my stomach, I can't help but agree.

Chapter 18

Cass

PINKY'S TUMMY IS FULL OF HOT DOGS, AND SHE'S IN THE TUB LEARNING to sing "Take Me Out to the Ball Game" with me while I wash her hair. She's as enthusiastic about singing as she is about everything, and I especially enjoy it because I know Alex loves to hear us.

"What are cracker jacks?" Her little nose wrinkles as she slides her hands over the soap suds.

"Caramel-coated popcorn." I take the spray nozzle off the side of the tub and use it to rinse the shampoo out of her strawberry curls.

"Why do they call it cracker jacks?"

"That was the brand. It came in a box with a little prize in it."

"I want a little prize!" Her blue eyes are round as she looks up at me.

Standing, I lift the towel off the rack and hold it out for her to jump. "I'll try to find you some. I'm not sure they even make it anymore."

Alex sits at the foot of her bed, waiting as I carry her from the bathroom. "I was so proud of you hitting a home run today, P." His voice is warm, and his daughter beams with delight.

"Uncle Adam says I learned to hit faster than anybody!" she brags.

"You're a natural." I slide the gown over her head and braid her hair so it doesn't get her pillow all wet.

Tucking her in and kissing the top of her head, I'm about to leave when Alex catches my hand. "Wait for me."

Heat blooms in my stomach. "Okay."

He moves to sit beside her against the pillow, and she puts her head on his chest with Piglet tucked under her arm. Tonight they read about Curious George playing baseball, and I watch a few moments as her eyes blink slower and slower to the sound of his deep voice.

It's cozy and perfect, and my heart warms as I watch them, dreaming of what it would be like if this were real. Only, it's not real, and I force myself to back away before I forget I'll be leaving in a few weeks.

On my own again, but at least I have a plan now.

I go to the kitchen to wait, and when Alex finally arrives several minutes later, I'm standing beside the bar, unsure whether to sit or stand. My heart beats faster, and all I can think about is last night and how incredible it was and how I ran.

He's a bit more casual, going to the refrigerator and taking out a bottle of water. "She was really something today. I had no idea she could do that."

The smile in his voice eases my tension. "Adam and I were both pretty shocked the first time she made contact. It was a foul ball, but he was pretty confident he could teach her to straighten it out."

He shakes his head. "My brother is always full of surprises."

"I remember." When we were in school, Adam would go from winning math awards on a Friday to being arrested on a Saturday night for breaking into a hotel pool with his buddies to swim. "I almost got in trouble with him a few times. He always covered for me, because he knew Aunt Carol would ground me for life."

"Dad threatened to leave him in that little jail cell overnight, but Mom wouldn't let him. Adam was a wild child, but he's working hard to be a good man."

"I think you're right." Lifting my chin, I smile. "Like his brother."

"We were never alike." He exhales a laugh, walking around to where I'm standing, pausing when he catches his reflection in the mirror behind the table. "Hell, I I do look like him though, with this mop. I've got to get a haircut."

He scrubs a hand through his soft, dark waves, and I go to him, plucking my fingers in the sides. "I think your hair looks nice, but I could shape it up for you."

"That's right." Hazel eyes meet mine, and it's electric. "I forgot *stylist* is on your résumé."

"Did I give you a résumé?" I squint one eye at him.

Before dinner, I showered and changed into a halter-top maxi dress with a network of laces across my back, and we're standing so close, the heat from his body radiates against mine, so inviting.

"I remember because you stopped doing hair before I could pay you a visit."

"You can visit me now if you want. All of my stuff is upstairs, and you can sit in the big tub."

"I want." The way he says it tingles in my stomach.

"Do you think Pinky will be okay if we leave her here?"

"I'll use this." He pulls out his phone and in a few taps, he shows me a night vision image of Pinky asleep in her bed with Piglet clutched to her side. "I haven't used it in a while, but it still works."

"That's a pretty high-tech baby monitor." Stepping back, I walk to the door leading to the garage. "Right this way, sir."

His eyes trace down my body, and I turn before my cheeks

flush. I've been dying for another chance to thread my fingers in his soft, thick hair, and tonight I plan to take my time.

"I like what you've done with the place." He looks around as we step into the cool loft apartment.

I've decorated it with a few oversized, beige throw pillows on the small sofa, a woven rug I found at a flea market, and twinkle lights strung along the wood ceiling. Candles and succulents are on the end tables, and my things are tossed around.

"I don't have a lot of stuff, but it comes together." I go to where the crates I used when I moved in are stacked, taking two and carrying them to the bathroom. "This bathroom is a real treat."

He follows me into the generous space. "Everyone appreciates a good bathroom."

"I couldn't agree more." I stack two crates in the center of the garden tub. "Sit here, and I'll grab my scissors."

When I return with my roll of scissors and combs, I stumble to a stop. He's sitting with his shirt off, looking up at me like a total snack. His hands are propped behind him on the crate, and the muscles in his arms are toned and flexed.

His broad chest is covered in a dusting of dark hair I remember tickling my sensitive nipples, and the lines in his stomach are mouthwatering.

A naughty smile curls his lips, and his eyebrow arches. "Should I have left my shirt on?"

"No." I shake my head, lifting a towel off the rack. "I'll just put this over your shoulders, and we can get started."

"Do I need to wet my hair?"

Lord, I don't know if I can handle seeing him wet again right now without bursting into flames. "I'll do a dry cut."

Catching the hem of my dress, I step into the tub in front of him. His clean scent of soap and warm woods meets my nose, and I thread my fingers all through his hair, gently pulling it out to measure.

"Cut it the way you like it." His voice is quiet, and I nod, lifting my scissors.

My fingers slide through his silky strands, and my palm caresses his cheek. I take my time, doing my best to guide the clippings away from his body as I study his profile, his straight nose and full lips. His face is so close to me, I could lean down and trace my lips along his forehead.

After a few heated minutes, he glances up. "What happened last night?"

It's a gentle question, not accusatory, and I thread my fingers in the back of his hair, my palm grazing his neck as I think about what my answer.

"We got too close." I move around so I'm between his legs again.

I could slide my fingers over his bare chest. I could straddle his lap and kiss his lips.

"Is that a bad thing?" His low voice tingles my core.

"No." I swallow the thickness in my throat and confess. "But I felt a little overwhelmed. I needed to get control."

"Did you?" I nod, and his hands move to the outside of my thighs, warming my skin through the thin material of my dress. "Is this okay?"

"Yes," I answer without hesitation, and his hands move higher, around behind me, sliding over my ass.

"You've been on my mind so long, but I don't know you. I want to know you."

His hands move to the small of my back. They move higher to touch my bare skin under the laces, and I shiver. I'm not wearing a bra, and his touch is making my physical response very obvious.

"What do you want to know?"

Lifting his chin, he looks up at me, his arms around my waist, and smiles. "Why do you learn to do all these things?"

My hands are on his shoulders, and I lift one to trace my thumb across the top of his cheek. "Curiosity. I like a challenge.

I like surprising people with what I can do." I tilt my head to the side, studying his perfect face. "I like knowing how to take care of myself."

"Are you finished with my hair?"

"I think so." I put my scissors and supplies away. "I didn't take off too much."

"Thanks." He takes the towel carefully off his shoulders and rolls it, dropping it on the floor, then returns his hands to my hips.

"I like having you here in my place. I like hearing you teach my daughter songs." His face is at my stomach, and he lifts my left hand. "I like you wearing my ring."

"I like it, too." My fingers are in his hair, and I think I like it too much.

"Is this okay?" He kisses my stomach then looks up, smoldering hazel eyes meeting mine. "I don't want you to run away from me again."

My tongue slides over my bottom lip, and my stomach trembles. It's *so* okay. "I won't run away from you again."

He stands off the crate, wrapping his arms around me. My breasts flatten against his bare chest, and only thin rayon separates my body from his.

He cups my jaw, leaning down to pull my lips with his. "What was that song you were singing in the ocean?"

"'I Have a Dream.' It was from…" I gasp as his mouth moves behind my ear, kissing and nibbling the sensitive skin there. "Broadway."

"It haunted my memory." His fingers slide along the laces covering my back, undoing them one by one. "The same way your body haunted my dreams."

Electricity skitters through my veins with every touch. "I love the way you touch me."

My dress falls, and he leans down, cupping my breast and pulling my nipple into his mouth with a firm suck. A loud moan rips from my throat, and he straightens, consuming my mouth again. This time he parts my lips with his, and his tongue sweeps in to find mine.

I clasp his cheeks in my hands, rising on my toes to meet him, chasing his lips with mine, tasting his tongue.

"No one has ever touched me like you do." I gasp as his mouth moves to my cheek.

"Come with me." He holds my hand as we step out of the bathtub, leaving my dress behind.

We're both topless. He's in jeans, and I'm in a tiny scrap of a thong. He moves quickly, guiding me to the bedroom, and turning me so my chest is against the wall.

"I have to be inside you now." It's possessive and hungry. "You have no idea how crazy you make me."

The growl in his tone soaks my panties. My elbows are bent, and my cheek presses against the smooth pine as he yanks my thong off my body. Dropping to his knees, he buries his face between my legs, and my back arches.

He only takes a few passes before standing. "I don't have a condom."

"We don't need one." I'm desperate and needy. "I have an implant. I'm clean."

"Me, too." His hands move swiftly at my backside, grazing my hypersensitive skin as he unfastens his jeans and shoves them down.

Arching my back, I whimper as he slides his hard dick up and down the seam of my pussy before slamming fully inside me.

"Oh, God…" I whimper. He's thick and fat and perfectly long.

"Fuck me…" It's a ragged groan. "You're so wet."

His hand fumbles up the front of my thighs, threading and circling my clit as he thrusts faster, going deeper in me. Wetness slips onto my inner thighs, and he circles faster, melting my knees.

"Oh, shit…" I grip the wall, doing my best to stay upright as he pushes harder.

"You take me so good." He groans, fucking me onto my tiptoes, driving so deep, he finds the sweet spot that rolls my eyes.

"Fuck, Alex." It's a quivering gasp, and my legs spread wider. I need more.

Pleasure tightens in my lower belly, and my body starts to buck. I'm arching my back, twerking and riding his cock, doing my best to match his relentless pace.

It's true, I've never been fucked this way. He devours me like I'm his last meal before dying, like I'm the first scent of water after crossing the desert, like I'm a promise of sunlight in the dead of winter.

I've never been so desired, so worshiped. I've never felt so safe.

"Come for me." His growl is low at the back of my neck, and chills race down my spine to my pussy. "Come!"

His teeth graze my shoulder, and when he bites me, I lose it. My eyes squeeze shut. The pleasure is overwhelming, and with another thrust, my body goes rigid. I let out a guttural noise I've never made in my life. Everything in me shakes and spasms as if I've touched an electric fence. Pleasure floods my pussy, which is clenching and pulling uncontrollably.

"Fuck, oh fuck," he gasps as he holds. "I feel you…"

He thrusts two, three more times as if by reflex. My core is still spasming around him, and he wraps two strong arms around my waist holding me securely. My fingers are weak against the wall, and I have the most ridiculous urge to laugh, which I don't.

Warm lips press against my shoulder blade, moving higher into my hair. "My perfect girl. We're just getting started."

It's a terrifying thought, but in this moment, I know I'll give him whatever he wants.

Chapter 19

Alex

"Oh, my God…" Cass is lying on her back on the bed with my face between her thighs. "I'm right there… I'm right…"

Her fingers curl in my hair, and her back arches off the bed. That animal sound enters her voice, and my dick aches to be inside her. Nothing feels better than her body erupting into orgasm around my cock.

I lave my tongue faster over her clit, and with my thumb, I feel when she shoots over the edge. Her voice shudders through a moan in time with her pussy, and I pull that hard little bud between my lips, sucking it.

She rises off the bed, clasping my cheeks in her hands as she laughs shakily. "Stop, I can't take it."

It makes me smile, and I kiss her inner thigh, which gains me another squeal as she falls back on the bed. Climbing between her thighs, I kiss the base of her ribs. Moving higher, I pull a nipple into my mouth as I slide my cock into her slick, wet heat.

"Mmm…" She sits up again, clasping my cheeks and pulling my lips to hers.

We fall back in a ravenous kiss, licking and biting, and I thrust quickly, so close to the edge it hurts. After fucking her like a madman against the wall, I wanted to take it slow and easy.

The problem is one taste, and we turn into ravenous animals. She pulls my neck, biting my lips as our tongues chase and twine.

"Harder," she gasps, and my head bows.

I'm feverish with need, driven by a seemingly insatiable lust she's awakened. Then every day she does something incredible that makes it grow fiercer.

Rising higher, I clasp my arm around her leg, bending her knee so I can go deeper. Tendrils of pleasure snake up my legs. A drop of sweat traces from my temple down my cheek, and she licks it away.

"Oh, fuck…" I arch my back, holding as eruptions of pleasure blind me.

My knees quiver and my ass tenses. I'm holding onto her for dear life as my dick pulses repeatedly.

"Cass." I drop my forehead to her shoulder, and she slides her hands up my arms, humming with pleasure.

"You're so sexy when you come."

Falling to the side, I gather her in my arms, her back flush against my chest, and I kiss the side of her neck. "I'd like to spend the night."

A laugh moves through her, and I love that she's so happy. "I can't really throw you out of your own home."

Hesitating, I relax my arms around her, turning her onto her back so she can see me. "You could." My voice is serious. "You always have that right, and as much as it would kill me, I'd respect your wishes."

Warmth fills her pretty blue eyes, and she places her hand on my cheek. Lifting slightly, she plants a brief kiss on my lips. "I want you to stay."

I drop my head to kiss her once more before returning to our spoon position and quickly slipping into sleep. I wake half-way through the night to pick up my phone and check on Pinky.

She's sideways in her bed, a foot hanging off the edge and Piglet over her head. Still, she's sleeping soundly. I exhale a soft laugh, glancing at the beautiful woman beside me.

Cass is on her side, her hand tucked under her cheek and her lids flickering as if she's dreaming. I wonder what it might be. I wonder if I might be in it.

For a while, I'm unable to fall asleep again, but it's not like last night. I'm awake, but I'm fucking happy. Lying on my back, I gaze up at the warm, yellow twinkle lights, and I think about being in heaven. I wonder how possible it might be to stay.

"Ultimately, as you can see, opening Redford Park on the land between the distillery and town maximizes the benefit to both." Drake stands in front of the town council with a sketch of the massive resort and golf course he's planning on an easel. "However, if we can't get the Stone family onboard, we have other options."

Aiden insisted we all attend this special town council meeting to present a united front of opposition to Drake's plan. I came over from work, and when I saw Cass standing with Britt, it was even harder than yesterday to keep my hands off her.

After last night, I wanted to scoop her into my arms and kiss her, ask her how her day went, ask her if my funny daughter had done anything else new and amazing. Instead, I put my hands in the pockets of my jeans and hung back, waiting for us to take our seats.

When I woke up this morning, the bed was sadly empty, and when I returned to the main house, I found Cass in the kitchen with Pinky making breakfast tacos. My daughter stood on the stepladder beside the stove in an apron, holding a taco shell, and Cass stirred scrambled eggs in a skillet.

They were so cute, chatting about baseball and making plans for the day, I left them to it and got ready for work. I was already running late from sleeping in, so the most I had time for was a stolen kiss behind the refrigerator.

Now we're in this meeting together, and I want to put my arm around her.

"How did he have time to make elevations?" Britt whispers to Cass.

The girls sit between Aiden and me. Piper is up front in the press section, and Adam has the kids across the street on the ball field.

Now that my little slugger has learned she can hit a homer, she's determined to do it again. Owen and Ryan are equally determined it *won't* happen again, but it won't stop her from trying.

"I know this is an unpopular opinion," Harold Waters smiles from behind the long desk, "but I think Drake raises some interesting ideas. Sorry, Mr. Redford, I should say."

A wave of muttered groans meets his suggestion, but there is also a smattering of applause. I glance at Aiden, and his brow lowers.

"I wouldn't expect you to know this, Harold, considering your background and all," Terra Belle, who represents the older part of town, leans closer to her mic. "Eureka doesn't aspire to be Hilton Head or Kiawah. Those places are designed to deal with the strain heavy tourism puts on a town."

While I'm not a fan of pulling rank, she has a point. Harold moved to Eureka from Chicago two years ago, and after opening the successful Popcorn Palace on Beach Road, he introduced the hilariously popular dog race at last year's Founders Day Festival. It made him a bit of a town celebrity, and he was elected to the council to represent newer residents who live on the outskirts of Eureka.

"I'm not saying it's a slam dunk." Harold holds up his hands like a true politician. "I'm just saying there are business interests to consider."

"Thank you, Harold." Drake's smug tone isn't helping him. "And you can call me Drake."

"What plans do you have for infrastructure to support this development?" Terra isn't letting him off the hook. "A development of this size requires additional roads, utilities, sewage…"

Loud applause breaks out, but my eyes are on Cass. A wavy lock of dark hair falls over her cheek as she looks down at her lap, and I want to hold her hand.

Leaning closer, I whisper in her ear, "I'd like to take you fishing on Sunday."

Her blue eyes slide to mine, and she smiles. "I've never been fishing in my life."

"I seem to recall you love a challenge."

"I never considered fishing a challenge."

"You'd be surprised."

Britt's eyes are on us, and I clear my throat, looking up to where Drake is answering the woman's question. "We have plans for all of that."

Nice non-answer.

Edna breaks through the noise, holding up her hand. "We'll conclude this preliminary hearing. We'll take up the matter at our next official meeting, since there does seem to be a definite interest in your proposal, Mr. Redford."

"Thank you, Mayor." Drake nods in an obnoxious gesture of subservience.

What an asshole.

Everyone stands, and Cass turns to face me. Our eyes meet, and it's the first time I've had a chance to really look at her since our love-fest last night. Do I have heart-eyes?

"What the fuck is going on here?" Britt grabs Cass's left hand, yanking her third finger closer for inspection. "Is this what I think it is?"

"Ahh…" Cass shoots worried eyes at me as Aiden steps up beside his wife to inspect the situation.

Somehow that fucker Drake is right behind him. "Are you two lovebirds still keeping that under wraps?"

"What is he talking about?" Britt frowns, turning her eyes on me.

Looks like we're doing this.

"We're engaged," I announce proudly. Cass gasps softly, and I put my hand over hers, threading our fingers.

"Love is not on my agenda, my ass." Aiden narrows one eye at me. "How long have you been hiding this?"

"We didn't want to steal your thunder at the wedding."

"So you're not really the nanny?" Britt turns her attention to her friend, who is blinking fast and starting to squirm.

I'm not having her getting cold feet. "She is Pinky's nanny—for now. That's all we're saying to Penelope. Until we set a date and make everything final."

"Looks pretty final to me if you're wearing a ring." A smile breaks across Britt's face.

"Yes," Cass quickly reinforces. "Don't say anything to the kids yet. We don't want them getting attached or getting hurt or anything."

"And to think I was worried about you." Britt jumps into Cass's arms, squeezing her tightly. "This is the best thing to come out of this silly meeting! I can't wait to start planning all the parties. Are you getting married at the distillery? Of course you are."

"What did I miss?" Piper hurries up to where we're standing.

"Cass and Alex are engaged!" Britt throws her other arm around Piper. "Isn't it amazing? Another wedding so soon!"

"Not so soon!" Cass squeaks, looking slightly squeamish.

"What's the problem?" Britt's brow furrows.

"It's all so sudden." Cass blinks down to our clasped hands

then up to her friend again. "We want to be sure, since Pinky's involved, and well, because it's always good to be sure."

"Cassidy Dixon!" The stern voice makes Cass jump, releasing my hand at once.

"Aunt Carol!"

"Is that your car in the parking lot, young lady?"

"If you mean the Subaru, then yes—"

"You were not raised to post profanity on your vehicle. There are children in this town, and I expect you to set a good example."

Cass's lips part, and utter confusion lines her face. "I don't know what you mean…"

Well, shit, talk about backfires. I step up to rescue my girl. "It's my fault, Mrs. Dixon, it was a joke."

"I don't find this joke very funny, young man. I would think with your family being in law enforcement you'd know the importance of creating a positive environment for our young people."

"Yes, ma'am. I apologize. It won't happen again."

Aunt Carol scrubs her arms over her waist muttering a begrudging acceptance, while Cass turns wide eyes on me. "What did you do?"

Rubbing my hand over my mouth, I swallow my laughter. "I got you back."

"Is this about the BBL?" Piper hoots a laugh before dashing for the exit. "I've got to see what you did."

Britt's on her heels. "What's the BBL?"

The room slowly empties, and it's just the two of us standing, facing each other.

"I guess we're officially in it now." Cass's voice is soft, and I want to pull her into my arms.

After last night, all I can think about is all the ways I want to claim her. "You asked me to help you until Drake left town. He's still here."

"I think it's safe to say this has gone so much further than I ever expected it would when I asked you that."

"Are you sorry? It's not too late to come clean. It'll be a little awkward, but I think our friends will understand."

She hesitates, and my insides clench. I don't want to stop. I like being with her. I want her to be my girl. I like being able to touch her in public, hold her hand, and no one questions it.

"I'm not sorry." Her pretty blue eyes lift to mine, and I step forward to catch her chin, covering her mouth with mine for a kiss.

Chapter 20

Cass

I'M A CLASSY BITCH. THE WORDS ARE IN A BRIGHT WHITE SCRIPT ON A fire-engine red background. It's impossible to miss.

"He really wasn't thinking, was he?" Using my thumbnail, I manage to loosen the corner of the bumper sticker so I can start to pull it off.

"To be fair, Pinky can't read very well, and definitely not in cursive." Piper is beside me, working on the other end of the sticker. "And is *bitch* really a curse word these days?"

"Yes." Britt has already snapped photos of everything. "Owen will not be saying that word if I have anything to do with it."

"When you put it that way, I guess you're right." Piper nods. "I don't want Ryan being disrespectful of women either."

"I can't believe you put that silly BBL bumper sticker on his car." Britt leans against the side of Roger. "I missed so much this week! You got engaged, you loosened up Mr. Grumpy Gills."

"Pinky does watch an unhealthy amount of *Nemo*. I need to find something else for her to love."

"Are you really the nanny? Or are you the *nanny...*" My blonde friend's eyebrow arches knowingly, and I decide to keep our extracurricular activities to myself.

"Yes, and I am very professional. I don't sleep with a man who's paying me." As I say the words, I get an icky feeling.

I really don't want to be sleeping with a man who's paying me.

Piper reads my expression at once. "Oh, for lord's sake, he's not paying you for sex. He's paying you for childcare!"

"Don't make it weird, Cass." Britt waves a hand at me. "You provide a service he would pay anyone else to do. It's only right."

"Yeah..." I think we'd better set up some kind of direct deposit situation ASAP. The first time he tries to hand me a check, or worse—cash, I'm moving out.

They're both watching me with so much happy expectation, my stomach sinks even further than it was when I was struggling with the thought I might be a hooker.

I hate lying to my friends.

Alex is right, they'll totally understand when I explain to them how it all came about. They'll probably make fun of me for being so insecure and dragging Alex into this mess. Still, I'm embarrassed at the thought.

"Whatever happened with the kindergarten thing?" Britt loops her arm in mine as we walk across the street to where the kids are packing up the baseball field.

"I filled out the application and sent the email to Dr. Bayer." I shrug. "Now, I guess I just wait."

"It's going to work out for you." She's saying the same words Alex said to me. "I bet you could go virtually, so you don't even have to leave Eureka!"

"I bet." I lean my head on her shoulder, wanting to believe it's going to work out for me, even if I'm terrified I'm in way over my head.

"Look, Daddy! I'm fishing!" Pinky stands on a floating platform in the middle of the marshy grass leading out to the ocean.

Her red hair is styled in two curly ponytails, and in her hand is a pink princess fishing pole with a sparkly rubber lure on it and streamers off the end of the handle. I'm not sure she's fishing, but she has something in the water.

"That's great, sweetie!" Alex calls from where he stands beside me, getting me started. "First you have to bait the hook."

He lifts an old coffee can full of soil, and my nose wrinkles. "What do I do with that?"

It's an overcast morning, and it's warm as an armpit. The humidity must be 100 percent. I sprayed bug repellant on all of us, otherwise we'd be running a free blood bank out here.

I had no idea when I said yes to fishing, it meant we'd have to be in the marsh before 6:00 a.m. Now I'm standing here in a tank top and jeans with my hair braided back, and sweat trickling down my neck and sides.

"Reach inside and take out one of these guys." He pulls a fat earthworm from a can, and my throat tightens. "Then you thread him on the hook."

Without even hesitating, he stabs the squirming piece of goo, and a thick stream of dark-red blood slides down his finger.

Holding out my hands, I take a step back. "Whoa, whoa, time out. You didn't say anything about mutilating worms."

"It's not mutilating." He holds out a fat one to me.

"Oh, no." My hand covers my mouth. "I'm going to be sick."

"What's happening?" Pinky cries from her perch across the shallow pool. "Why is Mama Cass going to be sick?"

"Also, I'm not so sure about that nickname." I nod to where Pinky is watching us with her little face scrunched.

Alex only snorts, but Pinky puts her fishing pole down like she's about to run to me. "Stay there, baby!" I call, swallowing the knot in my throat. "Don't come over here."

"I did not expect you to be so dramatic about this." Alex slants his eyes at me, his mouth drawn in a disapproving line. "It's just a worm."

"It's disgusting, then you stabbed it, and it freaking bled everywhere. That's just cruel."

"I'm pretty sure they don't feel pain."

"I'm not." He steps up behind me, and the warmth of his body eases my twisting stomach slightly.

"Well, it's done now. Time to cast." He slides his hand up my arm, lifting the rod behind my shoulder. "Now, just draw it back like this and toss it. Press the button when it gets over your head. It's very intuitive."

Following his direction, I cast the rod, sending the poor impaled earthworm sailing out into the brackish water.

"Good one." He smiles at me, speaking softly. "See, you're a natural. Now dial it back until you hear a click."

"I had no idea fishing was so gruesome. So much gore, and these fish hooks? They're just an accident waiting to happen. Didn't you see *There's Something About Mary*?"

"Yes, and it scarred me for life when his dick got caught in his zipper. And the jizz in her hair…" He starts to laugh.

"And the fishhook in the face."

Shaking his head, chuckles softly. "You change the oil in cars, change dirty diapers, cut matted turds off dog butts."

"That dog-butt thing only happened once."

"It's still too many times."

"I've never brutally murdered a poor, unsuspecting worm."

"I'll bait your hook for you. It can be our thing." The warmth in his voice tingles in my stomach.

I really love being with him this way, bantering... Pinky on the bridge pretending to fish, him taking care of me. We sit beside each other on the bank, and he casts his line so easily. I watch as the invisible strings wait in the quiet waters. It's hot as fuck, but it's peaceful with the bugs humming and the water lapping.

"Do you really think we'll catch anything?"

"Maybe." He nods to where Pinky is dancing around, misspelling words to the tune of "Fergalicious." "If my daughter doesn't scare everything away."

"She can't watch *Nemo* after this. Fish are friends, not food, remember?"

He shakes his head. "What do you suggest?"

"I'll think about it." Instinctively, I lean over, and put my head on his shoulder.

Last night he slept in my bed again, following another round of incredibly hot sex. I've never had so many orgasms with a man. He knows exactly how to eat my pussy.

My lips press together, and I grin at my dirty thoughts.

"Before my grandfather died, we'd come out here and fish almost every weekend." His voice is thoughtful, and I lift my head to study his profile.

"Just the two of you?"

"Yeah. He loved making whiskey and overcast days." He drops his chin in his hand and glances up at me from under his brow. "He taught me to wait for good things."

The tingle in my stomach spreads lower into my torso. "He seems like more of a dad to you."

Shifting in his seat, he gives his rod a little lift and turns the reel. "Dad never understood why I didn't want to be a cop. I never understood why he and Aiden did."

I copy his movement with the rod, giving it a little lift and turning the reel to take up the slack. "So you didn't get along with your dad?"

"It's not that we didn't get along. We just never really understood each other. Not like Pop."

"He sounds really special."

"He'd have loved you." Alex's eyes hold mine, and it's like we're in our own place.

I lean forward, forgetting Pinky, forgetting everything, ready to kiss him when my rod jerks violently in my hand, and I squeal. "Shit! Something's banging on my line!"

"It's a fish." He wraps his arms around me, grabbing the rod with both hands over mine. "Pull it back…" We pull my rod straight up. "And tighten the line." I turn the crank on my reel.

"Keep doing that." He steps to the side, staying close as I repeat the movements again and again until I lift a fish, wiggling and flapping out of the water.

"What do I do?" I hold the fish out of the water, swinging it around to where we're standing and let it fall on the grass.

Pinky squeals and claps from her little perch down below us, but when I see the large, silvery fish flipping all over the dry grass, I wave to her. "Stay right there for just a second, okay?"

"I want to see it!" She's running to the end of the boardwalk so she can circle around, up the bank to where we're standing.

"We'd better hurry." My eyes are large when I meet Alex's. "What do we do?"

He walks over to where the fish is flopping in the dry grass and lifts the line. "That's a good-sized one." Reaching out, he places his hand smoothly over the head and fins, gripping it tightly, and slides the hook out like a pro.

"I caught that." Awe fills my tone.

"I want to see! I want to see!" Pinky is charging through the grass to where we're standing. "Look at it! It's like those silver fish that do charades."

"It's a bluegill. We need to take a picture of you holding it."

"We do?" My nose wrinkles. "I don't think we do. We can just tell everybody what happened."

"You have to document it, or it's just another fish story." He cocks an eyebrow at me. "And who knows? You might never catch one again."

"Hold it up, Mama Cass!" Pinky jumps beside me, tugging on my arm.

I bite my lip to keep from telling her not to call me that, and a laugh puffs through Alex's lips. "Okay." I step over to where he's holding the fish that's slightly larger than his palm. "How do I do this?"

He holds my hand, positioning my fingers over the top and bottom fins so they don't cut me. Pinky stands in front of me doing a little victory pose with her hands, and I hold my rod and reel as Alex takes the picture.

Then I quickly dance over to the edge of the water to toss it back.

"Wait!" Alex holds out his hand. "Fresh bluegill is delicious."

"You can't eat it, Daddy! Fish are friends, not food!" Pinky stomps back to where she left her fishing pole, and I give him a "told you so" look.

"We definitely have to find her a new movie to watch."

Curled up on the sofa that evening, after showers and a meal of chicken nuggets for Pinky and an unidentified, grilled, flaky white meat for Alex and me (also known as fish), I pull up the streaming service and navigate over to a show featuring lots of fancy, pink pigs.

"*The Muppet Show*?" Pinky sits up beside me on the sofa, where I'm nestled into Alex's side. "What's that?"

Turning my head, I look up at him, "I can't believe you've never introduced your daughter to Miss Piggy."

"Miss Piggy!" Pinky bounces beside me, getting excited. "I want to meet her!"

I put my arm around her, and she puts her head on my lap again.

For the next hour we watch as frogs, bears, dogs, assorted monsters, and all the pigs dance, sing, and tell corny jokes alongside celebrities from decades past.

And it still works.

"I like your voice better," Alex whispers close to my ear as Julie Andrews sings to Kermit about loving him since he was a tadpole.

A little-girl snore rises from my lap, and I duck my head to keep from laughing. "I'll carry her upstairs."

"I'll wait here."

Chapter 21

Alex

I T WAS A PERFECT DAY.

It started when I woke up this morning with Cass in my arms, threading my fingers in her soft hair as I watched the sky turn from dark purple to light blue. Her soft cheek was against my chest, her soft breath against my skin.

Our fishing trip was *educational*.

Even now, I can't help a laugh at how squeamish she was. I did not expect it. I mean, sure the worms wiggle and bleed, and the fish have a slimy coating, but this is a woman who enjoys intimidating mechanics and isn't afraid to get dirty.

And she knows my daughter so well.

I loved seeing Pinky in her denim cutoffs and her pink *I'd rather be fishing* tee. The pink rubber boots and sparkly princess rod and reel set were the icing on the cake.

I have no idea where Cass found it all in two days, but my daughter couldn't wait to get out on the water, which satisfied an urge I didn't even know I had. It was like carrying on another tradition that meant so much to me, and even with her "Fish are friends, not food" motto, she asked when we were going again. Pop would be proud.

Then tonight, sitting on the couch with Cass snuggled at my side, my arm around her and Pinky's head in her lap...

We're only halfway through the month, and already I can't imagine Cass not being here.

A soft noise from above draws my attention, and I look up to see her on the stairs, beautiful as ever in a long, cream-colored dress, her dark hair hanging in a single braid over her shoulder.

Rising to my feet, I go to the stairs. I climb them until I reach her, then I cup her face in my hands and kiss her the way I've been wanting to do all day.

Her fingers wrap around my forearms, and she kisses me back. Her lips chase mine, and when our tongues curl, a soft whimper escapes her throat. It's a noise that registers straight to my cock.

Breaking the kiss, I lean down and lift her off her feet, carrying her down the remaining stairs, across the living room, and straight to my bedroom. I can't go another minute without touching her body.

Once we're inside, I place her on her feet and lock the door. Her back is to the wall like the first time, and her beautiful breasts, bare beneath her thin dress, rise and fall with her pants.

I think of that first night, the intensity. The pent up desire from wanting her for so long and finally being able to take her. This time is different. This time we know each other, and we know what we want.

Walking past her, I reach behind my head and pull off my T-shirt, then I unfasten my jeans, shoving them to the floor and stepping out before sitting on the bed.

My erection strains against my boxer briefs, and I watch her, not moving as her blue eyes devour me. She's not shy anymore. Now the hunger in her eyes mirrors mine, and it turns me the fuck on.

"Come to me." It's a low order, and what she does next makes me smile.

She pushes off the wall, sliding her hands under the straps of her dress, slipping them off her shoulders and letting the garment fall to the floor. My breath hisses as I admire her body, naked except for a thin scrap of underwear.

Dropping to her hands and knees, she crawls to where I'm sitting, making my dick harder with every move. When she reaches me, she glides her hands up my thighs, catching the waistband of my shorts and pulling. I lift my hips, allowing her to remove them.

The minute they hit the floor, her mouth is on my cock. She licks all over the tip before sucking it into her mouth. My ass clenches, and I lean back as pleasure snakes up my thighs.

"Fuck," I groan deeply, and her hand slides over my wrist.

Lifting my hand, she puts it on the back of her head as she deep-throats my dick. My hips lift off the bed, and I groan louder. She comes up, meeting my eyes and focusing on the tip, and I'm losing my ability to see.

My hand is in her hair, not forcing her head, and I'm completely at her mercy. Whatever she wants from me, I'll give her. She goes down again, and my mind blanks. My hand is on her shoulder, and my head drops back as indescribable pleasure rockets through my hips.

I thrust involuntarily, ragged groans tearing through my chest. She moves faster, and I can't hold back anymore.

"I'm coming…" I gasp, and she slides her hands to my ass, lowering her mouth all the way as my cock begins to pulse.

Gripping the side of her hair, I hold on as I come, as she holds my body, taking it all down her throat. When my vision finally returns, she moves her lips to my inner thigh, and the sensation makes me jump.

"Fuck, Cass." I cup her cheek. "You'll make me come again."

A little laugh huffs from her lips, and she kisses my lower belly, tracing a line over the muscles in my hips.

"I love this line. What's it called?" It's a sultry question.

"I have no idea. You blew my mind."

Another little laugh, and she continues kissing my skin, tracing her lips higher as I lie back on the bed. When she reaches the center of my chest, I catch her by the arms and roll her onto her back.

Her eyes are shining and warm, and her cheeks are flushed. She smiles, and her full lips are red and swollen from sucking my cock. She's the sexiest thing I've ever seen.

Sliding my hand over the top of her head, I lean down to kiss her gently, pulling those full lips with mine. Tracing my lips down, I cup her breast, sliding my tongue over the hardening nipple as a sigh slips from her throat.

"I dreamed of this body all through high school." Kissing my way across her chest, I repeat the movements, licking and pulling her nipple with my teeth. "These perfect tits."

Her hands thread in the sides of my hair, and a laugh ripples through her chest. "Why were you dreaming of this body?"

Lifting my head, I meet her eyes. "Your first is always special."

"Hmm, not always." Her eyes slide away from mine, and I don't like the sound of that.

I'm surprised by my desire to beat the crap out of any man who didn't treat her with the respect, the reverence she deserves.

"In what way was it not special?" My tone reflects my irritation, and her eyebrows rise.

She rolls onto her side facing me, and a little smile curls her lips. "You're the first time I haven't faked an orgasm. At least once." Shaking her head, she looks down at her hand resting on the duvet. "Usually more than once."

Reaching out, I slide my hand from her shoulder, down to the curve of her waist, and over her hip. "It's not hard to learn to please a woman. The info is out there."

"Too bad most men don't share your attitude. Or at least not your interest."

"Lazy assholes." I rise onto my elbow, placing my lips on the top of her shoulder and lightly following the path my hand just went. "They don't know what they're missing. The way your pussy clutches and squeezes my dick… it's incredible."

Her shoulder rises, and I kiss the curve of her waist before tracing my lips over her hip and rolling her onto her back.

"For instance, this right here…" I spread her thighs, putting my face directly above her pussy. "Is the quickest way to get there."

Sliding my finger under the front of her thong, I rub the back of it up and down over her clit, watching as her eyes heat and her tongue slides out to wet her bottom lip.

"You are so fucking gorgeous when you come." Tearing the fabric aside, I cover her with my mouth and slide my tongue over that hardened bud again and again.

"Alex!" My name is a high-pitched moan on her lips, and her back arches off the bed.

Shifting my position, I wrap my arms around her thighs, feasting on her soft skin, tugging at the hidden spot that makes her crazy.

Her body rocks, and I continue to tease her with my tongue. I put my hand between her thighs and sink my thumb into her wetness. Her body moves faster, her inner muscles beginning to spasm.

Looking up, I see the skin of her stomach tremble, and I lick her again, circling, focusing my efforts on that one place, the one that makes her…

"Oh, fuck!" She breaks with a yell, her fingers curling in my hair, her back jerking off the bed.

I don't let up as her thighs tighten around my ears, and her wails grow more persistent. I don't stop until she tells me she can't take it anymore. Even then, I move my mouth to her stomach, holding her and hugging her as she shivers through the last of her orgasm.

Rising higher, I wrap her in my arms, and she tucks her face against my chest. One slim arm circles my waist, and I swear, I could hold her like this forever.

I could never let her go. I could tell her it doesn't have to be a lie. It doesn't have to be fake. We could make this situation real and permanent, a place we never have to leave.

Only, I forgot another thing Pop told me, a quote from a book that said, "God made the world round so we couldn't see too far down the road."

Chapter 22

Cass

"Hi-YAH!" Pinky karate chops the air above her chips and salsa as we sit in the vinyl booth waiting for her dad to return with our drinks.

El Rio is the only restaurant in Eureka, and our special dinner is a reward for Pinky going a whole day without karate-chopping anyone in town.

She's been watching *The Muppet Show* nonstop since our fishing trip, and she's obsessed with her new favorite character Miss Piggy, which means she's been acting just like her.

Owen immediately declared if she karate chops him one time, he's pushing her down. Aiden told him boys don't push girls down, but I'm not convinced he won't do it. Pinky doesn't seem to be convinced either.

So far, she hasn't tried chopping her cousin or his friends. Yet.

"Here you go." Alex places a frozen margarita in front of me. "A lemonade for Miss Piglet, and a Modelo for me."

"Miss Piggy, Daddy! Piglet is Mr. Piglet."

"Ah, Mr. Stone, you don't have to serve yourself." Herve Garcia hustles up to the table, smiling. "Who is your waiter tonight?"

He looks all around, and when a young woman in an apron appears, he says something to her in Spanish.

Alex holds up a hand. "No worries, Herve, it's all good. I'm used to slinging drinks."

"Can I get you anything?" The girl's name tag says Gina, and I don't recognize her.

She must be new in town—a situation I still remember in a town where everyone seems to know everyone.

"I know what I want if you do?" My voice is light, and I meet Alex's eyes across the table.

"Steak tacos and street corn all around?" he asks.

"Street corn!" Pinky sits back on her feet, lifting Piglet's hoof in a cheering motion. "Hi-YAH!"

Gina nods, making a note before dashing away. "I'll get that right out."

Herve turns back to us, placing his hand on the booth behind Alex. "I've been keeping up with these development plans, and if they bring in a big resort, we want the people of Eureka to know we appreciate your business."

"I wouldn't worry too much about it." Alex shifts in his seat.

"We'll never stop coming to El Rio." I smile up at him. "We can't live without your steak and street corn."

"Sounds like just the kind of recommendation I'm after." A confident, female voice comes from behind Herve's shoulder.

My brow furrows, but Alex's expression blanks like he's just heard a ghost.

"I'm sorry!" Herve quickly steps to the side. "Are you joining them?"

A woman about my height with tightly coiled red hair and pale skin steps forward. She has big blue eyes, an even bigger smile, and I don't need Alex to tell me who she is.

My stomach jumps to my neck, then plummets to the floor.

"Jessica?" Alex stands slowly, almost cautiously. "What are you doing here?"

"Hi, Alex." She steps forward, pulling him into a hug, and a knot tightens in my throat. "I parked at the courthouse, and an older man in a sheriff's uniform was kind enough to tell me you were here."

Doug. Swallowing the knot, I stand as well.

"You're Jessica?" My voice sounds weird, so I clear it and try again. "I've heard so much about you. Won't you join us?"

"Really?" Her voice goes high, and I realize she must be as nervous to be here as I am to see her.

Alex clears his throat as well. "Of course, sit. We'll get you something to drink. We just ordered food, but I'm sure it's not too late—"

"God, no. I don't mean to crash your date."

"It's not a date. I'm the nanny. Cass." Alex's brow lowers as if he'll contradict me, but I extend my hand.

"The nanny!" She grabs it, giving me a generous, friendly shake, and her voice returns to its original, more confident tone.

She sounds like a news reporter, and she looks like she just came off safari. She's dressed in khaki cargo pants and Birkenstocks, and her short-sleeved shirt has a tiny floral print and those little loops that hold up the cuffs. I imagine her taking out a 55-mm digital camera and showing us photos of giraffes and zebras in the Serengeti.

I don't hate her.

I don't.

Maybe a little.

But she's Pinky's mom… Speaking of Pinky, I look over to find she's busy feeding Piglet a corn chip and making him talk like Link Hogthrob from "Pigs in Space."

"Have you met Penelope?" I ask.

Jessica's blue eyes widen almost as if she's startled. "Not in a long time."

Moving away, I motion to Pinky, and Jessica's eyes glaze. "She's so beautiful." It's a quiet observation.

Alex cuts in abruptly. "I think we should hold off on any… *connections.*" His voice has a very pointed tone. "Until I know what's happening right now."

"Of course." Jessica nods, dropping her chin and blinking rapidly. "I should've called first, but to be honest… I don't have your number anymore. I only found you because of the bourbon. I remembered when I left, you said you'd come back here and start the distillery."

My heart is beating so hard, and my emotions are swirling like a tornado in my chest. When she talks about their past, I remember they have one, and it's complicated.

While I want to stake some claim, the truth is, Alex and I have been playing a game. I told a lie, and he saved me from being embarrassed.

From the start, we said the most important thing is Pinky, and what's best for her.

I know what it's like not to have a mother, not to know her, not to feel like you matter to her. When I was a girl, I only prayed for one thing—my dream that one day she'd come back and want to be with me.

Then I'd be like all the other kids.

Then I'd be normal.

Pinky looks up to where we're standing awkwardly, and she crawls on her little knees across the vinyl, sliding her hand into mine and looking up at this new woman.

"Who are you?" Her voice is so direct.

Jessica's eyes widen with her smile. "Hello, Penelope. I'm Jessica."

P's rosebud lips twist, and she tilts her head to the side. "Do you like Miss Piggy?"

Jessica exhales a breath I recognize as relief. "Absolutely. I think Miss Piggy is an icon of humor and feminine strength."

Pinkie's little brow furrows, and I know she doesn't understand a word her mother just said.

Still, she nods. "Miss Piggy is not like Myrtle. Miss Piggy says, 'Hi-YAH!'"

Jessica laughs softly. "Yes, she does."

"Jessica's going to have dinner with us." I hesitate, glancing at her. "Where would you like to sit?"

"I don't want to intrude…"

"You can sit by Alex." I lean forward, speaking quietly. "That way, you can see her better."

Grateful eyes rise to mine. "You're very kind."

Forcing a smile, I don't feel kind. I feel jealous. I feel like a possessive intruder, and I want to fight for the family of which I've only had a taste.

My heart aches, and my stomach is tight, because I also feel like a grown woman who was once a little girl left behind, and if I can save Pinky from that insecurity, I will.

Because I love her.

She's not less than or broken. She's funny and strong.

We order another margarita for Jessica and steak tacos with street corn. Throughout our meal, her eyes continue to drift to Penelope, who's happily eating her street corn and bobbing her head side to side to the Spanish-style music playing overhead.

Alex's eyes continue to drift to me, but I can't meet his gaze. My heart might break.

I'm hot and cold and I'm not hungry and I have no idea what this new dynamic means.

When the bill finally arrives, I dip my napkin in the glass of water to wipe the sauce off Pinky's cheeks.

"We need to talk." Alex's voice is flat.

"Yes…" I quickly answer at the same time as Jessica says, "I agree."

My face flames red, and I have no idea who he was addressing just now.

"Right," is all he says.

I help Pinky out of the booth, holding her hand as we head for the door. We'll go back to the house, and I'll give her a bath like always. Then when she's in bed, I'll retire to my garage apartment so they can talk.

I'm the nanny, after all. My job is childcare, regardless of what's been happening after hours.

Jessica walks with Alex, following us to his car. I pause at the back door, helping Pinky into her booster as they talk quietly on the opposite side of the car.

"Where are you staying?" he asks, and I analyze his tone for any indication of interest.

"I thought I'd get a place in town, but it looks like—"

"Yeah, there's nothing here." I don't sense affection. "All the hotels and resorts are in Hilton Head or Kiawah."

She hesitates, and I linger a bit longer over Pinky's seat, holding my breath until finally he says, "I have plenty of room. You can stay at my place."

"I hate to intrude. I realize now I should've planned better."

"It's not a problem. You're here to see her, right?" He nods in our direction, and I straighten.

A warm smile lifts Jessica's cheeks, and she nods. "Thank you, Alex."

"I'll wait so you can follow us to the house." He opens his door.

"That's me." She gestures to the white Camry with out-of-state plates. "I see you got a Tesla. Funny, I never took you for the religious type."

"What?" His brow furrows, and she points to his bumper. "God is my copilot?"

For a split second he hesitates. Then his eyes flash to mine, and I quickly step into the vehicle. He walks around to the back of the car, and I see him shake his head in the mirror before slowly returning to the driver's side.

"Inside joke."

She laughs. "I'll be right behind you and God."

He gets in, closing the door and not smiling, and the pressure is seriously getting to me now.

The door closes with a solid thump, and he doesn't look up as he presses the start button. "That is seriously messed up."

My voice is quiet, and I study my hands clasped in my lap. "I figured it would be less offensive."

Is our game no longer funny?

Is everything we've done simply over now?

"It's probably more offensive." He puts the car in reverse, pulling out slowly as Jessica backs out of her space. "Shouldn't God be the pilot?"

When I look up, he gives me a ghost of a smile, and I can't decide if it makes me want to laugh or cry.

We say nothing more the rest of the drive. The muscle in his jaw moves back and forth as if he's thinking, and his expression is the same as the first night we got too close.

He's weighing every angle, and I know Pinky is his top priority. He's a father. He can never forget it's not only about what he wants.

Pinky's fingers trace the small bubbles as I drag the sponge down her back. Alex asked me to put her to bed tonight while he and Jessica talked, and I'm kind of dying to know what they're saying and where it leaves me.

We skip washing hair, and when I help her out of the tub, I notice her little expression is troubled. My throat tightens, and I wonder if she's going to hit me with another hard question— this time about Jessica.

"Everything okay, Miss P?"

Her small brow furrows, and serious blue eyes meet mine. "Owen said Miss Piggy is a bad role model. He said you can't karate chop your way through life."

Exhaling a quiet sigh of relief, I scrub the towel all over

her little body as I contemplate my answer. "He has a point," I start, and I see her frown deepen. "Not about the role model part, but he's right about not karate chopping everything. It's good to stand up for yourself, but hitting is never how you handle problems. That's just to be funny."

"I'm chopping to be funny."

"Yes, but you're not a stuffed animal. When she chops it feels like Piglet. When you chop, it's like a real hit."

Holding hands, we walk to the bed, and she climbs in, cuddling her stuffed animal under her arm. "So I can chop with Piglet's arm?"

"No…" I lean forward to touch my nose to hers, before scooting in beside her with a book. "We talked about this. Chopping is only for Miss Piggy. Not you."

Piglet is snuggled to her chest as I start reading *Madeline*, and tonight we have Platy the Platypus in bed with us as well. I'm halfway through the story when I notice her fingernail curling around the side of Platy's eye and picking.

I continue reading, but by the time I say "The End," she's not asleep, and Platy is almost blind.

I tap her finger. "What's going on here?"

She looks down, and her mouth pulls down at the corners. "I'm sorry."

"Why are you picking at Platy?" Her little shoulders shrug, and I put my arm around her. "Is something else on your mind besides Miss Piggy?"

She shakes her head no, but it's pretty obvious she's not telling me everything. What I don't know is why. I don't think Jessica is the cause of her anxiety. I'm pretty sure she doesn't know who she is.

One thing weighs on my mind, and I figure we'd better address it before things get awkward. "Remember how sometimes you call me Mama Cass?"

Her little chin moves up and down, and I shift in the bed to face her, tracing a red curl behind her ear. "Maybe you shouldn't call me that right now."

Round eyes meet mine, and a knot twists painfully in my throat. "Because I'm a bad girl?"

"No!" I reach out to smooth her hair. "You're a very good girl! This has nothing to do with anything like that."

She's quiet a moment, then her voice is small. "Because you don't want to have a little girl?"

Scooting further into the bed, I pull her closer, tracing my fingers along her back. I hate her feeling like I always did, like *why would anyone want me if my own mother didn't?*

"I would love to have a little girl, and if I did, I'd want you to be that little girl. I'm only worried… What if your real mom comes back?"

More silence, and I worry I might've let the cat out of the bag. Instead, she says, "I don't think my mom is ever coming back. She's in Africa."

Chewing my lip, I'm afraid to venture much farther down this road. "Sometimes people surprise you."

Her little finger moves, and I glance down to see she's picking at Platy's eye again. Guilt is a heavy weight in my stomach as I watch her.

I reach over and close my hand over hers. "You're still my favorite home-run hitter, and you can still talk to me when you need to. Nothing has to change."

She nods again, but it doesn't make me feel better. I feel like her heart's broken now, too, and I hate this whole situation.

"I love you, P." My fingers trace along her back.

"I love you, Mama…" Her breath catches, and she hesitates, finishing with, "MC."

"That's good." I kiss her head. "Let's sing our bedtime song."

We're back to the first night, and I hum my favorite lullaby, "Castle on a Cloud" from *Les Mis*. At first her brow remains furrowed, but as I sing it again slower, she starts to lose her battle with sleep. The little line in her forehead relaxes, and her breathing evens.

I don't sing it again, but I continue tracing my fingernails lightly along her back with a pain in my chest until I'm sure she's asleep. Then I kiss her once more, softly on the forehead, and carefully stand, easing out of the room.

Pausing at the door, I watch her sleep, chewing on the edge of my thumbnail. I hated correcting her, even if I didn't really like that nickname. Still, I didn't want to create any problems for her with Jessica if she's really here to stay.

Tiptoeing downstairs, I hesitate on the landing when I hear voices in the kitchen speaking low.

"Perhaps we should've discussed it more." Jessica's back is to me.

"We did nothing but discuss it for nine months." Alex's voice is tense, but he sounds more concerned than angry. "The entire time you were pregnant, it wasn't what you wanted."

"It was an accident." Jessica's tone is penitent. "I had a plan, and having a baby wasn't part of it."

"And now it is?"

"That was five years ago. Now I look around, and I see my job going away. I see A.I. coming in and drones and everything changing, and I realize the one thing that's constant is family."

They're quiet, and I start to take a step. I don't want to eavesdrop on their conversation, but there's no way for me to get from here to the door to the garage without bursting in on them.

"You said you didn't want domesticity. You never wanted to settle down, and it was fine." Alex exhales heavily. "It's still fine. We're fine."

"Well, maybe I'm not fine." Her voice rises slightly. "Maybe it's time for me to stop being selfish."

"I don't think it's selfish to pursue your dream. I think it's more selfish to come back, then decide it's not what you really want and leave again."

Movement fills the silence, and my throat tightens when

I realize she's gotten closer to him. "I won't leave you again, Alex. I want to try."

It's like a kick to the stomach. My eyes heat, and I put my hand over my mouth to silence my hiccuped breath. Forcing myself to step into the room, I do my best to smile, to appear calm, neutral, and not devastated.

"I'm sorry." I clear my throat hard, not making eye contact. "Pinky's asleep. I'm just headed out to the garage, to my room." I point to the door as I cross the space.

"Thank you, Cass." Alex's voice is sharp, which hurts.

Jessica comes to me and takes my hand. "Thank you so much for taking care of my daughter. I hope you'll help me get to know her now that I'm back."

"Of course," I nod, blinking up to her eyes before turning quickly.

I need to get out of here. I'm not strong enough for this.

Pushing through the door, I jog up the stairs, not stopping until I burst through my door. The window unit is on, so no one will hear the quiet whimpers huffing in my chest as I fight against crying.

I have no right to cry. Pinky is her child, and she deserves to know her daughter. It's the best thing for Pinky, and I'll do what I can to help her know her mother.

Taking off my clothes, I go through the motions of getting ready for bed. Pain pulses through my chest with every heartbeat, but I'm not doing this.

I'm an adult. Playtime is over.

Still, when I curl under the blankets in my bed, I do my best to stay awake, waiting to see if he'll come to me.

Closing my eyes, I think the words as hard as I can, *Come to me... come to me...* as I close my eyes, tucking my hand wearing his ring under my chin.

But I fall asleep alone, and no one comes.

Chapter 23

Alex

"**J**ESSICA'S IN TOWN." I'M STANDING IN MY BROTHER'S OFFICE, tension radiating through my shoulders.

I spent the better part of the night googling what to do when an estranged parent returns. I read several articles and even a how-to, but none of them were what I needed. What I need is something to tell me if this woman is going to leave in a week, right after we tell Pinky she's her mother.

Predicting female behavior has never been my strong suit, and by 7:00 a.m., I couldn't stay in the house any longer. I went out to the garage, hesitating as I glanced up to where Cass would be sleeping.

Deciding I couldn't drag her into this until I had a plan, I headed to town.

"What the hell?" Aiden's blue eyes flash, and I appreciate his grumpy response. "What does she want? Money?"

Aiden's solid as a rock, and he dealt with his own personal crises after his wife died, then finding out she'd cheated. It shook him to the core, but it gave us something in common. Neither of us has been very interested in starting relationships.

Until Britt came along.

And now Cass.

"I don't think so." Exhaling, I step to the window, looking out at the gazebo in the town square. "She showed up last night, and Doug was kind enough to tell her I was at El Rio with Cass and Pinky."

"Wow." He rises from his chair. "For a guy who always has a plan, you sure are full of surprises. What does Cass think?"

It's a question I've been avoiding for twelve hours. "I don't know."

"You haven't talked to her about it?" The astonishment in his voice makes me wince.

"I don't know what to tell her." Scrubbing the back of my neck, I turn to face him. "I don't know what to tell Penelope. Jessica's a flight risk, and the last thing I want is for her to swoop in, do a lot of shit, and then hurt my daughter."

"This is why you should've had lawyers from the start. If you had full parental rights, you wouldn't have to worry about her reappearing and fucking up your life."

Growling, I shake my head. "I don't want to take away her rights. Pinky's her daughter. I just figured we'd deal with this later on, when she was older."

Pausing, I take a beat. I put my hands on my hips and look down at my Italian leather loafers and inhale slowly, doing my best to get my head around this.

The one time I didn't plan things. The one time I was reckless, I slept with a woman I didn't know, and now I'm here, with a daughter I'm prepared to commit murder to protect and a woman who doesn't understand her power to hurt my child.

I glance up at Aiden. "I'm sorry. I usually talk to Mom when things come up with P."

"I'd talk to Cass. If she's going to be your wife, she needs to be a part of this."

"Yeah." He has no idea it's all fake.

Granted, things between Cass and me had started to feel more serious lately, more like it could turn into something… Now I'm facing baby-mama drama, and I wouldn't blame her if she's running for the door.

"I'll talk to Cass, but I have to make a plan for Pinky first. I won't let Jessica hurt her."

"I don't think you have a choice. She has a right to see her child. Where's she staying?" His blue eyes fix on mine, and he straightens. "Shit. She's in your house?"

"Don't look at me like that. You know there's nowhere to stay in Eureka."

"So she's in the house with Cass? This is going to blow up."

"Thanks, I appreciate the support." Sarcasm is thick in my tone.

"Look, I'm here for you." He walks over and puts his hand on my shoulder. "Tell me what you need me to do, and I'll do it."

Exhaling heavily, I shake my head. "I just needed a sounding board. I'll figure it out."

It's what I do. I'm always in control. I make decisions, and I plan for everything. It's how I turned Stone Cold into a top bourbon brand. Problems arise, and I solve them.

"You're welcome at our place if you need someone to run interference. I'm grilling burgers tonight. Bring the gang over for dinner around six."

"That's a good idea. I'll see you then." Now I'd better get home. When I left no one was up, but I'm sure that's changed.

Hustling out to my car, of course I run into Drake Redford, gloatey as ever.

"The people have spoken," he brags. "Eureka *is* ready to be developed."

I don't have time for this. "Curiosity isn't the same as interest."

"I'm really surprised by you, Stone." He steps closer as if he thinks he'll intimidate me. "Redford Park would benefit the distillery more than anyone. Hell, it would be the main attraction."

"The distillery doesn't need your help."

"Maybe not, but the young entrepreneurs in Eureka are hungry. You can't be the only big fish in this little pond."

He's such an asshole.

"I welcome the growth of business in Eureka, Drake." I take a step closer, pleased to be a few inches taller than him. "What I don't welcome is opportunists like you coming in trying to ruin the scenery and split our community so you can make off with a fortune."

His eyes narrow, and he takes a step back, making our height difference less obvious. "If it's not me, it'll be somebody else. At least I'm the devil you know."

"That should be your slogan. See how many people jump onboard with that approach."

"You listen to me, Alex Stone, just because your family owns the town, doesn't mean your word is law." His nostrils flare, and this jerk has no idea how willing I'd be to punch his lights out right now.

As it is, "My brother the sheriff is right inside the court-house if you'd like to file a complaint. In the meantime, I've got shit to do."

"Shit like Cass Dixon?"

My hand shoots out faster than I can stop it, grabbing him by the front of his shirt. "Insult my wife one more time, Redford…"

He holds up both hands, exhaling an arrogant laugh. "My bad. Just trying to figure out what you see in her. She never really did it for me."

"From what I hear, you never did it for her either." Releasing his shirt, I give him a little shove. "Stay away from Cass."

I'm halfway home when I realize what I said.

Chapter 24

Cass

"SO OUR FAVORITE BREAKFAST IS SCRAMBLED-EGG TACOS WITH fresh guac, sour cream, and salsa." I'm standing at the cooktop with Jessica, holding a bowl of beaten eggs.

"Mm, that sounds good. You think it's safe for her to be right there?" Jessica tilts her head to where Pinky is on the step-ladder in her pink apron.

"I hold the tacos!" She lifts a platter of hard shells.

"We're not cooking with grease, so there's no danger of splatter." I look at where she's standing, more over the counter than the stove. "She likes to be a part of the process."

"On Sundays, Daddy and I make penny cakes with maple syrup and powdered sugar!"

"That sounds healthy." Jessica laughs sarcastically, and I bite my lip.

"Why don't you take over here?" I pass the egg bowl to Jessica along with the spatula. "This part's easy, and P can help you."

"I'm the best helper," Pinky informs her, nodding.

"Okay…" Jessica seems nervous, but I give her a reassuring smile.

"You got this."

Walking to the bar, I set out three napkins and forks. Alex's car was gone when I emerged from my apartment at eight, and my heart sank. It's not like him to leave before I'm in the kitchen, but I guess if Jessica is here, Pinky's not alone in the house.

I don't know when he plans to talk to me about what's happening or how it changes things—if it does change things.

Of course, it changes things.

"You need to stir them more," Pinky instructs, pointing to the frying pan. "They'll stick."

"This isn't the first time I've made scrambled eggs." Jessica's tone isn't quite defensive, but it isn't entirely friendly either.

As always, Pinky is undeterred by anyone's tone. I don't say a word. I'm doing my best to let them get to know each other and stay out of the way.

"I think these are ready!" Jessica's tone is bright, and she takes the pan off the stove, shutting off the fire.

"You didn't add the cheese!" Pinky turns worried eyes to me. "She didn't add the cheese, Ma… MC!"

My lip is going to be destroyed with how much I'm chewing it. Thank God we had our Mama Cass chat last night, as painful as it was.

"That's okay!" Returning to them, I put my hand on Pinky's back. "The cheese can be added once they're in the shells."

"But that's not how we do it!" My little friend is adamant.

"I don't think it's really that big of a deal." Jessica's eyes are wide, and she laughs like this is so ridiculous.

It is ridiculous, of course, but we're dealing with a perfectionist almost five-year-old Leo.

"Hey." I bend down beside Pinky's ear. "Jessica is our guest. Let's be nice, okay?"

Pinky's tone is quietly urgent. "But she's not doing it like you do!"

"That's because she's not me." I give her chin a boop and pass Jessica the pouch of shredded cheese. "Ready to cheese it?"

"Sounds like I'd better be." I can't tell if she's offended, but I'm holding my smile.

My cheeks ache as bad as my chest does when Alex finally appears in the kitchen. "Looks like you guys are having fun. Breakfast tacos?"

He has no idea.

"Daddy!" Pinky jumps up and down holding her arms out, something she never does when it's just the three of us.

He steps over and lifts her onto his hip. "How's it going, Sweet P?"

"We tried to make the eggs, but Jessica forgot the cheese." She shakes her head sadly. "I don't know how they're going to taste."

Jessica's jaw drops, and I jump in fast. "They're going to taste the same as always, because we added the cheese while the eggs were still hot!"

"Good save." Alex gives me a brief smile. "Thanks."

My jaw tightens, and I go to the bar. "I only put out three place settings. We can move this to the table and all eat together."

"I'm good," he says, placing Pinky in her stool at the bar beside me. "If you've got this under control, I've got to take care of a few things at the distillery. Then Aiden invited us all to dinner."

"Hooray!" Pinky pumps her little arms over her head.

"Your brother Aiden?" Jessica's voice is tentative. "The sheriff?"

"The one and only." Alex turns, going to the coffee pot

and fixing a to-go mug. "I'll be back in time for us to ride over together."

My eyes widen slightly, and I'm ready to pinch him. Is he actually leaving like this without even talking to me? "You're going to work?"

"It's the end of the week. I have to take care of orders. Looks like you're all good here?"

"Are we… saying anything?" I nod towards Pinky, and his eyes go to Jessica.

"I think we can give it a few days, yes?" His tone is more of an order than a question, and Jessica immediately concedes.

"Yes! Of course." She walks up to where I'm standing. "We'll keep getting to know each other. It's all going to be fine."

I'm not so sure about that.

Pinky's busy filling her taco shell with eggs, guacamole, and salsa, completely oblivious to the tense adults around her.

A loud crunch breaks the spell, and I see a big blob of salsa dangling precariously off the edge of her taco over the front of her white dress.

"Whoa, easy there!" I grab a napkin to catch it at the same time as Jessica.

"I can do it." She goes for the blob, but our hands clash as I scoop it away.

"Looks like I'm in the way here." Alex steps back, going to the door and pulling it open. "Y'all have fun, and I'll see you this evening."

I'm going to murder him.

"Where's Adam?" We're back at the ball park, only today Pinky's uncle isn't standing on the pitcher's mound.

Today Ryan is pitching, and a new kid I don't know is on first. Owen is on third, and our usual catcher is behind the plate.

"They needed help at the Seamen's Center in Kiawah, so he drove over early." Piper stands beside me at the fence watching the kids. "I've got Owen today."

"Don't you need to work?" I look over at where the boys are setting up the tee for Crimson.

"I can take a day off. Not much breaking news other than Redford Park, which seems to be splitting the town between the old-timers and the newcomers. It'll be interesting to see how it plays out once Patricia gets back from Italy."

"I've got some breaking news." Stepping to the side, I gesture between my friend and the newcomer. "Piper Jackson, meet Jessica Meade."

Jessica steps forward. "Nice to meet you, Piper."

"Piper publishes the town paper, the *Eureka Gazette*."

"Publishes, edits, writes, photographs. I'm it." Piper's brow furrows, and she studies Jessica a beat before looking over to the dugout where Pinky is helping Crimson with her helmet. "Are you?"

"She's Pinky's mom." Another forced smile lifts my cheeks, but my friend knows me better than that.

"Well... that is breaking news. Does Pinky know?"

"No," I say under my breath. "We're keeping a lot of things from her these days."

"We think it's best to wait a few days." Jessica says it like she made the decision. "Get to know each other first."

"I see." Piper's eyes move from her to me again, and I can read her mind. *Are you okay?*

No, my mind replies. *I'm definitely not okay.*

"Hi, ladies! What did I miss?" Julia trots up breathless to where we're standing just in time to see Crimson at the tee. "Oh no, here we go again."

"I'm surprised you got her out there!" I step to the side, allowing her space at the fence.

"Pinky gave her a pep talk." Julia laughs. "I think it was

more along the lines of 'Don't be a baby' and 'Owen's just a boy' more than anything."

"Oh, no!" Jessica's eyes are wide, and she appears truly concerned. "I'm so sorry. She should be more sensitive."

"It was really hilarious and probably just what she needed." Julia's brow furrows. "We haven't met…"

"I'm Jessica." She shoots out a hand. "Pinky's mom."

Julia straightens fast. "Pinky's…"

"She just arrived in town," I explain quickly. "We're getting to know each other first."

"I see." Julia smiles tentatively, looking from Jessica to me. "So are you okay?"

"Oh my gosh, Cass is still the nanny! She's fine." Jessica quickly answers, then exhales a laugh. "Her job is *very* secure."

"That's not exactly what I meant." Julia's lowered tone is worried, and I squeeze her hand.

"Your daughter's up to bat!"

I cheer for Crimson, but I feel my friends' eyes on me. This time, the little girl doesn't spin around like a top when she hits the ball. She also doesn't make it to first base, and Pinky runs out to get the helmet and bat.

I'm pleased to see her hug her friend and pat her shoulder, but all that friendliness disappears when she enters the batter's box.

Ryan looks to Owen, and they exchange a nod. Owen motions to the kid on first base with two fingers, signaling to keep his eyes open.

Our little slugger walks up to the plate with her brow lowered and what looks like a ping-pong ball in her cheek.

"What is she eating?" Jessica asks.

"Big League Chew," I reply, my eyes not leaving P.

"We want a batter, not a broken ladder!" The kid on first base starts, and she cuts him a look just as Ryan pitches.

"Strike!" the catcher yells, and she turns on him.

"You're no umpire!"

"It's okay, Pinky," I call. "Don't worry about him. Keep your eye on the ball."

She gets back into position, her elbow up and her eyes lowered. Ryan takes a minute, and Jessica exclaims, "Is it always this intense?"

Piper whispers in my ear. "As intense as Alex's house?"

Ryan pitches an under-handed throw, and Pinky swings with all her might...

And misses.

"Stee-rike!" The catcher stands up and does a pulling motion with his fist.

The kid on first is back at it. "Keep swinging, the breeze feels nice!"

Pinky stomps at him, but I'm on her from the sidelines. "Remember to keep your eye on the ball!"

I'm also starting to realize how much Adam keeps the peace being on the field with them.

"Shouldn't she be using a tee?" Jessica's brow is furrowed. "She's not even five yet."

Nobody answers as the little players assume their positions. Pinky holds the bat over her head, elbow high, and Ryan stands in profile studying her little self.

He turns and tosses the ball underhand, and she rears back, lifting her leg and swinging with all her might...

It connects with a loud *Crack!* Only, the ball shoots straight up in the air. She's running as hard as she can to first, but Ryan positions himself under the foul ball, easily catching it.

"You're out!" the catcher growls, and Pinky charges at him on her way back from first.

He's twice her size, but she's not intimidated. Ryan races forward from the pitcher's mound, grabbing her around the waist and lifting her off the ground. "Easy now!"

"I'm going to pull that mask off his face!" Pinky yells, and I start to head out there and break it up.

Then I hesitate, glancing at Jessica. "Did you want to take this one?"

"No..." She pulls back startled. "Please take it!"

Relief washes over me, and I run through the fence, taking a struggling Pinky from Ryan and walking her back to the dugout. She's a little spitfire, and I love it. Still, in that moment, sitting with her in the dugout, making her drink water and walk it off, I realize with painful clarity.

Pinky is never going to know her mother until I remove myself from the situation. My stomach cramps, but I know what I have to do.

Chapter 25

Alex

"THAT DRAKE REDFORD IS MAKING A ROYAL NUISANCE OF himself." Britt's grandmother sits across the picnic table from me on Aiden's back deck. "I'd like to turn him into a donkey."

When my brother invited us over for dinner, he failed to mention that Britt's mother Gwen and grandmother Edna, a.k.a., Eureka's mayor, would be joining us.

Not that I mind. They're just a lot with all the magic and supernatural elements.

"I ran into him when I left your office this morning, Aiden," I quickly tell my brother, who's pulling hot dogs off the grill for the kids. "He was so stunned I didn't support him in all this."

Edna's brow furrows. "Why would you support him?"

"He's trying to use the distillery as the major attraction. What he doesn't know is I don't need him. I'm having a hard enough time meeting demand now that Ben and Chip are spreading the word."

"William Cartwright is good people." Edna nods. "He was always a friend of your father's and your grandfather's."

"I wouldn't worry about Redford Park." Gwen sits beside her in a swirl of paisley fabric and clinking gold bracelets. "I met with the Fireside Ladies Club this afternoon, and together we put a protective spell over the town."

A laugh coughs up from beside me, and the skin on my neck tightens.

"You don't really believe that, do you?" Jessica snorts in her beer.

Gwen levels cool hazel eyes on Pinky's baby-mama. "The spirit world has never let me down, no matter how many years it requires."

Jessica's eyebrows rise, and she holds up her hands. "I meant no disrespect. I guess I'm just confused about why everyone is so against having a hotel in Eureka. It would've come in handy for me last night."

"So Jessica, where have you been for the last five years?" Britt sits across the picnic table from her, smiling in that sunny way that removes the potential rudeness of such a question.

"Well, let me see." Jessica picks at the label on her bottle. "For the first three years I was in Africa covering the rise of the Sudanese rebels. Then the war broke out in Ukraine, and I made the trip north to document that..."

"Wow!" Britt's eyes are wide. "Was it for a particular paper or magazine?"

"I'm freelance, so I shop the photos around. Whoever offers the highest price wins."

"I had no idea that's how photojournalism works." Brit wrinkles her nose at me.

"It's one way," Jessica replies.

Britt looks at me. "I guess I see where Pinky gets her fearlessness."

"She's also four years old in a town where no one has ever

told her what she couldn't do." Adam walks up, joining us at the table.

That makes me laugh. "Not that we haven't tried."

He and Aiden swap a bro-hug. "Heard you had to drive to Kiawah today."

"They were short-handed." Adam leans down to me. "Heard you had a surprise last night." Then he holds out a hand to Jessica. "I take it you're it?"

"Jessica Meade." She gives his hand a firm shake. "I've heard a lot about Alex's brothers. You look the most like him."

"Seriously?" Adam gives me an incredulous look. "That's a first."

"I guess I was sort of channeling your energy the night we met." The night I slept with a woman I didn't know.

"Not me." My younger brother slaps me on the shoulder. "I might've been a player, but I always wrapped it." He leans closer to Jessica. "Not that I'd trade anything for that little girl. She keeps us all on our toes." Straightening, he looks around. "Where is she anyway?"

"I'm not sure." I answer. "She's with Cass somewhere, I think?"

That gets me a pointed look from Aiden, who puts a platter of hamburgers and hot dogs in the center of the table.

Britt hops up and heads for the house. "Be right back with all the fixins!"

"What brought you to Eureka, Jess?" Aiden asks. "We're nowhere near as exciting as Africa."

"Maybe not." Jessica exhales deeply. "But I don't want to bore you with my story."

"Nonsense." Edna smiles. "We're all family here. We're very interested in what brought you to Eureka, especially since it concerns Patricia's granddaughter."

Also known as my daughter, and speaking of which, I stand and scan the yard for her or Cass. They pretty much disappeared as soon as we got here, and I'd hoped to talk to Cass with everyone occupied. She's been distant all afternoon, and I'm sure she's wondering what's going on. I'd like to tell her I'm still figuring out what's going on myself.

"I guess I'm getting older." Jessica studies her thumbnail. "The world is changing. My jobs are getting harder to come by, and with all that's happened in the last few years, I felt like I needed to know my daughter."

"So you're planning to stay in Eureka?" Adam leans back, studying her.

She blinks up to him, shrugging. "I guess we'll find out."

His eyes twitch, and he nods. I can tell he doesn't like that answer any more than I do. It's the main reason I'm not telling Pinky this woman is her mother.

Not yet, anyway.

"Ready to eat?" Britt calls out, returning with a platter of buns and a big bowl of potato salad.

Behind her, Cass follows with giant squeeze-bottles of mustard and ketchup. She's also holding my daughter on her hip, and Pinky has her head on Cass's shoulder. She's carrying a plastic bottle of mayo, and her little lips are pulled down like she's upset.

I'm on my feet at once, going to where they are. "Everything okay?" My voice is quiet, and the sadness in Cass's pretty eyes is a punch to the gut. "What's wrong?"

Her lips press into a sad smile, and she passes the mustard and ketchup to me. "I'll tell you later. Let's eat."

I take the mayo from Penelope, and she puts her now-empty hand around Cass's neck, snuggling closer to her.

Cass slides her hand up and down my daughter's back. "Come on, now. It's time to eat."

"I'm not hungry." Pinky's pouty tone has me concerned, but I carry the condiments to where everyone is waiting.

We prepare hamburgers for the adults, hot dogs for the kids, potato salad and chips for all, and the remainder of the meal is spent discussing the upcoming school year, Adam's volunteer work, and the informal baseball team.

The boys are in the yard playing with Britt's bloodhound, and my eyes keep drifting to where Pinky has crawled into Cass's lap. The most interesting person at the table (to me), rocks my daughter gently, smoothing her hand up and down her arm. It's her left hand, and I'm relieved to see my ring is still on her finger.

When it feels like enough time has passed, I stand. "I don't know about you people, but I have to work for a living."

That gets me the response I expect from everyone—playful groans and *whatevers*.

"Are y'all coming to the movie in the square Saturday?" Britt is on her feet beside her friend, tickling Pinky's side. "It's *Finding Nemo!*"

Pinky nods her head, which is pressed against Cass's shoulder, and Cass gives her friend a kiss.

"I'll text you," I hear her say softly, and my stomach tightens.

"Is she sick?" Jessica's brows pull together like she's trying to read a foreign language. "She was so active at the ballpark today."

"She's probably exhausted." My voice is even, and I go to where Cass is holding her. "I can take her if she's getting heavy."

"It's okay." Cass blinks up at me and smiles briefly.

Fuck. This isn't good.

We don't speak on the drive home, and Jessica retires to her bedroom suite when we arrive. Cass takes my daughter upstairs, and I wait at Pinky's bedroom door as she brushes her teeth, changes her into her nightgown, and tucks her into bed.

She hangs at the bedside a moment longer, singing that sad lullaby I've heard so many times.

I think my daughter is asleep, but when Cass starts to stand, chubby arms wrap around her neck. Cass hugs her back, and I hear Pinky whisper, "I love you, Mama Cass."

"I love you, too, baby." She kisses my daughter, and stands, turning to me.

I cross the room to kiss and hug my little girl. "Goodnight, Princess."

"Night, Daddy." She turns away, pulling Piglet to her chest, and I feel like a failure.

Cass is gone, and I hustle down the stairs to find she's not in the kitchen. My throat tightens, and I charge into the garage and up the stairs to where I find her in her room, stacking her already-packed crates at the door.

"What's going on?" My voice comes out sharper than I intend.

Lifting a crate, her shoulders drop as she looks up at me. "I have to go."

I walk across the room and take the crate from her hands. "Where are you going?"

"Britt's apartment in town is empty, so I'll stay there for now." She turns and picks up another crate.

I put the one I'm holding down and take the new one out of her hands, stacking it on top. "Why are you doing this?"

Her eyes flash at me. "Are you serious?"

Clearing my throat, I take a breath to calm my emotions. "I know Jessica's appearance was sudden and unexpected, but it doesn't change anything."

"It changes everything!" Cass's voice rises, but like me, she looks down, doing her best to calm it. "Jessica wants to know her daughter. Penelope needs to know her mom. None of that's going to happen if Pinky's constantly running to me the minute things get hard."

"So you're leaving us?"

"I talked to Pinky about it tonight at Aiden's. I told her it was time for me to go. Patricia will be back in a week, and Jessica needs this time to get to know her daughter."

My chest is tight, and I want to smash something. I want to yell this isn't right. I didn't ask for this.

Instead, I slide my hand over the ache in my stomach. "What about us?"

Her chin drops. "There is no us. Not really. It was all pretend, and now it's time to stop pretending."

I wasn't pretending. Was she?

"I don't want you to leave." My voice is rough. "But if that's how you feel, I won't force you to stay."

"This needs to happen, Alex." Pleading blue eyes meet mine. "You know I'm right."

"I don't know that you're right, but I respect your wishes."

"Will you help me load my car?"

Reluctantly, I carry her suitcase to her waiting Subaru. She follows behind me with the crates just like the day she arrived. It feels so long ago. We've come so far. How can she say it was all pretend?

She hesitates before getting into her car, and I watch as she works the ring off her finger. "I should give this back to you now. I'll tell everyone what happened, and I won't let you be embarrassed."

"Keep it." Lifting my hand, I block her attempt to return the ring. "You can tell them what we agreed to say. I work too much, or I don't give you what you need."

"But—"

"I want you to have it."

It was meant for her.

"Thank you." Her voice is quiet. "You were wonderful to me. I'll tell them the truth. I told a lie, and you tried to help me."

I'm not sure that's the truth—at least it's not the whole story. The whole story is much deeper and longer than that.

Standing in the garage, I watch her drive out of our lives too soon after she drove into it, and an emptiness I can't describe expands in my chest. I've never felt this way in my life, not even when Pop died. The color faded out our lives, and now we're in cold sepia.

"She left?" Jessica's voice interrupts my thoughts.

Turning, I see her standing in the doorway in leggings and a long-sleeved shirt. Her curly red hair is tied at her neck, and I have zero interest in speaking to her.

"She said it was the best thing to help you to get to know P."

"She was wearing the ring." Jessica's voice is quiet, and I look up at her. "The one you bought in Hawaii... that you never gave to me."

"It was for her."

"Then why did you let her go?" Her brow furrows as if she's confused.

Pop once told me it's sometimes best not to say what you're thinking if it might cause more harm than good. I'm not pleased with my unexpected visitor, but standing here right now, I'm not ready to burn any bridges.

I'm also not ready to concede defeat when it comes to Cass.

So I walk past her into the house with a simple, "Good night, Jessica."

Chapter 26

Cass

MY PHONE BUZZES ON THE NIGHTSTAND, BUT I STAY HIDDEN under the covers.

I've been here since I left Alex standing in the garage.

Since he held my hand and told me not to give his ring back.

Since I took out my heart and tore it in two.

I had to go. It was the right thing to do.

I'm helping Pinky know her mom, and I'm taking responsibility for my own mess.

If only I could get this piano off my chest.

My lips press together, and I hug my knees tighter. Pretending was so easy, and he wanted to pretend with me.

But when Jessica came back and he didn't talk to me, I was reminded so vividly of my place. I wasn't his fiancée. I was only the nanny. Or worse, I was the nanny with benefits.

Squeezing my eyes shut, I don't want to believe that. I don't want to spoil my memories of him that way. So I stay under the covers, taking a time out until I can get back out there.

The noise of the door opening and closing stops my breath, and for a half-second I imagine Alex coming here to find me, to tell me it wasn't a game, and he can't live without me. Then he'll lift me in his arms and carry me back to his place.

Instead, I hear my best friend's voice.

"Mail delivery!" The door closes, and she crosses the space, crawling onto the bed and sitting on the covers. "Aunt Carol has been calling for you to stop by the house. Piper has been texting you for two days. Adam was organizing a rescue party, but I said I'd get you."

I don't move, and I don't answer.

I continue hiding from my sucky reality.

"Cass?" Britt pokes me through the blankets. "Paging Cassidy Dixon."

"No." My voice is as pitiful as my insides.

The covers rustle and lift, and Britt's light hair and bright blue eyes appear beside me on the pillow. "Why are you hiding under the covers in my old apartment?"

"I didn't want to go to Aunt Carol's." I sound pouty.

"Are you and Alex fighting?" She makes a sad face. "Aiden told me he didn't talk to you about Jessica. You know, sometimes it takes men a minute to realize they have to share things with us—even after you're married."

"He didn't do anything wrong." My voice is quiet. "He was good to me from the beginning all the way to the end."

Saying the words makes my eyes heat again. Can I call it the end if there was never a real beginning?

Her brow furrows, and she props on her elbow. "You broke up?"

"No." Sliding my hands over my face, I can't look at her when I confess. "We didn't break up because we were never together."

"I'm confused." Cool hands wrap around my wrists, moving my hands off my face.

"It was all a lie."

"What was a lie?"

"All of it."

"I can't breathe under here." Britt pulls the covers off us and sits with her back to the headboard. "Explain to me what you're talking about. The nanny job?"

"The engagement. We were never engaged. I lied, and he covered for me."

Her nose scrunches, and she tilts her head to the side. "You lied about being engaged to Alex? But why?"

"Ugggh!" I climb out of bed and stomp around the room. "It was at your wedding. Everyone was dancing and having a good time, and stupid Drake Redford showed up. I told you he was going to ruin the night."

"What does Drake Redford have to do with you and Alex?"

"Drake is obsessed with Alex. He thinks he's some kind of business genius, and he wouldn't stop talking about how much luck had to do with it. He was practically drooling all over himself."

"Gross." Britt's lip curls. "But I still don't see the connection."

"I said I personally knew it wasn't luck, that Alex worked very hard, and somehow Drake jumped to the conclusion we were a couple… and I didn't correct him." I cover my face with my hands again. "Then Alex appeared, and Drake congratulated him on our engagement. So Alex played along. It was only supposed to be that one night—just until Drake left."

"But he didn't leave." Britt's voice is quiet.

"So we kept pretending."

"Were you even Pinky's nanny?"

"Yes." I look down at my hand still wearing his ring. "That part was real."

Britt blows air through her lips. "I don't know, but it *all* looked pretty damn real to me. I've never seen Alex that way with anyone."

"He did it because he doesn't like Drake."

"Nobody likes Drake, but that doesn't make a man call you his future wife. Men don't play games like that, not even for friends."

The friend zone is not my lane. Alex's hazel eyes burning with desire sear through my memory, and I cross my arms, sliding my hands over my skin.

The heat between us wasn't fake. The things we shared were very real... but real what? A real fling? He told me before we ever started Penelope was his top concern, and the more I was with her, the more I wanted to protect her as well.

I don't want her to question everything like I always did growing up.

"My mom never came back for me." Lifting my eyes to hers, I see her confusion. "It took me a long time to get over believing if my own mother didn't want me, why would anyone else?"

"Oh, honey." Britt stands, pulling me into a hug. "You are so loved."

"I know that now, but I'm trying to explain." I stretch back. "Pinky needs to know her mother wants her, that she does care about her."

Britt takes my hand. "I get it. You know I do, but I think having two people who love her so much they'd put her needs over their own sends a pretty strong message, too."

"I wouldn't know." I study her hand holding mine. "I never had that."

"Get up." She gives me a pull. "You're coming with me to *Nemo* tonight."

"Oh, no..." Shaking my head, I'm ready to dive under the covers again. "I can't see them there, all being a family. I'm not ready for that."

"Let's go." She stands, pulling the blankets all the way off the bed. "You're coming with me. Now get dressed. I'll meet you in an hour, and don't make me come up here and get you."

Movies in the Square launched last summer as a community service project by the Little Miss Sunbeam Pageant winner. Britt disapproves of pageants in general, but I've looked forward to this town gathering ever since we had a girls' night, huddled up in lawn chairs with blankets and wine in our Yeti cups singing along to *Grease*.

Tonight, I'd pay to be anywhere else.

The sun is setting as everyone gathers around the large screen at the end of the grassy square across from the courthouse. Blankets and lawn chairs, portable play yards for babies, and dogs on leashes fill the space.

Events like these remind me how many people I don't know in Eureka now, and how much the town is actually growing. Drake is on the sideline handing out pamphlets promoting Redford Park, and I do my best to avoid him, lifting my chin when I see Britt waving from down front.

Owen and Ryan are throwing a frisbee to Britt's dog on the other side of the lawn, and a knot is in my stomach as I scan the area for Alex. I really don't want to see him, but I can't stop looking.

Before I came, I ran to the Pack-n-Save and picked up three boxes of Cracker Jack for the kids. They were all out of Big League Chew.

Picking my way through the crowd, I notice Britt hop to her feet. Her eyes are worried, and she's making her way towards me. The skin on the back of my neck tightens, and I'm about to turn around when I hear the loud voice I love.

"EmCeee!" Pinky yells from behind me.

Instinctively, I turn, dropping to one knee and holding out

my arms. She runs straight into them, wrapping hers around my neck like she might climb me.

"Hey, baby." I give her a tight squeeze. "Are you ready to watch *Nemo*?"

"Daddy said I had to sit with him, but he didn't know you were going to be here. So I'm sitting with you." She's talking fast, and I notice her hair is in one of Alex's cockeyed ponytails.

Sliding the scrunchie out of her silky curls, I re-tie it in the center of her head. "I like your shirt."

She's wearing cutoffs and a T-shirt with Nemo on it that reads, *Have you seen my dad?*

Nodding, she holds it out. "Jessica got it for me. She said it's funny because it's true."

"How's Jessica doing?" I don't really want to know, but I need to.

"She thinks I should use *kind words* at baseball." Pinky shakes her head. "It's like she doesn't know Owen at all!"

My lips press together. "She *doesn't* know Owen at all…"

"She said at this rate I'll have cavities in all my teeth, and she said Daddy lets me get away with murder." Her little brow furrows. "I don't even know what that means."

"I think it means you eat too much sugar."

Pinky frowns. "She never gives me lavender baths with bubbles, and she *never* sings to me."

"Not that anyone could sing like you." My heart leaps at the sound of Alex's smooth voice.

Standing quickly, I do my best to smile because I want to cry, and I will *not* do that.

"Hi…" My voice is breathless. "How's it going?"

His dark brow lowers, and he's so deliciously grumpy. "I've had time to think about things, and we need to talk."

"Okay…" I look around the lawn. "Where's Jessica?"

"We left her at the house." His voice is flat.

"Jessica wasn't in the mood for cartoons tonight." Pinky pulls my arm. "What's this?"

Swallowing my emotions, I drop to one knee again, handing her the small red-and-white box. "I got some Cracker Jack for you and the boys."

"Cracker jacks!" She jumps up and down, shaking the box. "Does it have a surprise inside?"

"Yes." I give her the other two. "Take these to Owen and Ryan."

She grabs them and starts to run. "Don't step on people's blankets!" I call after her.

When I look up, Alex is watching me, and the heat in those sexy hazel eyes takes my breath away. He's in jeans that stretch over his toned thighs and a short-sleeved navy tee that shows off his round biceps. He's so perfect.

His eyes slide down my body, like he's remembering me naked, and my bottom lip slips into my mouth.

Clearing my throat, I cross my arms over my chest. "What did you want to talk about?"

"Our arrangement."

I'm about to ask him to explain when Drake strolls up, gloating like he won some award. "Folks are getting really excited about Redford Park."

"Drake, would you give us a minute?" I can't keep the annoyance out of my tone.

"Always so warm, Cass." His eyes narrow. "I'm surprised to see the two of you together. I heard you got the boot from the baby mama."

Heat burns in my cheeks. "Who told you that?"

"It's so like you to lie about being engaged." Dismissing me, he turns to Alex. "You're a good man to put up with her shit."

"We discussed this." Alex's jaw clenches, and I see his arm start to rise.

Stepping between them, I hold Alex's wrist. "Don't. It's not worth it."

"It might be." Alex doesn't flinch. His muscles are tense and ready, and fire is in his eyes.

I can't help it, but I love him so much for it. He's always ready to defend me.

"Whatever." Drake exhales a huff as he starts to go. "I don't get you, man. We could've been good friends."

Alex watches him leave. "Like I'd ever be friends with that asshole."

His eyes lower to mine, and it's heat in my veins. His body is so close, our chests are almost touching. We're caught in each other's gaze, and I want to slide my hand into his, threading our fingers and holding on forever. I want him to kiss me.

I think he might, but Pinky's loud voice interrupts us. "Look at my surprise, MC!" She holds up a pink, plastic poodle, and I make a surprised face. Then she grabs my arm possessively. "Come on, the movie's starting!"

"MC?" A faint smile is on his kissable lips.

"I didn't think she should call me Mama Cass in front of Jessica."

His eyes tighten, but he allows his daughter to pull me away. "We still need to talk."

Nodding, I follow Pinky to the low chair Britt saved for me beside her. I take a seat, and my little friend climbs into my lap, turning to the side and snuggling under my chin.

Chapter 27

Alex

As usual, Jessica is nowhere to be found when we get home from the movie.

I carry my sleeping daughter from her booster chair into the house and help her brush her teeth before carrying her to her bedroom. Her eyes are closed as I help her out of her clothes and into her nightgown.

"When is Mama Cass coming back?" She's pouty, and I achingly agree.

"I'm not sure. I'm going to talk to her about it."

Tonight. I intend to talk to her about it tonight.

"She sings all the songs with me. I want her to sing me a lullaby."

"I know, Princess. Can you sleep now?"

Her eyes are closed, and her little chin nods slowly. I place my hand over her sweet face before kissing her head and leaving the room.

Jogging downstairs, I notice Jessica is in the kitchen, but I don't stop.

"How was the movie?" She follows me into the living room, and I pause.

"It was *Finding Nemo*, your daughter's favorite." I can't keep the annoyance out of my tone. "I've seen it a hundred times."

She nods, and her eyes drift away. "That makes sense. She likes fish, and you like fishing."

"Actually, it made things really complicated. Pinky didn't know fishing involves catching fish and eating them. It's why Cass introduced her to Miss Piggy."

"Right." Jessica nods, exhaling a laugh. "Talk about backfires. Then she started karate-chopping everyone—Adam told me."

"And Cass also helped her with that." Irritation is clear in my tone. "She's a preschooler. She doesn't know everything."

"Don't tell her that!" Jessica's eyebrows rise, and I've had enough.

"Did you need something?"

"No! I was just… making conversation."

"I have to go out. I'll see you in the morning."

Jessica's eyes fly wide, and she almost seems panicked. "What about Pinky?"

"She's asleep. She should sleep all night, but if she wakes up, just read her a story and tuck her in again."

Like a mother would do, I'm ready to say out loud, but I don't have time for a fight.

She starts to protest, but I'm out the door. She came back to be a part of her daughter's life. Time to step up.

The lights are still on in Britt's old apartment when I park near the courthouse. The workers have finished taking down the projection equipment. Most of the moviegoers are gone, but a few stragglers are strolling down Main Street.

The air is heavy, and dark clouds have rolled in from the

coast. It happens during the summer after hot days, and I taste rain on my tongue.

From a block away, a lively crowd is going at El Rio, but I'm not interested in any of it. I have one thing on my mind.

I quickly enter the code and pull open the glass door leading to the small foyer outside the Star Parlor. Heat burns in my veins as I jog up the narrow staircase.

Almost a week has passed since I touched her, and seeing her tonight in that dress with the setting sun casting a halo on her skin as she held my daughter in her lap…

It took all my strength to hold back.

Pausing on the landing at the top of the stairs, I take a deep breath to calm my surging need. I can't meet her at the door acting like a caveman.

In a swirl, the door opens, and Cass lets out a little scream.

"I'm sorry!" Reaching out, I hold her upper arms so she doesn't fall, and her scent of lavender and fresh soap surrounds me.

"Alex?" She places her palm against her chest. "You nearly gave me a heart attack. What are you doing here?"

"I told you we needed to talk." Releasing her smooth arms, I take a reluctant step back. "Were you going somewhere?"

"Piper just texted me. She and Adam are at El Rio." She frowns, looking past me. "Would you like to go with me?"

No. I don't want to go to El Rio. I want to take her inside and kiss her, tell her how much I miss her, and fuck her.

"Sure." I smile. "I'll have a nightcap."

"Hey, bro!" Adam pulls me in for a brief hug. "Didn't know you were joining us. Does this mean Jessica is finally acting like a mom?"

I don't say no. I don't want to badmouth Jessica. Instead,

I shake my head and order a Modelo for me and a margarita for Cass.

He laughs off my nonresponse. "I have to say, you two had us going. I honestly believed you were engaged."

"We weren't," Cass answers too fast, and my jaw tightens.

Piper's eyes are on me, and I know she's reading me like a book. She runs the *Eureka Gazette* for a reason—she has a nose for news.

"Something to say, Alex?" Her question hangs in the air as our drinks appear.

My brother holds his glass aloft. "To Cass!"

Piper raises her glass, and Cass appears self-conscious. "Guys! Stop it."

"Don't be shy. It's a big accomplishment." Adam holds her arm, lifting her glass.

I raise my bottle. "I'm out of the loop. What are we toasting?"

"Your ex-fiancée is officially a college student," Piper explains. "She got her admission letter this week."

My stomach sinks. "You're going to college?"

"Mrs. Priddy is retiring at the end of the year, and the school needs a kindergarten teacher. So I applied." Her tone is apologetic, and I feel like an ass.

Forcing a smile, I clasp her elbow. "That's wonderful. You'll be an amazing teacher."

"Not in time for Pinky, but that might be for the best." Adam laughs.

Piper is still watching me like a hawk. "You didn't know?"

"No." I shake my head.

"I didn't tell anyone but you and Britt," Cass explains. "It was such a long-shot."

"It was not a long shot," her friend argues. "Dr. Bayer couldn't write his recommendation letter fast enough. You're amazing with kids."

The old elementary-school principal has known us all our lives. "I'm sure he knows how good you'll be."

"Thank you, Alex." She still looks guilty, so I lift my glass, toasting her again.

An acoustic band starts up with "Hotel California" in the style of The Gypsy Kings, and Piper and Adam drift closer to listen. Cass and I linger at the bar.

"I'm sorry I didn't tell you." She stabs her straw in her margarita. "I really didn't know what to expect."

"You don't have to apologize." My stomach cramps at the thought of her leaving Eureka, and while I'm happy for her, now I really feel like I'm losing her. "Where are you going to school?"

"It's a community college in Ridgeland. I'll commute, so no big deal."

"That's kind of far for a commute. Is it very expensive?"

"Dr. Bayer helped me get a tuition waiver. Apparently there's a teacher shortage in our area."

Nodding, I think about all this information. "I need to pay you. You'll need the money for books and supplies."

"You don't have to pay me." She smiles, shaking her head, and it's so Cass.

"I hired you to help me with my daughter. I'm going to pay you for your work."

She inhales, and discomfort lines her face. "I can't take money from you for that. We were… *together*. It wouldn't feel right."

Frustration tightens my lungs. "I'm able to separate what we did in the bedroom from what you did with my daughter. You didn't have to be her nanny, but you were. Your time has value."

"I love being with Pinky. I was glad to spend time with her." Placing the drink on the bar, she pulls away. "I don't charge the people I care about."

It's what I've been waiting to hear from her, but she's gone before I can say what I need to say.

Without a word, she plunges into the crowd, weaving through the bodies until she's out of the restaurant.

Turning quickly, I fish out my wallet, removing two tens and signaling the bartender we're leaving. He takes the cash, and I fight through the growing crowd, doing my best to get to the door before she's too far ahead of me.

The rain has started to fall when I step out into the night, and I see her jogging up ahead. I don't have a jacket either, so I duck and run, doing my best to catch up to her.

We're both soaked by the time I meet her outside the door to her building. She's entering the code, but I stop her, holding her hand.

"Why are you running from me?" My voice is rough.

"I don't want your money, Alex," she cries through the rain. "I want you to leave me alone."

We're both breathing hard, and the rain is beating down on us. "I can't leave you alone."

Her wet dress is transparent, and I can see the dark circles of her areoles rising and falling beneath the fabric. It's fire to my burning need. Palming her breast, I step closer, ready to take this to the next level when I notice her eyes are pink and misty.

My hand moves from her body to her face, sliding my thumb across the wetness on her cheek. "Why are you crying?" She tries to turn away, but I pull her back. "Answer me."

She hiccups, stretching out of my grasp. "You hurt me, Alex."

It's a punch in the stomach. We're on the landing, water dripping from my hair onto my cheeks, and all the frustration twisting inside me rises to the surface.

"I'm sorry." It's more of a growl. "I always have a plan, and when Jessica showed up, I was fucking blindsided. All I could think about was protecting my daughter, and I guess I thought you were strong enough to wait."

"Right." She takes another wobbly breath. "I don't rank. Message received."

Fuck. I hate this.

The rain grows harder, and I gather her in my arms, pulling her through the door. "Dammit, Cass, the only message I ever want you to receive is you belong with me."

"No." She shakes her head. "I'm done pretending. I have to have value."

Dropping to my knees, I wrap my arms around her waist, pressing my cheek against the fabric of her dress, against her stomach. "How can you think you have no value to me? From our first kiss, it was real. Before that… from the moment I saw you swimming in the ocean, when your voice wouldn't leave my mind and your body lived rent free in my head. You were my angel. That ring is yours because I bought it for you, and when I gave it to you, it was from my heart."

Her hands grasp my arms as if she'll push me away. "And you shut me out like I was nothing."

My arms tighten, and I look up into her pretty, pretty eyes. "You're everything to me. You're the wind and the sea when I'm the rocks and the sand. You're the calm, the soothing. You quiet the storm and make me whole. You're the song in my head I never want to stop hearing. You're beautiful and smart and kind. You're priceless."

She sniffs, and I rise slowly. Her nose is a light shade of pink, and I reach for her, cupping her face in my hand.

"I've only ever wanted to dry your tears, Cass. I've only ever wanted to hold you. I will never leave you behind."

Her eyes blink faster, and another tear wells onto her lash, falling when she looks down. Her nose wrinkles, and she rolls her eyes away, fighting a smile. "How do you know what to say to me?"

"Because you're mine." Sliding my hand behind her neck, I draw her face closer, tracing my lips along her cheek. "I want to kiss you."

It's a hot murmur against her damp skin, and she exhales a

whimper. Her fingers curl in my shirt, and she pulls me closer, lifting her chin.

Our mouths chase, and hunger takes over. She fists and jerks my shirt higher, but I catch her hands, guiding her to the stairs then lifting her off her feet.

Thunder rolls outside, as we enter the small apartment. My shirt is over my head, and I let it fall to the floor. I grip the sides of her dress, trying to get it off her.

Her fingers fumble over the buttons, unfastening them quickly so her wet dress can slip from her body. We kiss, and I pull her flush against me.

My mouth is on her shoulder, and I taste fresh rainwater on her skin. Her hands trace the lines of my body, and my cock is hard and desperate to be inside her.

Cupping her cheeks, I consume her mouth, curling my tongue with hers and nipping her lips with mine. She holds my hands, leading us to the bed, and I stop to shove my wet jeans down, stepping out of them.

"We're making a mess…" My voice is quiet.

She puts my hands on her body. "We'll deal with it later."

Lifting and kneading her breasts, I turn her around so I can slide my fingers between her thighs. Her back arches against my chest, and her head is on my shoulder as I massage her clit.

I kiss the side of her neck, biting her skin gently as I roll a hardened nipple between my thumb and forefinger. She writhes and moans, and her hand slides behind her back, rubbing and pulling my cock.

"You're going to make me come." I groan as her hand moves faster, drawing me closer to the edge.

Pushing her forward, I line myself up at her entrance and thrust fully into her slippery, wet heat. We both hold with a moan, but I can't stop.

Primal instinct takes over, and I'm moving fast. She's on all fours on the bed, and I'm behind her, thrusting vigorously, chasing that intense release.

She gasps and moans as I reach between her thighs, as I kiss her between the shoulder blades, tracing my lips higher to her ear. Another loud moan, and orgasm flashes in my cock.

"I'm so fucking close," I groan. "Come for me, Cass."

Moving my hand faster between her legs, I breathe raggedly as my hips jerk and my thrusts drive deeper. I couldn't stop if I tried.

A shuddering cry ripples from her chest, and her arms tremble. Her pussy breaks into spasms, and I let go, groaning loudly as I hold, my skin flush with her ass. My cock jerks and pulses, and I groan again, filling her sweet body as she trembles beneath me.

Several seconds pass as I hold her, fumbling back to Earth with the woman of my dreams in my arms.

Chapter 28

Cass

MY CHEEK IS AGAINST ALEX'S BARE CHEST, AND HIS FINGERS SLIDE through my damp hair. He gently kisses my forehead, tracing his lips over my eyebrow, and my eyes close.

I'm so deliciously satisfied, so incredibly happy.

"Do you forgive me?" His voice is warm and deep.

"You have to ask?" Lifting my chin, I kiss his jaw.

His face lowers, and our mouths seal together. It's a rush of dopamine straight to my brain. My eyes close, and I've never been so happy.

"Will you tell your friends we're a real couple now?" A tease is in his tone, and I lift my upper body, grabbing my phone.

"I'll text them all right now."

"It's only midnight. I'm sure they won't mind you waking them."

"I guess you're right." Grinning, I tuck my head under his chin again. "I'll wait until the morning. Do you need to get back or can you sleep over?"

"I informed Jessica I would be gone for the night, so you're stuck with me." He traces his fingers slowly, lovingly up my back, and I exhale a hum.

"I love being stuck with you. We can be stuck together."

"I like the sound of that."

Wrinkling my nose, I prop my chin on my hand to look at his gorgeous face. "If I'd known you were into me in high school…" Shaking my head, I remember the quiet, bookish boy who was always so attractive and always so distant. "Why didn't you ever say anything?"

His brow furrows, and the problem-solving expression I love appears. "In the beginning you seemed too young."

"Didn't stop you from looking." My eyebrow arches.

"It was an accident." His fingers trace my back. "But you're right, I couldn't tear my eyes away from you. As we got older, it was always you were dating someone or I was."

Warmth tightens my stomach. "It wouldn't have mattered who I was dating. If you'd said one word, it would've changed everything."

A low chuckle vibrates in his chest. "Pop used to say everything happens in its time. I think he was talking about bourbon, but it fits."

Resting my cheek on his chest, I think about the future, Pinky. "What happens now?"

"We get married for real, make a few more babies, and live happily ever after."

Electric sparkles radiate in my veins. "You still want to marry me?"

His hand slides under my chin, lifting my face to look at him. "I love you, Cassidy Dixon. I most definitely want you to be my wife."

My heart squeezes, and I slide forward to kiss his full lips. "I love you."

It's a timid whisper, and he rolls me onto my back, looking straight into my eyes. We don't speak, and his expression is so serious, my heart aches.

Cupping my cheek, he covers my mouth with his, kissing me slowly, fully. Our tongues trace and curl, and he moves between my thighs, parting them and inserting his hard cock into my heated core.

My chin lifts, and I exhale a moan as he moves faster. I'm cradled in his arms, so close, I don't know where we begin and end.

We rock like waves on the sea, and I lift my knees, riding the impact of his dominating thrusts.

His hand lowers, cupping my ass, and I tilt my hips, allowing him to claim me in a way he never has. He finds a place deep inside me, and with every stroke, my body heats. Pleasure twists tighter in my core.

Faster, harder, we chase our shared release, and when it happens, I cling to him like he's the only thing that matters. He is my match, my home.

It's still drizzling when I open my eyes again. Alex sits on the edge of the bed getting dressed. "I should've set an alarm. It's late."

Turning, I see it's after eight, and I sit up quickly. "You've got to get home. No telling what's happening in that kitchen right now."

He grins, and he's so damn handsome. I spent all night blissfully wrapped in his arms. Half-asleep, I felt him get up at some point and collect his jeans and tee and put them in Britt's small clothes dryer. He hung my dress in the bathroom before returning to hold me close as we drifted away again.

Sitting in bed on this overcast morning, I want to pull him to me and disappear under the covers. "What happens now?"

He stands, pulling his jeans over his toned ass, and my bottom lip goes between my teeth.

"I'll stop by the house and make sure nothing's on fire. Then

I'll get Pinky, and we'll come back to take you home with us. I'll ask Aiden what everyone's doing for dinner…"

Resting my chin on my bent knees, I love listening to him making plans for us with so much confidence, like I'm one of his family. Just like that.

A shadow passes over my sunshine. "What about Jessica?"

"I'll take care of it." His shirt is over his head, leaving his dark hair a sexy mess.

Leaning over the bed, he gives me a light kiss, hesitates, and comes back for a longer one that sends a charge to my core.

A naughty grin curls his lips, and my stomach squeezes. "I'll text you when we're on our way back."

He leaves me basking in the happiest glow, and I snuggle deeper in bed, reliving everything that happened last night. My head is still spinning.

It started so miserably. Being in El Rio, toasting my college admission, I knew I should've been happy. I *was* happy. I'd made a plan for my future, and it was all coming together. I was surrounded by friends… And Alex, was impossibly sexy with his broody, square jaw and those sexy eyes all conflicted and sad.

I kind of snapped. After the way he'd done me all week, I was furious he'd act like his dreams were shattered. I couldn't pretend not being with him wasn't killing me. My feelings were too real.

Then he chased me in the rain like I was Audrey Hepburn in *Breakfast at Tiffany's*, and when he got on his knees… He held me so close, his warm face pressed to my stomach, begging me to forgive him. My eyes heat at the memory. My heart completely melted.

I'll never forget the words he said to me. They're imprinted on my memory forever. It was the most beautiful moment of my life. He changed me from the little girl nobody wanted to the woman he can't live without.

He made me cherished, coveted, desired… *loved*.

Holding out my hand, I kiss the angel ring. I smile so hard

my face hurts, and my heart beats so loud in my chest, I could laugh and cry and float up to the ceiling.

Instead, I hop up and take a quick shower and wash my face. Sorting through my clothes, I take out a pair of black leggings and a V-neck tank. It's not cold, but the drizzle makes me grab a thin cardigan. A quick dash of makeup, and I'm on my way out the door.

I'll grab a coffee and head over to his place, no need to wait around. But when I reach the bottom of the stairs, the door to the Star Parlor opens, and Piper's mom steps out onto the landing.

"Martha, hey!" My voice is nervous, and I glance up the stairs from where I just came.

I didn't realize until this morning the windows were open all night, and Alex and I didn't give a shit about how loud we were. Hell, I was making animal noises at one point.

"Good morning, Cassidy." She steps forward to hug me and kiss my cheek. "You're glowing today."

Shit shit shit. "Did you sleep here last night?"

"Here? No." She glances at the neon purple sign with the little gold stars around it. "I just dropped off my special tea for Gwen. She likes to brew it when she's doing the readings."

"I remember…" The tea has a strong scent of ginger and herbs, and it creates a mystical vibe in the room, almost like incense.

Martha's eyes narrow, and she tilts her dark head to the side as she studies me. "You remind me so much of your mother these days. It's amazing how alike you are."

Normally, the comparison pisses me off, but for some reason, after last night, it stirs a longing I didn't know I still had. "You were friends with her, weren't you?"

"I was best friends with her. The summer she brought you here, we grew very close."

My brows pull together, and I study this woman with her straight, dark hair hanging in a long, thick braid down her back.

A stripe of white is in the front, threaded through her braid, and her eyes are pale blue. She's dressed in jeans and a black T-shirt with a long-sleeved plaid shirt on top.

Martha has always been suspicious and careful. She has a cellar full of food and tools, gasoline and supplies for the end of the world, and I've never known how to take her.

I can't imagine her being best friends with anyone—at least not the way Britt and Piper and I do it.

"I never really knew my mom. She dumped me here and never came back. Then she died, and that was the end of it."

Martha's lips tighten, and she nods. She almost appears sad. "Your mom had dreams, and she tried to manifest them. Her bravery inspired me... but the ones you love hurt you the deepest."

It's a haunting remark, spoken as if she is well acquainted with deep hurt.

"Piper and I have been friends for so long, I wish you'd told me." My voice is quiet. "Aunt Carol acted like my mother was a shameful secret."

Martha gives me a warm smile. "What would you like to know?"

"Can we step inside?" I motion to the glass door, and she opens the tarot studio.

I follow her to the gold velvet sofa in front of the empty fireplace. A small, cherry-wood coffee table is in front of us, and a stack of intricately decorated arcana cards is positioned in the center.

I used to do readings here, but I'm not interested in the future. Today, I'm ready to dig into the dirt, and I'm going straight to the heart of the matter.

"Why did she have me if she didn't want me?"

Martha's expression flinches. "Crystal would never call you a mistake. You were a 'happy accident'... but that didn't make her right for you. She wasn't equipped to be a mother, but she hated to let you go."

"After she left, I never heard from her again. Not once."

Martha reaches out to pat my hand. "I think she thought a clean break would help you forget her, but she asked me about you all the time."

"It wasn't enough." Pulling away, I remember my dreams, swimming in the ocean, pretending I was a mermaid. "She never said 'I love you.'"

"Love takes different forms. Carol is a lot of things, but she was better for you than Crystal. You couldn't live the way your mother lived."

"Aunt Carol watched every move I made, like I was always on the brink of evil. She never showed affection… Try living that way."

Martha nods her head. "Carol clings to a lot of fear."

Disgust twists my lips. "Fear of what?"

"Fear that maybe what happened to your mother was somehow the family's fault, like they made her be what she was."

"What was she?" My stomach is tight, but I need to know the truth from someone who won't hide it from me.

"She was a dreamer." Martha hesitates, as if she's turning this over in her mind. "She used drugs to expand her creativity, but that road often leads to the worst outcomes."

My throat tightens, and my eyes squeeze shut. "So she was a junkie?"

"She was alone."

"She chose to be alone." Anger tightens my throat, and tears burn my eyes.

Martha grasps my hand firmly, holding me with her gaze. "You are the best parts of her. You're brave and you have dreams, but you have strength and a foundation she never had."

Quiet falls between us, and the anger and the sadness and the grief I've carried so long spill onto my cheeks. Martha scoots closer, putting her arm around me and pulling me into a hug.

Resting my head on her shoulder, I turn her words over in

my mind. I'm tired of carrying this anger and pain, but the explanation doesn't make things easier.

"It's hard to see our loved ones clearly." Martha's voice has that tone again, like she's speaking from experience. "When you're strong enough, forgive her. Then you'll be free."

Forgiveness.

I sit for several minutes contemplating the word. It's the second time I've been asked for it in less than a day. The first time was so easy, but this time?

Martha's hand slides up and down my back, and I sit up, drying my cheeks with the backs of my hands.

"I grew up feeling worthless because I never had a mom, but now I realize I had two. One left me behind. The other was always with me... She drove me crazy, but she was always there."

Martha's lips poke out, and she nods. "Carol means well."

The statement pushes a laugh through my lips. Shaking my head, I can't let it go unchallenged. "She's a judgmental old cow."

When Martha doesn't respond, I feel self-conscious.

I think about this situation, and I think about the stories I've heard so many times in this very room, working with Gwen. I remember holding people's hands and feeling their pain. So many of them were so lost. So many of them were trying to rebuild with broken tools.

Gwen said I was an empath. I could connect with these strangers and give them what they needed, comfort and forgiveness.

Lost. Alone. Broken.

I could forgive them; can I forgive the people I know?

The fist in my chest loosens a notch. "I want to forgive her. I'm not sure I can, but I want to."

Both of them.

"That's good." Her eyes are distant. "They say time heals. They just don't say how much time."

She's pulling away again. I can see her doing it in front of me, back to that place of distance and hiding. She starts to rise, but I catch her hand.

"Thank you."

She nods. "Your mom asked me to look out for you, so I tried. I think Alex Stone is a good man."

"I love him…" It's the first time I've said it out loud to another human. "And it scares me to death."

"Why?"

I think about everything she just told me. "I was afraid I was like her."

"You have dreams, but you're not selfish. You take care of the ones you love." Sliding her hand over my cheek. "You're not her."

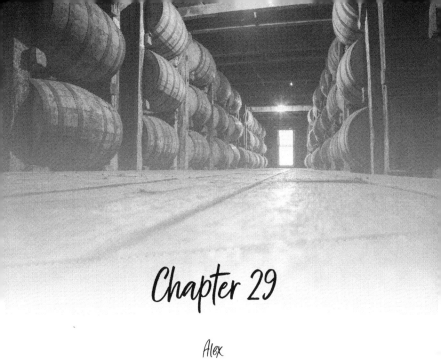

Chapter 29

Alex

"ON SUNDAYS WE HAVE PENNY CAKES WITH MAPLE SYRUP AND powdered sugar!" My little princess is arguing in the kitchen when I open the door from the garage.

"That's too much sugar." Jessica's voice starts to rise. "Your father isn't here, so we'll have our own tradition. Apples and peanut butter!"

"Eww!" Pinky's arms are crossed, and her eyes are squeezed shut when she turns around. She's dressed in a pink tutu with her *Have you seen my dad?* shirt and a crown on her head. "You can't make me eat that!"

I cover my mouth with my hand to hide my smile. The noise of the door closing breaks the impasse. My daughter's eyes fly open, and her entire demeanor changes.

"Daddy!" she yells, running to me as fast as her legs will move. "Jessica's trying to feed me dog food for breakfast!"

"I am not!" Jessica's eyes are wide, and her hair is a mess. She looks like she's been on the battlefield.

Lifting my little terror onto my hip, I narrow my eyes. "I doubt that, honey. We don't even have a dog."

"She's trying to make *me* the dog!"

"I'm trying to make you healthy." Jessica's tone is sharp. "Your father spoils you."

"*You're* a banana!"

I swallow my laugh, forcing a frown. It's possible I'm still basking in the afterglow of last night. It's going to take a lot to get me down after what Cass and I shared.

"Why did you call Jessica a banana?"

"One of the bananas at Uncle Aiden's house was all black and had little flies on it and Owen said it was spoiled. Jessica said I'm a bad banana, but she's the banana!"

"I'm done." Jessica throws up her hands, storming out of the kitchen. "Eat all the sugar in the house. Get a swimming pool and roll around in it."

She stomps up the stairs, and my mood deflates slightly. This isn't how I want my daughter to act.

Carrying Pinky to the kitchen, I sit her on the bar in front of me. She crosses her arms, and her fingers pick the skin near her elbows.

"I think we can include apples with our special breakfast."

Her blue eyes flash to mine. "It's not what we do, Daddy."

"Jessica has a point about eating too much sugar. It's not good for you."

Her little lips twist, and she doesn't answer me.

"Also, I want you to be nicer to Jessica. She wasn't trying to feed you dog food, and she didn't call you a bad banana." Hooking my finger under her chin, I lift her face to look at me. "I want you to say you're sorry and invite her to breakfast."

"She doesn't do it right." Her little voice is quietly firm.

"She hasn't been here very long."

"Mama Cass hasn't been here very long, and she does everything right."

Exhaling slowly, I can't argue with that.

Still, "Jessica and Cass are different people, and I know Cass would want you to be nice to Jessica. She'd definitely want you to treat adults with respect. I want you to treat adults with respect."

"Daddy…" She exhales a frustrated sigh. "I don't know what that is!"

"It means being considerate of other people." She still looks confused. "It means to be polite. Remember how Gran taught you to ask nicely? That's using good manners. Now come with me."

I lift her off the bar, and holding her hand, we climb the stairs to the room Jessica occupies. Allowing her to take the lead, I hang back as she knocks, and when Jessica says we can enter, I'm surprised to see her duffel bag is on the bed.

She's sitting at the computer, and her lips are set. I'm not sure what to make of this, but I give my daughter a nudge.

Her little shoulders drop. "I'm sorry I called your special dish dog food." Jessica's eyebrow arches, and she leans back, crossing her arms as she studies Penelope. "Would you like to have breakfast with Daddy and me?"

"I accept your apology." Jessica's tone makes me wince, but I hold back. "I can't join you for breakfast, but I appreciate the invitation."

My stomach is tight, and while I know Pinky can be a bit much, I had hoped Jessica might be a little warmer.

Penelope doesn't seem to mind at all. "Okay!" She looks up at me with a smile, which I return.

Leaning down, I pat her back. "Head on down. I'll be there in just a minute."

She turns on her heel and skips out the door singing a little song. Hesitating, I glance to where Jessica's eyes have returned to her computer screen.

"It's possible I do spoil her."

"You think?" She doesn't look at me, and I let the sarcasm in her tone pass.

"Everything okay with you?"

"It takes a lot more than a rambunctious five-year-old to upset me, Alex."

"I'm sure you've seen a lot worse." I motion to the bed. "Your bag is out."

She stands, walking to the dresser and opening it. "Yes, I got an email from a friend… He's working on a documentary about the plight of women in Afghanistan and wants me to join the team."

It's the announcement I've been waiting for since the day she showed up here. "Sounds right up your alley."

"We have a Zoom chat in ten minutes." She meets my eyes for the first time since I entered her room. "I was on the fence about even talking to him, but it's a compelling story. The Taliban has practically erased women from society there."

"I see."

"Did you know about the situation?" Her voice takes on that impassioned tone I know so well.

"I can't say that I did."

"That's the problem. No one does. Someone has to shine a light on what's happening."

"I'm sure it's very important."

"It's a way to make a difference in the world."

Nodding, I have no response to her. I'm only glad I trusted my instincts and didn't make a big deal out of Jessica returning to be a part of her daughter's life.

"Are you mad at me?" Her voice changes, and it reminds me of when I watched her packing for Africa, when my daughter was only six weeks old.

Now, my only concern is protecting that little human. "I never expected you to stay."

"I'm sorry, Alex. I've seen too much to sit in one place and let atrocities go unreported."

"Of course." Straightening, I go to her door. "I'd like to draw up papers. I want to have full custody of Penelope."

Silence fills the space between us, and she looks at the computer a moment, nodding her head slowly. "What will you say to her?"

"I'll think of something."

"I trust you." Blue eyes meet mine, and she knows I would never let Pinky think her mother was a bad person. "Send me whatever you need, and I'll sign it."

"Take care of yourself."

"It's a good thing I came back early!" My mother's eyes shine as she sits at the picnic table on the deck at Aiden's house while the grandkids surround her with hugs.

"You were gone a long, long time Gran." Pinky informs her. "I learned to play baseball, and I hit a homer, and Owen says I can't do it again, but I bet I can."

"Take a breath, Sweet P," I chuckle, watching her crawl into her grandmother's lap.

Owen lets out a groan. "It was beginner's luck."

"Was not!" Pinky argues. "I hit a stinker before that. Uncle Adam said so!"

Mom squeezes my daughter, laughing. "I have to see my Pinky hit a baseball!"

"I'll show you after dinner!" Penelope's so happy, surrounded by the kind of love I want in her life—unconditional, constant.

Cass stands beside me watching them, and my hand rests comfortably on her waist. When I picked her up at her apartment this afternoon, something had changed in her eyes. It was subtle, but I've watched her so long, it was unmistakable. It's a sense of calm, like a problem has been solved or a decision made.

I'd like to think it's because we defined our relationship

and set it in stone. *Finally*. But we'll talk more tonight. In the meantime, my mother's eyes catch mine.

"I see something else happened while I was gone."

Adam takes a seat across from her, shaking his head. "I swear, I'm getting whiplash. Eureka's supposed to be a quiet little town where nothing ever happens."

Mom shakes her head. "It's never been that."

After everything that happened last year with Britt and Aiden, I have to agree with her. This year hasn't been as tumultuous, but a lot has happened—some more monumental than others.

"Piper told me you got your acceptance letter!" Britt walks out to where Cass stands, pulling her into a hug. "I'm so happy!" Her green eyes slide between the two of us. "And I'm glad to see this is all sorted. Are we allowed to talk about it now?"

Cass glances up at me, and I give her a wink. "Give us a few more days. We haven't discussed it with the little princess yet."

"I think she's a few steps ahead of you, with all that Mama Cass business." Aiden passes us on his way to fire up the grill.

"She always is."

"Has Edna told you about Redford Park?" Piper takes a seat at the table beside Adam, and I notice my brother making room for her. *Interesting.*

"She did." They launch into that annoying discussion, and Owen jumps up to go play with Ryan.

Pinky chases right behind them as usual, and Mom gestures for the girls to join her at the table. Britt grabs Cass's hand, and the two of them walk over to where she sits.

Taking my beer, I walk over to where my brother is loading everyone's personal pizzas onto the large grill. Before we walked out, we each topped small, round flatbreads with different fixings for him to grill.

"So it's official?" Aiden arches an eyebrow at me, and I laugh.

"It always was. She just didn't know it." My eyes drift to where Mom holds Cass's hand, inspecting the ring. "Pinky loves her, and that was pretty much the last thing I needed to know."

"It's like you've been planning it for years. Like one of your special bourbons." He's teasing, but he has no idea.

Soft squeals from the table draw our attention, and I see Mom and Cass hugging Britt. Mom's eyes shine with what looks like tears, and Cass is beaming, touching her friend's stomach.

"Does that mean what I think it does?"

"Yeah, Britt's expecting."

"Didn't waste any time did you?" I pull my brother in for a bro-hug. "Congrats."

"We weren't really trying, but we weren't really *not* trying." His blue eyes shine like they always do when he talks about his wife.

"That's fucking awesome, Aiden." Adam walks up to where we're talking.

"Yeah, Britt wanted a baby, and we didn't want Owen to be too much older than his siblings, provided we were lucky enough to get pregnant."

"I'm really happy for you." My eyes travel from him to Britt to Cass, who is watching me with a dreamy look.

Images of her pregnant with my baby fill my mind, and the pull of desire is in my chest. I hadn't thought about it until now, but I want the same thing.

Adam grips my shoulder. "What's the latest with your baby mama drama?"

I put aside my visions of impregnating Cass for later. "Jessica's leaving again, as expected."

"Seriously?" Adam's brow lowers.

"She actually stayed longer than I thought she would. Pinky put her through the wringer."

Aiden chuckles. "That little girl is a pistol. I can't imagine what she'll be like all grown up."

"Yeah, good luck with kindergarten," Adam teases.

Rolling my eyes, I groan. "We're lucky to live in a small town where everybody knows everybody."

"Mrs. Priddy knows how to handle kids like her." Aiden pulls the pizzas off the grill and arranges them on the platter. "She handled Adam, after all."

"Hey!" He tries to act offended, but he knows it's the truth.

We gather around the table, and I take in my oldest brother with his arm around his glowing wife. Adam is across from me making sure Ryan has everything he needs, as always, only this time I also notice him subtly making sure Piper is taken care of as well. Cass is beside me, tucking a napkin into my daughter's shirt. When she sits up, I slide my arm around her waist, kissing her temple.

This is what I want. It's where I want to be, and I can't imagine making a choice that would take me away from it.

Pinky's asleep when I carry her to her booster seat. She did her best to hit another homer for her grandmother after dinner, but Owen was determined it was not going to happen. Several rounds later, we finally called it a night.

It wasn't long before my princess was asleep in Cass's lap.

Closing the door, I pull my lady into my arms. "Are you staying with me or…"

"I'll stay at Britt's old place tonight. Jessica needs a chance—"

"She's leaving."

I don't mean to say it so bluntly, but it's the first time we've had a chance to talk when Pinky wasn't listening.

Cass's brow furrows. "Did something happen?"

"I don't know." I open her door for her. "I don't know what provoked her to come here in the first place, but I've been waiting for this since the first night in El Rio."

When I climb in on my side, she's looking back at Pinky with a worried expression. I close the door quietly and start the short drive to town.

"Honestly, I don't think she'll be upset about it."

"You know her better than I do." Cass turns to face front. "Still, I'll give her these final days with her daughter."

"My daughter misses you." Placing my hand over hers, I lift it to my lips. "So do I."

Her pretty blue eyes meet mine, and she smiles sweetly. "I miss you both, too, but it won't be long before we're together always."

"It's already too long."

Chapter 30

Cass

D O YOU FOLLOW JESUS THIS CLOSE? THE BUMPER STICKER GLARES AT me from my back window, white lettering on a bright red background, and I snort a laugh.

"Alex!" I call out in the empty parking lot.

Last night he called to ask if I'd help them shop for kindergarten supplies today. Of course, I couldn't wait to help. Looking at all the school supplies is the best part of fall, and kindergarten has the cutest stuff.

Piper and Britt do not share my enthusiasm for back-to-school shopping, but I'm already planning to have feathers and sparkles and Miss Piggy everything for our little Sweet P starting kindergarten.

I do not expect to bump into Jessica loading her white Camry in the driveway. Pulling my car to the side, I walk up slowly, stopping when she slams the hood and starts for the driver's side door.

"Are you leaving?" I'm guessing she already told Alex and Penelope goodbye.

"Oh! Cass." She puts a hand on her chest. "You startled me."

"Sorry. Looks like I got here just in time to say goodbye."

"Yeah, I'm headed to the airport." She shrugs. "I can honestly say I tried."

I'm not sure how to respond to that. "Alex mentioned you were headed to Afghanistan? It sounds like really important work."

"I didn't think he approved of my decision."

"I think he doesn't understand your decision." I'm doing my best to be diplomatic.

"I'm sure he's never had to try." She exhales a disgusted laugh. "No one makes a big deal when a man pursues his dreams, but let a woman do it and no one understands."

Chewing my lip, I carefully reply, "I think it's more about having a daughter and being a part of her life."

She crosses her arms, leaning against the car to face me. "When I was pregnant, Alex and I had this conversation. The world is on fire, hatred is out of control, society is breaking down. Bringing a child into this mess is selfish, but that's just my opinion."

"Yes, it is." An edge is in my tone, but I'm doing my best to stay cordial.

I don't want a combative relationship with Pinky's mom, but broken world or not, I wouldn't trade that little girl for anything.

"Well, those problems still exist, and I can't live with myself if I sit at home and do nothing about them." She pushes off the car. "I have to shine a light."

"I think raising an honest, responsible, kind human is another way to shine a light."

"She's only one. I can reach thousands with what I'm doing."

Nodding, I look down at my feet. "Have you ever heard the starfish story?"

"About how it made a difference for that one? Yeah, I've heard it, and I get it. That life just isn't for me." Walking around to get in her car, she pauses. "I'm glad my daughter has you."

"I'm not sure you'll be able to call her your daughter if you leave." I think about my own feelings about my mother and the way she left me behind for her dreams.

"I guess I'm one of those people who aren't meant to be mothers." She pulls the car door open. "I have to make the world a better place in my own way."

I think how lonely her life would be to me, and sadness fills my chest. And I remember she and I are very different people. I remember my conversation with Martha, and I realize I'm here, and Alex and Pinky are already my family.

"Good luck." My voice is calm.

With a resigned smile, she's gone.

Pinky is unusually quiet throughout our entire shopping trip, even when I showed her the Miss Piggy lunchbox and pencils with feathers on the tips.

My mind immediately went to her mother leaving, since that was my experience, and on the way back to Eureka from our road trip to the nearest big box store, she fell asleep in her booster seat, giving us a chance to talk.

My hand is threaded in Alex's, and I glance back to be sure she's sleeping. "Did you ever tell her who Jessica really is?"

The muscle in his sexy square jaw tightens. "I didn't see the point. She left without even saying goodbye, so why bother?"

"She didn't say goodbye?" My eyes go wide.

"If you hadn't told me, I wouldn't have known until we started looking for her."

Sitting back hard in my chair, it's my turn to clench my teeth. "I don't want to say bad things about Pinky's mom…"

My voice breaks off, and Alex exhales a short laugh, lifting my hand to his lips. "I love how much you love my daughter."

His scruffy beard tickles my knuckles, and I finish my

thought. "She should've said goodbye. She should've at least given her that much to remember."

"I don't want to defend Jessica's behavior…"

"Then don't." Now I'm really mad.

"My little spitfire didn't hold back on her behavior." He gives me a tight smile. "She was a bit of a brat."

"Jessica deserves it. She didn't even try to meet her on her level. She just barreled in like Pinky was a grown-up and they'd have an adult relationship. So many times I wanted to say something." Exhaling a sigh, I shake my head. "But I didn't. It wasn't my place."

"Next time it will be." His voice is so smoothly calm, it warms my stomach.

"You think there'll be a next time? She seemed pretty confident in her decision to tap out to me."

"I've stopped trying to predict Jessica's behavior. I never would've expected her to show up here." He shakes his head, looking out the window. "She almost fucked up everything."

He adds the last part under his breath as he pulls into a parking space on the square across from the Star Parlor.

Turning to me, his hazel eyes capture mine. "Will you come home now?"

Heat fills my stomach, and I smile, leaning across the console to kiss his lips before answering. "Yes. I can't wait to come home."

"You're sleeping in my bed this time. No more garage apartment for you."

My hand is on his cheek, and I slide my thumb over his full bottom lip. "Then we are definitely having a conversation with P. I want her to know what's happening before she catches me sleeping in your room."

"We'll tell her tonight." He catches my arm as I step out of the car. "I'll come back and help you pack."

"I've got it. You take care of her." I give his hand a squeeze. "I'll be home for dinner."

Saying the words warms my stomach, and a smile splits my cheeks as I trot up the narrow staircase.

"You're marrying Alex Stone?" Aunt Carol's jaw pulls back as if she's stunned. "How did this happen?"

"Well…" I'm not sure where to begin. "We've sort of known each other all our lives, you know. I was friends with his brother Adam."

"But how well did you know Alex? Marriage is a big step."

"It's true…" My thoughts trail off.

I can't tell her how he saw me naked then I saw him naked, and I guess he saw me naked again.

"We kind of got to know each other better while I was planning Britt's wedding…" It's a total lie. I barely saw him that entire month. "Then he hired me to be his daughter's nanny, and we really got to know each other better."

She doesn't need to know how much better.

"You're marrying him for his money?" Her chin lifts, and I swallow the burn in the back of my throat.

Closing my eyes, I see Pinky and me singing "Paper Rings" at the top of our lungs in the car. I'd marry Alex Stone if he had nothing at all.

"I fell in love with his daughter first. Penelope Stone? I'm sure you've seen her around church."

"I've seen her." My aunt sniffs. "She's a little terror from what I've heard."

"She's four." Defensiveness rises in my tone. "She's a strong, independent little girl."

"Her father spoils her, I'm sure. Single dads always spoil their children, especially daughters."

Inhaling slowly, I remind myself I'm working on forgiveness.

"Alex loves her very much. He might not be as strict with

her as he could be, but what's wrong with a father doting on his only child?"

"A lot." She waves a hand, shaking her head. "Never mind, it's none of my business to tell you how to live your life. You've always known better than me."

I won't be baited. "Anyway, I just wanted to stop by and let you know what was happening." Hesitating, I think about how I want to say this. "And I wanted to thank you for taking care of me. After my mother left, I mean. I'm sure it wasn't easy, and having an extra person adds expense…"

Her back stiffens as if she's surprised. "It's what family does."

"I know." Nodding, I carefully close the space between us. My aunt and I have never been affectionate, but I carefully extend my hand. "Still, I wanted to say thank you. And I love you."

Clearing her throat, her shoulders move as if she's unsure what to do. "Well, of course. I love you as well."

I don't know where to go from here, so I pat her back. "I'll keep you posted about the wedding details."

"Thank you." The smallest hint of softness enters her voice. "Best wishes, Cassidy. Your mother would be very proud of you."

It hurts my chest, and I look down, blinking away the heat in my eyes. "I appreciate that."

Chapter 31

Alex

POOPED TODAY! The bumper sticker is a black circle with a white stick figure doing a spread-eagle jump, and I almost snort coffee through my nose.

Looking around the empty parking lot, I retrace all my steps since leaving the house this morning. With a cringe, I remember stopping by the school to drop off Pinky's vaccination records before heading to the distillery.

Swiping up my phone, I tap out a quick text. ***I pooped today?***

Her reply is quick. ***Regularity is so important.***

What happened to Buckle up with Jesus? It's where I expected her to go after my last one.

Gray dots precede her reply. ***It was time to give religion a rest. You're in trouble, Cass Dixon.***

Maybe you'll have to spank me?

My dick twitches, and I shift in my seat. ***Maybe I will.***

I can't wait. Are you picking up my stuff?

Yeah, see you in a bit.

Sliding my phone into my pocket, I see Doug holding a

ladder outside the Star Parlor. Britt is on top photographing a small white sign hanging above the entrance that reads *Everything in its time*.

"That is not from the eighties." I hold the other side of the ladder, watching my sister-in-law lean around to get a close-up of the nails used to fasten it.

"If it was, it wasn't famous." Doug shakes his head. "Sounds more New Age to me."

"So Madonna and Kevin Costner are off the hook?" I squint one eye, wondering if that joke is played out yet.

He quietly chuckles, and I guess it isn't. "I imagine they've got pretty busy schedules, after all."

"Hey, Alex!" Britt waves at me before climbing down the ladder.

"Should you be up on ladders in your condition?" I reach out to hold her back as she descends.

"Don't you start, too." Her tone is fussy. "Aiden treats me like I'm made of glass, and I'm not even showing yet."

Her feet are on the ground, and I motion to the sign. "Still no leads?"

"To be fair, we're not really pursuing it very hard." She scrolls through the images on her camera. "It's not like they're threatening messages."

"It is criminal mischief," Doug notes thoughtfully.

"Is it?" Britt's nose wrinkles. "They don't leave any marks once we take them down. It's not like graffiti."

"Let's see, we had *Open your heart* at Bud's garage, *Dreams do come true* at the ball field, and now *Everything in its time* at the Star Parlor." Doug counts off the messages on his fingers, then he shrugs. "I just don't see a connection."

"Bud's been married for years," I muse, "Otherwise, they kind of go with the locations."

"I think it's nice," Britt counters, putting her camera bag over her shoulder. "It's a fun little town mystery, and it doesn't hurt anybody. I'll take one of those any day."

"Same here." Doug holds up a hand.

"What are you doing, anyway?" Britt studies me. "Not coming for a reading?"

"Nah, Cass left one of her crates behind, so I'm picking it up for her."

Stepping forward, she gives me a tight hug. "Have I mentioned how happy I am you two are getting married? I like to think I had a teeny-tiny role in making it happen."

"I think that's fair to say." She has no idea how much her little apartment kick-started the process, along with her wedding.

"Let me know the minute you set a date. I want to do all the things. Do you think you'll get married at the distillery like we did?"

The frenzy begins, and I shake my head, grinning and holding up both hands. "I'll do wherever and whenever Cass says, just as long as she meets me at the altar."

"Oh…" Britt's eyes warm. "You're just the sweetest. Now all we have to do is find someone for Adam, and the family is complete!"

"Right." She's not catching me on that one either, despite my suspicions. "I'll tell Cass to text you."

What is it about married women wanting to marry everyone off?

"You're kind of young to be worrying about regularity." Doug chuckles, nodding to my parked car.

Shit. "Don't ask." I pull the glass door open, leaving the two of them snorting behind me.

When I'm finally at the house again, I grab the razor tool off the counter and carefully scrape the bumper sticker off my car. She kicked it up a notch, but I'm here for it.

Inside, my little princess is standing on the step stool at the bar with her red hair in a bun on top of her head and a cupcake tin in front of her. Cass is at the stove, stirring ground meat in a pan. It smells delicious.

"Daddy!" Pinky yells when I walk through the door. "I'm making cheeseburger cups! Look!"

Walking over to the counter, I see she's mashing what looks like flattened bread into the muffin cups. Beside her are bottles of mustard, ketchup, and small containers of shredded cheese and pickles.

"That's creative." I kiss her head, continuing past her to Cass. "Where do you find these recipes?"

"Google." She turns to kiss my lips, and I pull her closer, nuzzling my face into her neck and making her laugh. "Stop, you're going to make me spill."

Lifting the pan off the stove, she carries it to the sink to drain. Pinky watches her with fascination, and I can't wait another minute.

"Penelope?" I lift her off the ladder, putting her on my hip. "How would you feel about making Cass part of our family?"

"She's already part of our family, Daddy." Pinky props her little elbow on my shoulder, threading her fingers as she studies my chin. "She's more like my mama than Jessica is."

The pan clatters on the stove, and Cass's eyes are wide when she turns to face us.

Catching my daughter's chin, I lift her gaze to mine. "What do you mean, baby?"

"Jessica said I was her daughter, but she wasn't like a real mom. She was like Drizella, so I picked Mama Cass instead."

"Who's Drizella?" My forehead wrinkles.

"Cinderella's step-sister," Cass answers quickly, joining us and taking Pinky's hand. "Jessica told you she was your mother? When?"

"She told you, 'Thank you for taking care of my daughter' when she got here." My little girl uses a nasally, affected tone, and I can't help a chuckle.

"You heard that? Why didn't you say anything, Sweet P?"

"I didn't want her to be my mama." Bright blue eyes meet mine. "I want you to marry Mama Cass and have a carriage and live happily ever after like the princesses."

Cass slides her hand over Pinky's back, and my daughter reaches for her. "Will you do that?"

"Actually, that's what I wanted to tell you. I asked Cass to marry me, and she said yes." Saying the words warms my chest. "We wanted to be sure that was okay with you."

Pinky nods, her little lips pursed. "It's okay with me, because I already said it was, and we're already a family."

I don't know where she's getting all this, but I can't argue. It's a fact that's only grown stronger the more time has passed.

"You're right." Reaching out, I pull Cass to my side, and the three of us share a hug. "We just have to make it official."

"I don't want to wait," my voice grinds out, and I'm doing my best not to come until she's with me.

"So close..." Cass's voice has turned into a growly moan, and fuck me, I love that sound.

She's on my lap in a straddle, and my cock is buried balls-deep in her clenching core. She's riding fast, and her breasts bob right at my mouth. Pulling a hardened nipple between my lips, I give it a firm suck.

"Oh, God!" Her back arches, and I feel her break.

"Fuck, yes," I groan, lifting my hips as my orgasm surges through my pelvis, releasing at last in pulsing jets.

She jerks on my cock, exhaling shaky whimpers, and I hold her, closing my eyes as the sensation rockets through me, as her hot body pulls and milks me.

Wrapping my arms around her waist, I sit up so we're chest to chest, never wanting to let this feeling end. We're both breathing hard. A bead of sweat trickles along my eyebrow, and I kiss her shoulder, making my way up her neck with salt on my tongue.

"You are so fucking sexy." Finding her mouth, I push her lips apart, curling my tongue with hers.

She exhales a soft moan, another little spasm grips my cock, and I groan into her mouth. Shit, it doesn't get any better.

We drop onto the bed sated and happy, and she props her pretty head on her hand, tracing her finger along the side of my face, moving my hair off my forehead.

"Sorry I made you wait." Her lips press into a smile, and she almost seems embarrassed.

For a moment, I'm lost. Her timing was perfect.

Then I remember. "No, that wasn't what I meant. I don't want to wait to get married. I want to do it as soon as possible."

Her pretty blue eyes blink, and she reaches for my neck, pulling her face to my chest and inhaling slowly. I'm not sure if this is happiness, frustration, or something else.

"If that's okay with you, of course," I quickly add.

She nods against my skin, and I smile, wrapping my arm around her and pulling her body closer to mine.

Her head is tucked beneath my chin, and I lean down, kissing the top of her shoulder as I smile. "I've waited my whole life for you. I don't want to wait anymore."

"Paper rings." It's a soft whisper.

"What?"

"You waited your whole life for this."

I kiss the tip of her nose. "And if you hadn't come to me, I'd have spent it alone."

"I think we can be married by Christmas."

"What would you say to Halloween?"

Her eyes lift, and she laughs. "A Halloween wedding?"

"November first?"

"I think we can make that happen." Her voice is happy and full.

It's the best thing I've heard all day.

Chapter 32

Cass

"I SHOULD STAY HOME WITH YOU." PINKY'S HAND SQUEEZES MINE, and she pulls us to a stop on the sidewalk.

Alex takes a few steps before he realizes we're not moving and turns back. "What's wrong?"

I take a knee beside our little girl. "What's wrong, Sweetie? I thought you were excited about kindergarten."

She's all dressed up in her black leggings with sparkles and her feathered Miss Piggy shirt. Her iridescent backpack is on her shoulders, and her curly hair is arranged in two ponytails behind each ear. She looks adorable, and ready to own her first day of school.

Her chin drops, and she studies her light-up glitter Sketchers. "What if I don't know anybody?"

I slide the backs of my fingers over her cheek. "You know Crimson. And Owen will be down the hall in the fourth-grade room."

"Owen always tells me to go away." My heart twists, and I hug her close.

"Owen's just grumpy at home. When you're not at home, he'll look out for you. And Ryan's here, too. He's sweet."

Alex squats beside us, taking her hand. "You'll probably know more kids in your class than you think."

She puts her hand on his shoulder. "What if they don't like me?"

His jaw tightens, and I know the idea anyone wouldn't like his daughter is like fighting words. I feel the same.

Still, "Find Crimson, and the two of you can meet people together. You'll make friends. You're a very fun person."

"Owen said I'm not Little Miss Thing at school like I think I am at home, and I have to behave." Worried eyes meet mine, and my lips part.

It's like my first day as a nanny all over again, and I am not prepared for family drama. My eyes fly to Alex, and he steps in at once.

"I think Owen was trying to warn you not to come on too strong." Her little brow wrinkles, and he continues. "Like don't karate chop your classmates."

I'm not so sure it's what Owen meant, but I'm happy to go with this explanation.

Pinky's forehead relaxes, and she gives her daddy a look that clearly says *duh*. "I know not to do that, Daddy. Mama Cass told me a long time ago, and I got to eat El Rio when I stopped, remember?"

As if we could ever forget that night.

"Yes." He nods. "You did a very good job, and that's why you're going to have a great first day of class. Ready?"

She nods quickly, her smile returning to her cheeks. I'm about to collapse against the wall from the adrenaline leaving my veins, when a familiar little voice yells from behind us.

"Pinkeeee!" Crimson runs to where we're stopped.

She's all decked out in a white dress with the alphabet all over it and bright red Converse sneakers. Her brown hair is styled in two braids on each side of her head, and her brown eyes widen when she sees her friend.

"You're Miss Piggy!" She throws her arms around Pinky's neck.

Pinky hugs her back. "Crimey, you're here!"

The two little girls join hands and start walking towards the school, leaving us behind.

My head swivels around to Alex. "What the heck was that?"

"Kid stuff." He chuckles, taking my hand and helping me stand. "You have no idea how Aiden used to mess with me, and I messed with Adam."

"Cass!" Julia hugs me, gripping my hand. "I don't know if I'm ready."

"We're better now. I'm glad the girls are here together."

"They're so dramatic," she laughs. "You'd think they've been separated for months."

Alex steps up beside me, sliding his hand over my waist. "They're good little soldiers."

My hands cover my cheeks, and I inhale slowly. "It's hard to believe they're old enough to do this."

The three of us hesitate as we watch them, hand-in-hand, marching up to the school. Their backpacks are as big as they are, and they're just so small. I can't help thinking this is how it begins, and I'm so thankful I'll be a part of it next year.

Walking through the hall, observing all the children talking and greeting each other, I make mental notes. Next year, this will be my workplace—and I can't wait. I've found everything I was looking for.

The girls join their classmates, sitting on the floor with their backs to the walls, and the tiny kindergartners watch wide-eyed as the older students file past in a line on the way to their classrooms.

Mrs. Priddy steps out of her door and smiles at me, walking over. "Cass." She takes my hand. "I can't tell you how happy

I was when Dr. Bayer told me the news, and you'll be assisting me after Christmas?"

"Yes! I'll complete my basic courses this fall, then I'll do my student teaching."

"Extra, extra, read all about it." Piper slides up beside me, giving me a hug. "We need to do a story on Eureka Elementary's newest teacher. How does it feel?"

Alex is standing by the wall chatting with Adam. The contrast between the two is striking. Adam is relaxed, like he's done this four times already. Alex has his arms crossed over his chest like he's putting on a brave front.

"It's the strangest thing." My voice is quiet. "I didn't raise her, and I still think I'm going to cry."

"Oh, girl, I was on the couch sobbing when Ryan started kindergarten. Adam had to take me out for mimosas."

"That's nice." My eyes narrow, and I glance from my friend to her ever-present protector. "Adam always looks out for you."

"Yeah, he's been great since Rex died."

"That was nine years ago."

I'm ready to make her talk when Britt skips up behind me, giving me a hug. "How's it going?"

"Everybody keeps asking me that," I stage-whisper. "I'm going to cry, okay? Let's all just accept it."

"Aw, sweet Cass." Britt strokes the side of my hair. "You're such a good little mama."

"Before I forget, Pinky's birthday party is tomorrow at noon at Patricia's house. We'll have hot dogs and cake and they can swim, and all the things."

"We'll be there!" Britt sings. "Her gift is wrapped and ready. Now I have to get back to the courthouse. Aiden says I'm babying Owen walking him to school on his first day."

"We'll keep on babying them as long as they let us," Piper argues. "They'll be graduating high school before we know it."

The bell rings, and my heart squeezes. Pinky is sitting on the floor with Crimson holding hands and watching everything with wide eyes, but as soon as that noise sounds, her eyes fly to mine.

The flash of panic in her expression knots my throat, and I press my lips together, forcing an encouraging smile. Alex steps up beside me, taking my hand, and Mrs. Priddy steps out with her arms extended.

"Today is the day, it's the first day of school!" She sings the song from *CoComelon*, and a few of the children start to sing along with her.

Pinky's attention is diverted to the teacher, and Alex gives me a little pull. "Let's go."

My chest tightens, and the heat fills my eyes. Holding my smile steady, I wave as the teacher helps them line up to file into the colorful classroom.

She's not looking as we slip out the side door, and the minute it closes with a metal clatch, I press my face into Alex's chest as a tear sneaks onto my cheek.

His arms are around me. "Are you crying?"

"She's so grown up…" He moves me back, and his astonished face makes me cover my mouth with my hand. "I can't help it. It's a big step!"

Hugging me close again, he kisses the side of my cheek. "You know I love you, right?" I nod, and he laughs gently. "I think I fell in love with you even more just now."

"Piper said Adam took her out for mimosas after Ryan's first day of kindergarten." Arching my back, I reach over my shoulder to kiss his jaw. "I like your way better."

We're back at the house, and we only made it a few steps through the door before he bent me over the couch. His pants were down and my skirt was over my ass faster than I could say *fuck me, Alex*. Now I'm wrapped in his arms, buzzing from a full-body orgasm.

"I don't like to see my girl cry." His low voice behind my ear sends a sizzle through my legs.

"I'm just glad it's Friday. We have the weekend to get over it." I turn, going to the bathroom to clean up. "You men are clearly made of stone."

After cleaning up, we're in the kitchen where I take out all the ingredients for the snickerdoodle cake I'm making for Pinky's birthday.

"A lot has happened since the last time you made this cake." He leans on his elbows on the granite countertop. "But I knew we'd get here that day."

"You manifested our fake engagement?" I give him a skeptical wink.

"That was all you, my love." Walking around, he catches me by the waist, pulling me flush against his chest. "There was nothing fake about my feelings for you. I saw you as my wife, and when we were at Aiden's last weekend, I saw you having my baby."

A thrill moves through my chest, and I turn to slide my hands around his waist. "Your baby?"

He reaches up to slide my hair off my cheek, behind my ear. It's a possessive move that melts my insides.

He's so confident. "What do you think about that?"

"I think I like it very much. I think maybe next year we can start trying."

"Is that too soon?" His sexy brow furrows. "You'll just be starting with teaching, and we've got plenty of time."

"Always so patient." I rise on my toes to kiss his jaw. "Teachers get pregnant and have babies all the time, and I'd like Pinky to be close to her little siblings."

"Siblings?" The heat in his hazel eyes tingles in my core. "As in more than one?"

"Definitely." Wrapping my arms around his neck, I lean forward to kiss him. "I want all your babies."

His hands gather the back of my skirt, finding my bare ass beneath the fabric, and I'm ready for round two.

"We're very good at practicing." It's a low rumble against the side of my neck, below my ear.

"So good." It's a needy gasp.

His lips cover mine, and I think we're pretty good at kissing, too.

We're even better at building, and I think we should keep building the family we've made. The family I sang about in the ocean the first day he found me.

Epilogue

Alex

"Aw," Britt walks up the driveway at my mom's house carrying a fun pack of potato chips. "Hot dogs are your love language?"

My brow quirks, and I glance to where she came from—where all the cars are parked, and where Aiden is carrying a large gift and grinning.

Damn it. She got me. "Is that what it says?"

"You two are crazy." Britt kisses my cheek as she passes. "Don't ever change."

"Everybody's out at the pool." I'm getting Pinky's gift out of Mom's garage, a kid-sized pink beach cruiser with a basket.

According to Cass, it's just like the one Miss Piggy rode in *The Great Muppet Caper*. At this point, she and my daughter have watched every Muppet movie ever made.

I even caught them crying last night during *The Muppet Christmas Carol*. Apparently when the little Kermit sings, it makes my soon-to-be wife cry.

"Cute." Aiden stops, waiting for me as I straighten the bow on the basket. "It's a lot like Mom's old one."

"The one she gave to Britt?" I'm calculating how long it'll take my little slugger to learn to ride a bike.

"I'll see about getting it for Cass to use."

My brother's pretty good at reading my mind. When the two of us arrive in the backyard, Adam is at the grill making the hot dogs, and Cass is filling a large, silver bucket with boxes of Cracker Jack.

I park the bike behind the presents on the table and go to where she's standing. "I think you know my love language better than that."

A naughty grin is on her lips, and she tries to act innocent. "Whatever do you mean?"

"The bumper sticker. Britt told me."

"My future sister-in-law has a big mouth."

I lunge forward, lifting her off her feet and tossing her over my shoulder. "That does it."

"What are you doing?" She slaps my back, squealing as I head for the pool. "Alex! No! I have to finish prepping for the party!"

I get close, but right before I toss her in the pool, I set her on her feet. Her face is flushed, and her pretty eyes are wide in her face. Reaching up, I smooth my hands down the sides of her now-messy hair and kiss her lightly.

I lean into her ear and whisper, "I still owe you a spanking from the last one."

Her shoulder rises with a little shiver, and it hits me right below the belt. I want her so much right now, but we have a birthday party to throw.

"Daddy!" Pinky is jumping up and down on the diving board. "Don't throw Mama Cass in the pool!"

"I won't, Baby." I lift Cass's hand, kissing her fingers as I walk to where the kids are all swimming.

"Mama Cass." Adam snorts from the grill. "Gets me every time."

"Watch me do The Pencil, Daddy!" Pinky calls, and I nod, watching as she holds her little arms straight down by her sides.

Striding to the end of the board, she walks right off, dropping like a post into the cool blue water. Her little red head quickly bobs up to the surface as she kicks hard to the ladder.

"Did you see me, Daddy? Did you see me?" She really does sound like that little turtle in *Nemo*.

"It was a perfect ten," I call to her. "You barely even made a splash."

"Just like the real divers!"

"I want to do a pencil, Mama!" Crimson bounces on her toes as Julia fastens a hot pink vest over her bathing suit.

"Okay, but you need to do it in the shallow end here." She sits on the side of the pool with her feet in the water.

Owen and Ryan are throwing a ball back and forth from the deep end to the shallow, and classic rock is playing on the radio. I hear Meat Loaf singing about a Coupe de Ville not being in a Cracker Jack box, and I nod approvingly.

Britt walks over to where Adam is taking the hot dogs off the grill, and she motions to Cass.

"Time to eat, everybody!" Cass waves to my daughter in the pool. "Come eat, Birthday Girl!"

Pinky makes an immediate U-turn from where she was headed to the diving board, and starts running to where the kids are lining up for food. I'm impressed by how quickly the five-year-olds have learned to form a line.

"No running!" Mom calls, walking out the door with a cake stand, holding Cass's famous snickerdoodle cake.

Pinky jumps up and down. "Cake! Cake! I want cake!"

"Eat a hot dog first." Cass lifts her onto her hip, carrying her with a paper plate to the picnic table where the rest of her little friends are pigging out.

"I heard there was a new sign out today." Piper hands Ryan and Owen two hot dogs as she squints up at Britt.

"It said, *Trust Your Instincts*." Britt puts a small bag of potato chips on each child's plate.

"I swear, sometimes I feel like this sign bandit is reading my mail." Piper follows her friend, giving each kid a juice box. "The messages always speak to me."

"I wonder if we'll ever find out who it is." Cass wipes a blob of mustard off Pinky's cheek. "If they ever stop, we'll have to cross-check the obituaries."

"That makes me sad." Britt pokes out her lip.

"I think my wife doesn't want to find out who's behind them." Aiden's gruff voice joins the conversation.

"Maybe I don't." She kisses his cheek, and he wraps his arms around her.

"Is that more of our wedding cake?" He nods to where Cass is putting five candles in the large beige cake sprinkled with cinnamon.

"It is. Are we ready to do this?" Cass looks over to me, and I scoop up the princess, standing her on her feet in a chair beside the cake.

Pinky lets out a loud squeal, and I give her squeeze. "Five years ago today, you changed my life forever…"

"Daddy! You say that every year!" Pinky fusses. "Let's eat cake!"

"The birthday girl has spoken," I finish, and everybody laughs as Cass lights the candles.

We sing, the candles are blown out, and just as my mother begins handing out pieces of cake, Drake Redford's annoying voice cuts through the festivities.

"Sorry to crash the party. I came to drop these off for Patricia." He's carrying a folder containing paper and pictures. "We're planning a splash pad and pavilion in Redford Park. It would be a great place for summer birthday parties."

"We're fine having summer birthday parties here with our family." Aiden stands straighter, crossing his arms.

"Not everyone is as fortunate as your family to have such a place."

My throat tightens, and I know he has a point. I also know it's a point that will get a lot of traction among the younger families in town.

"If that's all you needed to do…" My tone is final.

"Keep your shirt on. I'm not planning to stay." Drake holds up a hand before passing the papers to my mother. "I look forward to seeing you at the next town meeting, Patricia."

My mother's lips purse, and she takes the folder from him, looking briefly beneath the cover. "Yes, I've heard as much."

"Happy birthday, little lady. Maybe you'll have a bigger party next year at our new facility." He nods to Cass. "I see you're still climbing."

My fist clenches, and my arm starts to rise.

Cass steps to my side, quickly wrapping both her arms around mine. "Not in front of the children."

"One of these days, she won't be here to stop me." My jaw is set, my eyes locked on Drake's.

"My lawyer will love it." His grin is smarmy as he makes his way to the exit.

"Not as much as I will."

I'm ready to go after him, but Cass holds me tightly. "Don't give him the satisfaction."

"It's me who would get the satisfaction."

She laughs, adding softly, "I would too."

Hours later, the sun is disappearing on the horizon, and the sky is bathed in red-orange fading out to deep purple. I'm chasing her through the palmettos, feverish with need, running along the path through the marshes, over the wooden foot-bridges, until we reach the little lagoon that leads out to the ocean.

In the shade of the Walter pines, the air is cooler, although it's still muggy from the hot August day. The thick, briny air is laden with the scents of pine straw and the ocean.

When we reach the sandy beach, Cass's white tank flies over her head. She pauses only a moment to push her khaki linen shorts down her long, smooth legs, along with her underwear.

I stop a few paces behind her, unbuttoning my shirt and toeing off my topsiders. My eyes drink in her mouthwatering form. Her long, dark hair hanging down her back in waves, her narrow waist and full hips, her round ass.

I've been here before, but only in my dreams.

My dick is a steel rod pointing straight to her as I shove my shorts down, stepping out of them and wading into the warm water. She hops and does a small dive, disappearing beneath the brackish waves and moving farther out from the shore.

I do the same, swimming freestyle until I reach her, catching her around the waist and pulling her naked body flush against mine.

Our mouths meet, and we slide our lips together. Salt is on my tongue as I pull her mouth with mine, chasing our kisses as the light breeze wraps around us. Her breasts flatten against my chest, and I lift her, sinking my hardened cock fully into her heated core.

"Yes," she whispers in my ear, and her legs wrap around my waist.

Her thighs tighten, and she's riding me. I lift my hips meeting her with my thrusts. The gentle waves grow bigger with our movements. We're lost in sensation, chasing that fantastic release as we cling to each other.

My eyes squeeze shut, and it feels too good. "I've been waiting for this all day."

"Me, too." She slides her lips to my ear, biting and pulling my skin with her teeth.

Pleasure snakes up my thighs, and my orgasm is driving me now. I'm thrusting faster, my fingers cutting into the skin of her ass.

"Fuck, Cass," I groan. "You feel so fucking good."

She moans loudly, and her grip tightens on my neck. "That's it," she gasps. "Harder."

My mind blanks, and heat erupts in my pelvis, tightening my balls. "I can't stop." It's a low groan, and her pussy squeezes around me.

With a shout, I break, holding as the pulses of my orgasm take over, flexing and jerking my hips. My knees almost collapse, but I hold us, guttural groans ripping through my chest as my climax fills her trembling body.

All my muscles are spent, and we're breathing hard as we come down from that insane high. Her arms loosen over my shoulders, and a lazy smile curls her lips. I kiss her cheek, loving the feel of her in my arms.

She exhales a sigh, blinking up at me. "I was just thinking… I have to get a job now."

"You have a job. You're Pinky's nanny."

Her nose wrinkles, and she shake she head. "I'm not letting you pay me for that."

My arms tighten around her waist. "You never let anyone pay you for anything. You're a full-time student in an accelerated program, you're Pinky's nanny…"

"Future mom," she interrupts, and I don't argue. I love it.

"*And* you're the new events director at Stone Cold."

Her eyebrow arches. "I am?"

"At least until you become the best kindergarten teacher at Eureka Elementary."

"The only kindergarten teacher at Eureka Elementary."

"I'm putting you on the payroll at the distillery."

Her lips twist, and she nods. "I'll allow it. At least so I can pay rent and buy food—"

"You're never leaving my house again."

She snorts a laugh. "Are you kidnapping me?"

"If I must."

Her arms tighten around my neck, and she presses her soft body against mine. "You can't even cook."

"We'll learn together." I slide my hands down, under her ass, ready to go again.

"Sounds like you have it all figured out." Her voice is sultry. "One thing I've been wondering."

"What's that?"

"Are we friends now?"

Exhaling a chuckle, I shake my head. "God, the friend zone is the worst. You see what happened to my brother."

Winking one eye, she frowns. "I think there's more to that story than any of us knows."

I think she's right, but I'm more interested in her. "Sing for me."

She traces the hair off my forehead with her finger. "What do you want me to sing?"

"Sing the song you were singing the first time I saw you naked."

Leaning forward, she presses her cheek to mine. Soft lips graze the skin of my ear as she sings the first lines of "I Have a Dream" from that Broadway musical she told me all about. I've never forgotten that day.

I hold her as I listen. My eyes close, and her body is soft against mine. She finishes, and I smooth her hair back, looking into her gorgeous face.

"You're so beautiful."

Her eyes blink quickly, and a bashful smile curls her lips. "No one has ever made me feel like you do."

"How is that?"

"Like you can't be without me."

I kiss her left cheek. Then I kiss her mouth. I place my thumbs along her jaw, memorizing the feel of her, this woman who completes me.

"When we were still pretending, you kept saying I saved you." My voice is low, thoughtful.

Her eyes shine with her smile. "You did."

I return her smile. "No, beautiful girl, it was you who saved me. You restored my passion and my joy. You fueled my hunger, and you sated it. You were the missing piece that completed my family."

Sliding her hand up, she places her palm on my cheek. "I never knew I could want someone this much. I never knew this kind of love was possible."

"It is." Leaning down, I kiss her lips. "With you."

Rising higher, she kisses me again, wrapping her arms around my neck. "Thank you for loving me, for giving me the life I was searching for."

We've both found what we were seeking. Because as good as we are at building things, as talented as she is in so many amazing ways, we're also very good at making dreams come true.

Thank you for reading Alex & Cass's romance!

Adam & Piper's romance *A Little Luck* is *coming Dec. 14, 2023*.

Have you had A LITTLE TASTE?

Keep turning for a short excerpt of Aiden & Britt's romance, available now!

A Little Taste

Aiden Stone is a **six-foot-two former Marine** with a **permanent scowl**, dark hair, and **dreamy blue eyes.**

He's the oldest of **the Stone brothers**, and his "by the book" family has battled mine for control of **our small town** for generations.

The last thing I should do is **sleep with him.** Or nearly run him down with my truck. Especially since he's sort-of **my new boss**…

It doesn't help that my grandmother (the mayor) is a former magician, and my mom is a psychic (sort-of)… And my dad died in a failed escape-artist attempt (that my mother is convinced was a murder).

Trust me, **I know crazy**, but I'm just plain ole Britt Bailey, Shania Twain-loving, non-magical forensic photographer. Yes, I take pictures of dead things, but I don't see them in my bedroom at night.

I only want to see one thing in my bedroom at night, and when I'm called home to help Sheriff Stone on an investigation, he actually stops frowning for a minute, and **my teenage fantasies get very real.**

It's a terrible idea. We work together, he's **seven years older** than me, he's **a single dad**, he hates all things magic, but *a little taste*, and **we can't say no**.

Until the town crime wave turns personal, putting everything on the line, and we'll need more than a magic bullet to get our happily ever after.

(A LITTLE TASTE is a small-town, grumpy single-dad romance with a touch of light suspense and lots of tasty spice. No cheating. No cliffhanger.)

Chapter 1

Aiden

"YEP, HE'S A GONER." DEPUTY DOUG HALLY STRAIGHTENS WITH a groan, holding the squashed cucumber out for my inspection.

I nod grimly, and Terra Belle throws up her arms in distress. "My entire pickle farm is destroyed! Who would do such a thing?"

We're standing in the middle of the two-acre field now riddled with large, circular ruts and damaged fruit still on the vine. The pattern of the tire tracks reminds me of that movie about the aliens making crop circles, but this damage was definitely done by a vehicle of some sort.

"My money's on them no-good Jones boys." My sole deputy tosses the damaged fruit to the side, lowering his brow in a knowing way.

"You think it was Bull and Raif, Dad? Are you going to arrest them? Can I go?" My son Owen blinks up at me, his seven-year-old eyes wide, and I hesitate.

If he weren't here, I'd say this looks more like asshole teenagers who watched that movie and wanted to play a prank. The

Jones boys were probably too drunk or high last night to do something this precise, but it's important to me to be a good role model, even when I'm tired.

Placing my hand on Owen's shoulder, I summon my dad, the former sheriff of Eureka's calm wisdom. I think about what he'd have said to me at Owen's age.

"It's not our job to decide who's guilty, son. We have to collect the evidence and make our best determination, then we'll get a judge to issue a warrant."

"Oh, you know it was those Jones boys." Terra drops to a squat, holding up a vine of crushed cuke after cuke—it looks like a sad party favor. "I'm tempted to gather up the rest of these and beat them to death with 'em."

"Now, Terra," Deputy Doug cautions. "Two wrongs don't make a right."

"Yeah, don't go there, Terra," I add. "Then I'd have to arrest you, too."

"So you *are* going to arrest them?" She stands quickly. Her dark hair is tied up in a red handkerchief, and she's wearing faded overalls and from what I can tell, nothing else. "This kind of vandalism can't go unpunished. It's trespassing, destruction of property, murder…"

With every charge she shakes the pickle vine at me, and I stand straighter, rising to my full six-foot-two height and lowering my voice. "Take it easy, Terra."

It's my standard way to diffuse tense situations, and sure enough, Terra deflates.

"What am I going to do about my existing orders?"

"You've got insurance, don't ya?" Doug squints as he walks to where we're standing.

"Of course I do!" she snaps at him, but I let it pass.

She's facing a pretty significant loss, which has her understandably emotional. I have no clue how long it takes to grow a crop of cucumbers, and Terra Belle's Pickle Patch is regionally famous, which I guess might make her a target. Of what, I don't know.

Exhaling slowly, I maintain my calm. "I'll head back to the office and get you a police report to send to the insurance company. Hopefully, that'll get you some money pretty quick." She starts to argue it's not enough, and I nod. "I know you want justice today, but I can't go arresting people without evidence. It'll just get thrown out, and that's not how we do things."

"Well, maybe it should be," she grouses.

I'm tired. I haven't had my first cup of coffee. The call to come out here had me out of bed before the sun even broke the horizon. Now it's climbing higher in the sky, and I'm ready to head to the office and possibly have breakfast.

"Doug, you finish up here, and I'll get Terra's report ready." I'm not sure the correct way to phrase my next question. "Before I go, do you have any enemies or rival... picklers?"

"Oh, I've got plenty of rivals, but no one would stoop to this level." She wipes a tear off her cheek. "Destroying my *babies*."

Pressing my lips together, I nod. I'm not good with tears, especially tears over "baby pickles," which in reality are called *cucumbers*.

"All the same, send me any names that come to mind, and take plenty of pictures. I'll have that report to you by lunchtime."

I whistle to my son, who's holding a squashed fruit with a stick and examining it. He drops it at once and takes off running to my truck. I let Doug drive the cruiser. In this town, I'm fine with a black Silverado and a light on the dash when necessary.

Terra can work this out with her insurance company, and I'll have Doug inspect every teenager in town's vehicle for traces of cucumber vines. It won't take long in Eureka, South Carolina. I'll include the Jones boys to cover all the bases.

We're halfway back to town, the radio playing some old country song. Owen's beside me, buckled in and bouncing Zander, his tattered, stuffed zebra on his legs. "Why would anybody drive a car in Ms. Belle's pickle patch?"

My hand is propped on the top of the steering wheel, and I think about it. "The older I've gotten, the less I understand why people do anything. I guess that's why towns need sheriffs."

"I'm going to be a sheriff when I grow up!" He smiles up at me, pride in his eyes. "Just like my dad."

My stomach tightens, and warmth filters through my chest. I'm generally considered something of a grumpy badass, but this little guy... He's a lot like I was at his age, thinking my dad was the greatest and wanting to grow up to be just like him.

I thought I'd have a chance to work right alongside him, but a heart-attack took him two days after I graduated from college. I've missed him every day since. Especially when life hits hard. Especially when I need advice.

I went from being a student, to being a Marine, to being a sheriff, and now Owen wants to follow in my footsteps.

"You'll be one of the best." I glance at him before returning my eyes to the road.

He sits straighter, lifting his chin, and I almost grin. I had no idea when he was born how much he'd carry me through the dark times.

He was barely old enough to remember his mom when she was killed four years ago on her evening walk. I'd mourned her and pledged to find the person who hit her and drove off without even looking back.

Then a year later, when I'd finally worked up the strength to go through her things, I found a box of love letters from Clive Stevens, who happened to live on the very street where she was hit.

He'd even had the balls to attend her funeral before he moved back to wherever he was from. It never occurred to me to be suspicious of her evening walks, but after that, I pretty much swore off anyone not related to me by blood. They're the only ones you can trust, and even then, it's good to keep your eyes open.

"Do you know what a zorse is?" Owen looks up at me, bouncing Zander on his leg. "It's a cross between a zebra and a horse!"

"Is that so?" I park the truck in front of the courthouse, which houses the mayor's office and our headquarters.

"A group of zebras is called a dazzle. I wonder if a group of zorses would be called a zazzle?"

He looks up at me like I would know. "Forget sheriff, you should be a zebrologist when you grow up."

"That's not a thing!" He groans as he climbs out of the truck, slamming the door and trotting up beside me, slipping his little hand in mine.

It warms my chest, again almost making me smile. I don't smile often, and I definitely don't hold hands, but with Owen, everything is different.

"You can be the first." I scoot him through the glass doors ahead of me, hoping Holly, our secretary and dispatcher, ordered breakfast—or at least has a pot of coffee ready.

"Aiden, I heard you were at Terra Belle's Pickle Patch." I'm met at the door by Edna Brewer, longtime mayor of Eureka, and unfortunately my boss. "My intuition tells me something sinister is afoot."

"Terra would agree with you. She left her house without her wig on."

Edna's dark brown eyes widen. "You saw Terra's real hair?"

"She had a handkerchief around her head, and she was in overalls."

"Only something truly sinister would cause Terra to leave the house in such a state."

"I suspect it's nothing more sinister than teenagers." I start to walk past her, but she pulls me up short with her next words.

"Owen, your father is a good man, despite his lack of faith."

My jaw tightens. We were almost having a nice moment, and she had to go there. "I prefer sticking to the facts when doing my job."

"Magic has never let me down, Sheriff, which is more than I can say of people."

She'll get no arguments from me when it comes to people, however, "Where was magic when Lars needed it?"

Her eyes narrow. "What happened to my son-in-law was a tragic accident, but escapologists are not magicians."

Neither are you. The retort is on the tip of my tongue, but I don't say it. We're fighting old battles, and we only go in circles.

The Brewers and the Stones declared a truce after my father died, and I've done my best to honor it since starting as sheriff—as long as Edna keeps her hocus pocus to herself and out of my work.

Placing my hand on Owen's back, I give him a little pat. "Why don't you run see if Holly got donuts on her way in." He takes off with a little whoop of "Krispy Kreme," and I turn to the mayor. "I apologize for saying that about Lars. It was insensitive."

She lifts her chin. "I accept your apology."

"And I'd appreciate it if you didn't put ideas in my son's head."

"Your son is very bright, Aiden."

"Thank you."

"And children are very sensitive to spiritual things. Owen's fascination with zebras is a clear indicator. They're remnants of a time when the world was shadows and light."

"No." My tone is firm.

She waves her hands. "I'm not trying to start a fight. I simply wanted to let you know I've been monitoring this rise in crime lately, and I think we need to bring in some backup."

My brow furrows. "What does that mean?"

She starts for her office, and I follow. Edna is almost seventy, with silver hair that hangs in a bob to her chin. She's dressed in a white silk blouse and tan pencil skirt with matching pumps, and in this conservative disguise, you'd never know she's a former magician and matriarch of the town's resident band of carnies.

She believes in premonitions and psychics and *vibrations* as much as cold hard facts when making civic decisions. It drove my dad nuts, and it doesn't make me too happy either—particularly when she drags her "psychic" daughter Guinevere into the mix. Gwen is a real space cadet, and sneaky as fuck.

You'd think Edna would be ready to retire by now, but this crazy town keeps voting her back in office every time she runs. If the town of Eureka were a zebra, she'd be the black to my white—and I'm sure she'd say the exact opposite.

"Someone has been nailing messages on telephone poles for a month. Last week, Holly said three of her hens were stolen. Now Terra Belle's prized pickle patch has been demolished. I think we need someone with special training in this type of work."

Heat rises under my collar, and a growl enters my tone. "You're not to call in additional officers without consulting me."

"I'm consulting you now. Doug's pushing sixty, but even if he was younger, you know he isn't up to this type of work. You could use the help."

I'm annoyed she's right. Still, the last thing I need is some new person coming in, getting in my way, asking a bunch of questions—or worse, another kooky mystic reading tea leaves and being totally loyal to Edna.

"Who did you have in mind?"

"That's the best part." She claps, rising to her feet and smiling like she's about to pull a rabbit out of a hat. "My granddaughter Britt has been working in Greenville, training at the crime lab at Clemson. She's got the best possible credentials."

My stomach tightens. "Britt said she wasn't coming back to Eureka."

The last time I saw Edna's granddaughter—at her going away party, which my youngest brother tricked me into attending—she'd said she wanted to define her life outside this town and her family's reputation.

"Oh, poo." Edna waves her hand. "Guinevere will call her. She'll want to be back in her hometown with her best friends and family."

I'm not so sure of that. I'm also not so sure about her working with me. Britt Bailey is too young and too pretty, and on the night of her farewell party, things got a little too blurry on the back porch of her friend's home.

We somehow wound up out there alone, and we started talking about her life in Eureka, my time in the Marines, her dreams, my son. It was the first time I'd seen her as the only sane member of her family.

Our bodies had drifted closer until we were almost touching, and the conversation faded away. She blinked those pretty green eyes up at me, and the starlight shone on the tips of her blonde hair. She smelled like fresh flowers and the ocean, and her pink lips were so full and inviting. It had been so long since I'd lost myself in the depths of a beautiful woman…

Obviously, I'd had too much whiskey.

"I can tell by your pleased expression you like this idea." Edna nods. "I'll have Gwen call her today, and I'll let you know how soon she can get started."

"That wasn't what I was thinking." My expression was *not* pleased. "Is she even old enough to work here?"

"She's twenty-eight, Aiden. Don't be ageist."

Seven years younger than me.

"But this would be her first actual job as a crime scene investigator?"

"She's an experienced forensic photographer. You can get her up to speed on the rest. She's a fast learner." Edna picks up her phone, excitedly tapping on the face. "Trust me, once you have my granddaughter at your side, you'll wonder how you ever survived without her. The vibrations are shifting already."

I'm sure they are, and it's exactly what's putting me on guard.

Read *A Little Taste* Today, available in paperback, ebook, and on audio!

Books by
TIA LOUISE

THE BE STILL SERIES

A Little Taste, 2023★

A Little Twist, 2023★

A Little Luck, coming Dec. 14, 2023★

(★Available on Audiobook.)

THE HAMILTOWN HEAT SERIES

Fearless, 2022★

Filthy, 2022★

For Your Eyes Only, 2022

Forbidden, 2023★

(★Available on Audiobook.)

THE TAKING CHANCES SERIES

This Much is True★

Twist of Fate★

Trouble★

(★Available on Audiobook.)

FIGHT FOR LOVE SERIES

Wait for Me★

Boss of Me★

Here with Me★

Reckless Kiss★

(★Available on Audiobook.)

BELIEVE IN LOVE SERIES

Make You Mine

Make Me Yours★

Stay★

(★Available on Audiobook.)

SOUTHERN HEAT SERIES

When We Touch

When We Kiss

THE ONE TO HOLD SERIES

One to Hold (#1 - Derek & Melissa)★

One to Keep (#2 - Patrick & Elaine)★

One to Protect (#3 - Derek & Melissa)★

One to Love (#4 - Kenny & Slayde)

One to Leave (#5 - Stuart & Mariska)

One to Save (#6 - Derek & Melissa)★

One to Chase (#7 - Marcus & Amy)★

One to Take (#8 - Stuart & Mariska)

(★Available on Audiobook.)

THE DIRTY PLAYERS SERIES

PRINCE (#1)★

PLAYER (#2)★

DEALER (#3)

THIEF (#4)

(★Available on Audiobook.)

THE BRIGHT LIGHTS SERIES

Under the Lights (#1)

Under the Stars (#2)

Hit Girl (#3)

COLLABORATIONS

The Last Guy★

The Right Stud

Tangled Up

Save Me

(★Available on Audiobook.)

PARANORMAL ROMANCES

One Immortal (vampires)

One Insatiable (shifters)

Acknowledgments

Huge thanks and so much love to my husband Mr. TL for helping me create my new families—real and fictional.

Thank you to my beautiful daughters, who made me a mom, and who I love with all my heart.

Thanks so much to my alpha readers Renee McCleary and Leticia Teixeira for your funny notes and highlights, and for falling in love with Alex.

Huge thanks to my *incredible* betas, Maria Black, Corinne Akers, Amy Reierson, Courtney Anderson, Jennifer Christy, Jennifer Kreinbring, Heather Heaton, Michelle Mastandrea, Jennifer Pon, and Tina Morgan. You guys give the *best* notes!

Thanks to Jaime Ryter for your editing skillz and hilarious notes and to Lori Jackson and Kate Farlow for the killer cover designs. Always love my dear Wander Aguiar for the *perfect* cover images, and the amazing Stacy Blake, who makes my gorgeous paperback interiors!

Thanks to my dear Starfish, to my Mermaids, and to my Veeps for keeping me sane and organized while I'm in the cave.

Thanks to the incredible Booktokers who help me so incredibly much, in particular Paige, Glav, Jime, Maria, Kayla, See, Kenzie, Morgan, Kate & Ali, Nikki, Jessica, Katarina, Katie, Leah, and I have to stop—you all mean the world to me!

I can't begin to put into words how much I appreciate the love and support of my author-buds. We're all so slammed, and your support means the world to me. In particular, thanks to Avery Maxwell, who has become such a dear friend, and to Laura and Elizabeth.

I hope you all adore this new romance. Thank you for helping me do what I do.

Stay sexy,

<3 Tia

About the Author

Tia Louise is the *USA Today* and #4 Amazon bestselling author of (*mostly*) small-town, single-parent, second-chance, and military romances set at or near the beach.

From Readers' Choice awards, to *USA Today* "Happily Ever After" nods, to winning Favorite Erotica Author and the "Lady Boner Award" (*lol!*), nothing makes her happier than communicating with fellow Mermaids (*fans*) and creating romances that are smart, sassy, and *very sexy*.

A former journalist and displaced beach bum, Louise lives in the Midwest with her trophy husband, two teenage geniuses, and one clumsy "grand-cat."

Visit **TiaLouise.com** for signed copies, book news, and more!